AN UNEXPECTED PATH

RIGHT PLACE, RIGHT TIME BOOK 1

MEGAN MCSPADDEN

To my family who have cheered me along on every unexpected path I've ever ventured down.

&

To those who remain hopeful in the face of adversity.

CONTENT WARNINGS

This is a book about an animal sanctuary and there is talk about the past lives of a couple of the dogs. Nothing is too graphic but some may find it upsetting.

War and discussions about things the main character has seen, again things are not overly graphic.

PLAYLIST

AVAILABLE ON SPOTIFY

Looking At Me Like That - Vance Joy
Mess Is Mine - Vance Joy
I'm with You - Vance Joy
Lover Come Back - City and Colour
Closer to You - Brandi Carlile
Before It Breaks - Brandi Carlile
Until You - AHI
Let Light Be Light - Lizzy McAlpine
We're Going Home - Vance Joy
Honey Hold Me - Morningsiders
Missing Piece - Vance Joy
Every Side Of You - Vance Joy
Sunscreen - Ira Wolf
First Light - Hozier
Keeps Me Going - BANNERS
Clarity - Vance Joy
Mess - Noah Khan
Nights Like This - St. Lundi
Someone Like You - Noah Khan, Joy Oladokun

Someone You Loved - Lewis Capaldi
What I Wouldn't Do - Serena Ryder
I Get to Love You - Ruelle
Soul Mate - flora cash
Wait for You - Obie Elliott

ONE

I cannot believe this is how I'm going to die.

Mauled to death by a vicious pack of two hundred canines all because I needed to clear my head on a hike. Fucking fantastic.

Okay, I'm being dramatic because there are only about twenty dogs, and they don't actually look all that vicious. I'm pretty sure the leader is one of those Taco Bell dogs. Even so, I'm wondering why I decided I had to travel an hour from home to think about my future? I like hiking, but there are a hundred trails near my apartment. Why the hell did I pick the one inhabited by feral beasts? *Go for a hike to decide if you still want to work in actual war zones, Marley. You'll be able to think in peace without the threat of an air raid or sniper fire, Marley.* Not only did I manage to talk myself into mental knots instead of finding clarity, but I twisted my ankle and accidentally made myself prey.

The pain in my ankle practically disappears as the dogs burst through the tall ferns surrounding me. I throw my arms up at the last possible second to cover my face, applying the long-disproved ostrich logic that if I can't see them, they won't be able to see me. Astoundingly, the feeling of hundreds of teeth piercing my flesh doesn't come, and for the briefest of moments I wonder if I did in fact disappear—that is, until I notice that I'm wet. Tongues and noses make contact with every inch of exposed skin, and I'm almost shocked to realize I'm laughing. It feels like I'm being tickled, possibly to death, which, I suppose, is a far more pleasant way to go than mauling.

"Off!" a deep, commanding voice booms.

Just as quickly as the tongue-lashing begins, it stops, all except for one rather persistent tongue. A dopey-looking little white dog is going to town on my left shoe.

"Yogurt!" The voice sounds exasperated now. I finally look up from the white dog in the direction the other dogs are all staring. I've never been one to cower from a man simply because of his size, yet I can't help doing so now. But then something comes to me.

"I'm sorry, did you just call that dog Yogurt?"

The man doesn't smile so much as smirks down at me. "That's his name," he says as he bends to pick the little dog up. Yogurt proceeds to lick the man's neck with the same enthusiasm he'd shown for my shoe. And while I should probably be worried about my current, rather vulnerable state, I find that I'm somewhat jealous of Yogurt.

I'm not too proud to admit that my love life is seriously lacking in the companion department right now, but going very strongly in the self-love one. One could even say I've mastered that one. I am the self-appointed Chief Orgasm Officer, the COO of the company at this point. Not that I want a companion; I'm happily single by choice. But I also know a good-looking man when I see him, and the man standing in front of me is making me think things I normally wouldn't think in this or any other situation. Things like, *Hey you, want to come home with me for Christmas to meet my family?* Which is wild since I don't even spend Christmas with my family.

I'm not sure how long I've been watching Yogurt lick the man's neck, but he's clearly tried to ask me something a couple of times because he's squatting beside me with his brow furrowed. I absently wonder if he would relax his face a bit if I licked it too? I give my head a shake and tell myself to pull it together. I've been in some pretty intense situations, and I've never allowed myself to zone out like this. I'm happy no one I know is here to witness it.

"Sorry?" I ask, instinctively pulling my knees up, which as it happens, is the worst thing I could have done. My vision goes white, and I let out a sound that has all the dogs perking up.

"You *are* hurt!" The well-licked man inches closer, holding his hands out as if I'm a wild animal and he doesn't want to frighten me. Years of working in dangerous places have taught me to not judge people by how they look. Some of the nicest-looking people will take out an entire village without dropping their smile. Heavily tattooed and pierced bikers will give you the shirt off their back, drive you to the closest hospital, and wait around to make sure you're okay while expecting absolutely nothing in return. And here I am in the middle of the forest with a very badly sprained ankle, a not-so-vicious pack of dogs, and a man who is coming off as a gentle giant. Once the pain dulls again, I open my eyes and meet intense hazel ones.

"Is it your ankle?"

I nod again because apparently the part of my brain that transmits words to my mouth malfunctioned when my ankle did.

"Do you mind if I take a look? It would mean touching you." I'm starting to nod when he adds, "I need a verbal yes."

"Yes, you may touch me." Which sounds a bit more like, *Oh*

yes god, please touch me, so I quickly add, "My ankle, I mean. You may touch my ankle." My libido, which had started to rev up, brakes hard, and I release a slow steady breath as he reaches for me.

His touch is gentle as he traces his fingers over my skin, and a pleasurable sensation fires in all directions.

"I'm going to turn it a bit. It's probably going to hurt." I nod again, then immediately wish the dogs had mauled me to death when the pain that shoots through my body manages to force the contents of my stomach to empty onto my lap and his left shoe. He looks down at his shoe, then my lap and back at my ankle. "Seems pretty conclusive that you've got a bad sprain."

I drag my eyes back to his, ready with a smartass reply, but the look on his face is so earnest that I swallow the words down. He gives me a soft smile and then turns his attention to the tree line.

"I'd offer to take you to the hospital, but my road is out." He looks over at me with so much guilt, like he'd caused the rain last night that had likely led to that happening. "Where did you come onto the trail?"

I reach for my phone and zoom in on the trail map I had saved. "Um, I came in at Hanlan Point." I'm not even sure I managed to stay on the right trail. I'd veered off at one point because the creek had overflowed.

He takes my phone and winces. "You're eight klicks from where you started." Holy shit! I must have said it out loud because he laughs. "I'm guessing you weren't really paying attention to the map?"

"I tend to zone out a bit when I'm hiking." This is a half-truth; I'm dyslexic as fuck, and maps are not always my friend. Zoning out plus eye-to-brain communication issues equals a recipe for disaster—or in my case, a sprained ankle far from my car, in the company of a stranger and his band of merry mongrels.

"Well," he says, handing my phone back and squeezing the back of his neck, "you're welcome to come back to my place. I'm not sure how long it's going to be until the road is fixed, but at the very least we can get some ice on your ankle."

"I'm not sure I have much of a choice at this point. I don't think I could get back to my car, and even if I could, there's no way I could drive it."

"If I squat down, do you think you could climb onto my back?"

A tiny voice somewhere inside me squeals, *He wants you to climb him.*

"Oh, I don't think that's necessary. Maybe if we just find a big stick?" This man is tall, and he looks like he'd do just fine against hurricane-force winds. But I'm 5'10" and on the curvy side of athletic, and while I'm a confident independent woman, society has trained me to shy away from being carried for fear of breaking someone's back. And let's not forget the whole vomiting on myself thing.

"Have you tried putting weight on it?"

I wince. "Tried and failed."

"So your options are to stay here and be tormented by mosquitoes and raccoons, go for a piggyback ride, or—and I won't lie, I've always wanted to do this—be thrown over my shoulder in a fireman's carry."

"You've always wanted to throw me over your shoulder?" I ask, confused.

"Well, not you specifically, but I've always kind of wondered what it would be like."

"That's some weird strong-guy shit to wonder about," I say, putting my phone away and swinging my bag onto my back. I should probably be a bit more concerned that he's always wanted to throw someone over his shoulder. Maybe I should dive deeper into this desire of his. Is the person conscious or unconscious? Are they a willing participant?

He shrugs. "There are probably weirder things."

"I guess it is on the low end of weird." I look up at him and bite my lip. I try not to notice the way his gaze follows as it disappears between my teeth and stays there for a second longer than is appropriate. The transition is going to hurt, and I feel like no matter where I end up on this man's body, I'm going to be all kinds of uncomfortable. That alone is disappointing because, in a very different situation, I'd imagine being on his body would be satisfying.

"So? What's it going to be?"

I huff. "Piggyback, please." I'm rewarded with that lovely smile again before he turns and drops into a deep squat. Somehow I manage to manoeuvre myself enough to avoid putting my right foot down at all. Large hands cup my thighs, and my arms instinctively wrap around his neck, effectively cutting off his air supply. I'm very good at this damsel-in-distress thing, clearly. I quickly readjust my position and apologize as he hoists me up a bit higher. "I'm Marley, by the way."

"Bennett," he says, turning his head slightly, causing his beard to brush my cheek.

"Well... I guess take me to your home, Bennett."

This is either going to be the best or worst thing that has ever happened to me.

<h1 style="text-align:center">TWO</h1>

This is not how I anticipated ending today's pack walk; trying not to trip on the dogs weaving in and out of my path while carrying a beautiful woman on my back. I am surprised by the direction the day has taken, but I find that I'm not upset about it.

We've only been walking for roughly five minutes when I hear Marley clear her throat. "So, um, come here often?"

I chuckle. "Is that a pickup line?"

"No, 'If I squat down, do you think you could climb onto my back' is a pickup line," she says, forcing a real laugh from me.

"Touché. You could say I come here often. I don't often go home with a woman I met on the trail, though." I can feel my face heat.

"That's shocking, actually. I've heard of guys using a dog to pick up women, and you've got so many I'd expect women to just be drawn here by some unknown force."

"That makes me sound like a predator. Not my style."

"That's a relief because I'm kind of at your mercy right

now." It hits then that despite the chatter and the calm demeanor, she's in a pretty vulnerable situation. Her legs tense, and I'm guessing it's dawning on her too.

I stop abruptly. "I really have no ill intent here, just so we are crystal clear. I'm just a guy helping out an injured hiker."

I can feel her relax. Other than being a man, I hope I have done absolutely nothing to make her question her safety. "Bennett? Ben? Benny?" I have to hold back a shudder when she says Benny, only one person ever got to call me that. "I trust you," she says, sounding genuine.

"Besides," I say as I start walking again, "how do I know this isn't some ruse to get me to take you into my home so you can case the place?"

"I guess you'll just have to trust that my injury is real and that I have never quite mastered vomiting on demand," she says innocently.

After about five more minutes of silence, she leans to the left, and I can feel her eyes studying me.

"Did you play football?" she asks.

"I did."

"I knew it."

"I also played hockey, soccer, and basketball," I add.

"Oh, well, that makes sense, I guess."

"Why's that?"

"I don't know, you seem sporty."

"I was a small-town kid. To field a team in anything, everyone had to become sporty, whether they wanted to or not."

"That sounds... fun." She says "fun" in a way that makes it obvious that fun is not the way she'd describe having to be sporty.

"Well, I *was* sporty, so it was for me. Although, it's hard when half the team doesn't want to be playing the game, and the other half wants to be winning," I reply, sounding a bit more winded than I feel.

"Do you want to take a break? I can't be that light. Honestly, if my ankle didn't hurt so badly, I would have crawled back to my car and taught myself to drive with my left foot just to avoid being carried."

"I'm definitely glad you didn't attempt that," I say, readjusting again. "We're almost there, and you're not that heavy."

"You are too kind," she scoffs.

"Remember that when I'm making you ice your ankle in about ten minutes." I chuckle.

"I'll have you know that I'm a damn good patient."

"In need of medical care often, are you?"

"Not exactly often but enough, and I've had no complaints."

"Do you give the medical staff a caregiver experience survey?"

"As a matter of fact," she begins, and I involuntarily let out a bark of laughter. "Let's just say this isn't my first unfortunately timed injury."

"Sounds like there's a story there somewhere."

"Probably..." she says, sounding distracted. "Holy shit," she murmurs as my place comes into view.

"Home sweet home," I say, appreciating her reaction.

"Truly," she says in wonder. "My apartment is... I don't know, like a comma in my life. A place where I catch up on sleep. I don't know what I was expecting, but it wasn't this."

"Oh yeah? And what had you been expecting?" I ask, curious to know her answer. What type of home did Marley expect a guy like me to live in?

"I don't know." She laughs. "Some run-down hunting lodge type thing, or a modern monstrosity."

My home is neither of those things. But I can imagine why

she'd think that; it does seem to be a theme out in the middle of nowhere. My house, on the other hand, is somewhere in the middle. Old but well-kept, large but not excessive, although perhaps too large for a single guy like me, even with all the dogs.

"It's beautiful," she adds as we get closer and the finer details come into view. The stonework and the window trim and accents scream English manor, but the porch that wraps around, surrounded by the fall garden, is all Ontario.

"Maybe hold off declaring your undying love for it until you see the inside," I add as I open the door and step across the threshold.

THREE

Once inside, Bennett slips his boots off, careful not to jostle me too much, then walks into a cozy-looking living room. This is a room true to its name—you can tell a lot of living is done in this space. The couches are plush, and there are blankets thrown haphazardly on every seat. I'm going to assume most of the living here is done by the dogs.

"I'm going to put you in that chair in the corner, slide the ottoman over, and stack some pillows to elevate your ankle," Bennett explains as if I have any choice at all here. Which I suppose I appreciate.

He squats in front of the chair, and I do the reverse of what I had done in the woods, dropping my small day pack beside the chair in the process. Then I watch as Bennett slides a large ottoman over and stacks a couple of pillows. "Mind if I—" He gestures at my leg, and I nod. "This is probably going to be the worst part," he says as he begins untying my boot, and I know exactly what he means as the pressure of the boot loosens, and I swear I feel my ankle swell in real time. It's unpleasant. He takes off my other boot faster, then tells me he'll be right back.

I hear the front door open and close, followed by a sharp whistle. I can't see much through the window from where I'm sitting, but I do catch a few dogs running by. About five minutes later, I hear another door open and close and the sound of wet boots on the floor. I can also hear Bennett speaking quietly to someone. My heart sinks a little at the thought of it being a woman. Which is beyond ridiculous. I have officially crossed into unfamiliar territory.

"Ice, ibuprofen, and some water." Bennett declares, walking into the room, carrying all three in one hand while he balances Yogurt in the other. The dog, not the food, although I kind of wish it was the food because I am a bit hungry. And then I remember that the last thing I ate is on my shirt, and to my horror, on the back of Bennett's.

"Um, I hate to ask, but you wouldn't have a spare shirt and pair of pants, would you? Maybe something of your wife's or girlfriend's?" It couldn't be more obvious that I was fishing for information. I may as well be wearing one of those hats fly-fisherman wear and a pair of fucking waders.

Bennett is much cooler than me and avoids the fact-finding mission like a seasoned politician. "I'm sure I can find something for you," he says as he wraps the ice in a tea towel that I didn't realize he'd thrown over his shoulder. Then he's squatting next to my ankle again and gently lifting and adjusting the ice for maximum contact. I can't control myself as a hiss escapes me, and I toss my head back, breathing in deeply. "Sorry," he says with such remorse that it hurts my heart a little.

"S'ok." I breathe, trying to smile in a way that doesn't scream "I will end you." Because that's not how I feel, but it is also very much how I feel. I'm dealing with some very complicated feelings at the moment.

He stands and puts his hands on his hips, and I so badly

want to make a Brawny Man joke. He just looks down at me but doesn't say anything. I'm in a male-dominated industry, and I'm often in areas that are off-limits to most women, so being looked at is something I can usually ignore. But I don't know how to ignore Bennett looking at me. The looks I usually get say, "What are you doing here?" I don't know how to interpret this look of his.

"You've got vomit all over the back of your shirt," I say, wincing.

His brows furrow for a split second before he nods and mutters, "Right. I'll be right back." Then he turns and heads up the stairs. I watch as his legs disappear and let my body relax. I didn't realize how tense I'd been the whole time. It's as though my mind and body were dealing with two different situations. My body has been on high alert while my brain has been ogling Bennett. I'd be the first to die in a slasher movie if the bad guy looked like him. However, now that the tension is gone, the pain has made itself known again. I try to focus on the space I'm in instead of the pain.

There is a saving grace in not being able to walk around: I won't be caught snooping, which is good because I can rarely forgo a good snooping opportunity. From where I sit I can see a wall of shelves, absolutely brimming with books. Across from it is a wall of framed pictures. An older couple makes up most of them, but I think there are a few of Bennett as a child. From this angle, I can just make out what looks to be a graduation picture. There is a TV above the fireplace, and I can imagine curling up in this room with a good book or movie on a rainy day, absolutely buried under a heap of dogs. It's a pleasant thought.

Eventually, I let my mind return to the man who has so graciously brought me into his home. Bennett is the type of guy you'd expect to see on a promotional poster for milk. Milk-poster good looks with his hazel-green eyes and wholesome smile. He's got light brown hair and a well-groomed beard a shade darker. His nose has a small bump that's only really noticeable from the side; I assume he broke it playing one of the many sports he was forced to participate in. He has a light dusting of freckles, and I can imagine that they were much darker when he was a kid, probably like mine after I've spent lots of time in the sun. His lips are, to put it bluntly, entirely kissable, and I can't help but wonder what they would feel like against my own, how his slightly fuller bottom lip would feel between my teeth.

"You're going to be swimming in these, but at least every-thing is clean." Bennett's voice brings me back to reality. He's holding up a sweatshirt and a pair of dark sweatpants. He's also changed his entire wardrobe and is now in a tight Henley with the arms rolled up and dark grey sweatpants. It's incredibly rude of him. I'm caught off guard that this man, who carried me out of the woods so I wouldn't be consumed by mosquitoes, could be so thoughtless.

"Hmmm." I pretend to be deep in thought, tapping my mouth to ensure I haven't drooled down my chin. "I think swimming may be preferable to the vomit." He doesn't bring them to me though; instead, he looks from my outstretched leg and back to the clothes. It takes me a minute to realize that while my shirt will be easy to change, maneuvering out of my leggings may be a challenge.

He gestures towards my legs. "Do you need help?"

Truthfully, I think I can get my pants to my ankles. It's the sliding them off my right leg that I'm dreading. I do some calcu-lations, looking from my ankle to the pants and back again. "Um, I think I'll be ok. I may need help with the end bit, but I'll try first."

Bennett nods and places the clothes where I can easily reach them. Then he points with his thumb somewhere outside the room. "I'll just be out there. Yell if you need help." Then he's gone so fast that I can practically see one of those cartoon dust trails.

FOUR

As it turns out I can, in fact, still undress and redress myself. I may have nearly blacked out a few times, but I did it.

"I'm decent!" I call out to Bennett when I've pulled the sweatshirt down over my body. I am indeed swimming in the clothes, but I'm also not complaining because they're clean and cozy. I have spent the better part of the past decade in very uncozy situations, so I'm choosing to view this as a silver lining.

When Bennett comes back in, his eyes do a quick sweep of my body before quickly looking away and sitting on the couch across from me. I expect him to lean back and get comfortable, but instead he leans forward with his forearms resting on his thighs, looking only marginally more comfortable than he had in the woods. And now I'm wondering if I look too comfortable like I'm enjoying sitting in this cushy chair, swimming in a sweatsuit, utterly basking in this impromptu lounging session. I push myself up a bit so I'm sitting a bit straighter and try to think of something intelligent to say.

The problem with trying to think of something intelligent to say is that it often leads to me putting my foot directly into my mouth, and because I've already made an incredible first impression, I continue down that path. "You've got a nice home. I mean, I haven't seen beyond this room and the kitchen could be a dump, but it seems nice."

Bennett laughs a little and finally sits back. "The kitchen is, in fact, a dump. My grandfather was in the middle of renovating it when he passed away, and I'm so busy with the dogs I haven't done much to it."

"Oh, I'm sorry." *Very on brand, Marley.* "Was it recent?"

"Three years ago."

"Oh." I know for some three years is recent but for others, it's forever ago. Navigating one's own grief is tricky; navigating someone else's is a fucking minefield. I have a complicated relationship with grief—it's how I keep ending up in shelled-out buildings taking pictures for media outlets to cash in on. "Were you close?" I ask.

His brows knit together like he's trying to find a diplomatic way to say what he's thinking. "It was not an easy relationship. But not uneasy enough for him to have left all his earthly possessions and money to someone else."

"Well, that's good, isn't it? I mean, have you seen the cost of things nowadays?" I laugh thinking about what I pay for an apartment I've barely lived in to store stuff I barely care about. "Did he leave you a bunch of dogs or..." I trail off as Yogurt appears out from under the couch. Yogurt is not a large dog by any means, but I cannot for the life of me figure out how he managed to get under the couch.

"Nah," Bennett says, bending to pick the dog up and plunking him in his lap. *Don't you dare think it,* I tell myself as Yogurt spins a few times before finally curling up with his head resting on Bennett's thigh. "He couldn't stand dogs." A slow, somewhat evil smile pulls at his lips while he looks down at Yogurt.

"So are they all revenge dogs or something? Or is this a 'I went a little off the deep end when I moved away from home' situation? You know, the kind that usually involves drinking too much or drugs? I guess that could work with dogs too."

He laughs, and I decide I want to hear that rich, smooth sound as much as possible while I'm stuck here. "I had two before he died. Then a friend called maybe a month after I moved back here and said she had found a dog wandering around her neighborhood. The shelter nearby has a high kill rate so she begged me to take her. I figured I had the room now so why not, and I guess things kind of escalated."

"How many are there?" I have heard the odd bark since the start of this little adventure, but if I hadn't seen all the dogs, I would be shocked to discover there are so many running around.

"Twenty-one," he says, looking guilty like he's been caught sneaking cookies or something.

"That's..." Insane? Bold? Too many dogs? "That's a lot of dogs," I say. "Is this your job then? Is this place like a shelter masquerading as a fancy country retreat for canines?"

"Sort of." He shrugs, and I'm starting to realize this is all feeling like a job interview.

"Do you have a phone charger I could borrow?" I ask, changing the subject and reaching for my bag to pull out my phone.

"I do, but it's for an Android," he says apologetically.

"Oh." I unlock my phone and see that I have 15% battery left. I'm usually really good at keeping things charged, but I had been listening to an audiobook in the car on my way up to the trail, and it was only when I arrived that I noticed my cable wasn't charging. "I'm just going to text my friend to let her know I'm alive."

"3087 Fire Route A, Harcourt," Bennett says.

"Sorry?" I look up from my phone.

"That's where you are."

"Right," I probably should have asked that earlier. I'm starting to wonder if I hit my head at some point and don't remember. "I'm usually better with being aware of my surroundings." I laugh nervously as I text Izzy, grateful for the app that helps make my dyslexia seem nonexistent.

> I'm alive and at 3087 Fire Route A, Harcourt.

IZZY

Why wouldn't you be alive?

> Long story. I sprained my ankle on the trail. A nice man and his dogs rescued me and took me back to his place.

IZZY

Excuse me? I'm asking Tom to google the address now and we'll come pick you up.

> You can't. The driveway was washed out. Bennett will take me to the hospital when there's road access again.

> At least I think he will? We haven't established anything beyond that his house was my only option and some clean clothes. Oh, and that he has nearly two dozen dogs as a big fuck you to his grandfather.

IZZY

Mar, do we trust this guy?

> He has given me no reason not to. He's been a perfect gentleman.

IZZY

Most are until they aren't.

I ignore that and let her know my phone is dying so I'm going to turn it off unless I absolutely need it.

This, unsurprisingly, does not go over well with Izzy.

IZZY

Marley Diane Cunningham, you cannot just turn off your phone! This is how horror movies start!

I sigh because it's all I can do at this point.

"You can give her my number too. That will probably put her mind at ease."

"It's not that, she's just… Yeah, that's probably not the worst idea." Of course, I didn't think of it because I'm on a hot streak of poor choices.

I tell her again not to worry and type out the number Bennett recites, then I power down my phone and slip it back into my bag before turning my attention back to my host.

"I bet you're used to having strangers in your home."

"Probably as accustomed to it as you are to being in a stranger's home." I have to laugh because I am actually very accustomed to that. He looks confused at my reaction.

"I'm a conflict photographer. I often find myself in strangers' homes, or what were once their homes."

Bennett's face tells me he thinks I'm full of shit. And honestly, why the hell wouldn't he? I haven't exactly given the impression that I'm prepared to be tossed into a hostile environment, I sprained my ankle on terrain I'd describe as "barely uneven" and threw up all over myself less than two hours ago. When people think of conflict photographers, I am not the ideal candidate, in my current state anyway. But that is what I do, and it is who I am. I mean, I *think* it is. I was properly lost in thought about my future when I snapped, crackled, and popped my ankle like a human Rice Krispie.

"You don't believe me?" I ask.

He shakes his head slowly. "It's not that. You just caught me off guard."

Now it's my turn to do the not-believing thing. "Mm-hmm." I purse my lips and scrutinize him. "What kind of job would you expect me to have?"

"I don't know." He lifts one shoulder and contemplates for a minute. "A teacher, maybe?"

"What kind of teacher?"

"Hmmm." He studies me for a beat. "An English teacher?" When I say I bark out a laugh so loud it could wake the dead, I am not exaggerating. "So, not an English teacher?" he smirks while rubbing at his temples.

"No." I cackle, trying to pull myself back together. "Most definitely not an English teacher. But I cannot wait to tell Simon."

"Simon?" he asks, his head tilting. And if I was delusional I may convince myself that his expression is reading as slightly disappointed with a touch of worry.

"Oh, he's a journalist, the pen-and-paper kind. Simon keeps me sane. He's like..." I try to put into words what the guy is to me outside of our professional world. "A wise uncle, older brother, and father figure rolled into one." Bennett is nodding but has gone back to pressing on his temples, and now that he's not looking at me, I notice the strained set of his mouth and a slight flair of his nostrils.

"Headache?" I ask quietly.

He nods and moves Yogurt off his lap before standing slowly, "Probably just dehydrated. Can I get you something else to drink? I've got water and"—he thinks for a minute—"well, basically just water."

"Water sounds great," I answer quickly, not wanting to prolong his suffering.

Before he leaves he removes the ice pack from my ankle and says he's going to pop it back into the freezer. Then he grabs my empty glass and leaves the room, Yogurt trailing at his feet. Honestly, I don't know what the hell I'm going to do for the next little while. It's too early for bed. Shit. My eyes snap open, and I stare at the ceiling. Am I sleeping in this chair? Is this my home now? And oh my god, what happens if—no, *when* —I have to go to the bathroom? Maybe we can create a set of makeshift crutches. Those can't be too hard to construct, right? Certainly no harder than Ikea furniture. There are fewer pieces than the Hermawhatever in my bedroom. Bennett strikes me as the type of person who could not only forage but would enjoy looking for some strong sticks or branches.

I take a few deep breaths and remind myself that I have been in far worse situations. Hell, two weeks ago, I was sleeping on a grass mat in Tunisia next to a gassy camel and a rookie American journalist who was distraught over a broken nail. I'm not sure I'd say I was in my element there, but if I really examine things, it was more my element than my present time-line. That is to say, I know how to handle whiny reporters and gassy camels far better than nice, handsome men who dedicate their lives to rescuing dogs and injured hikers. I'm also questioning why everything has felt so easy. In the field, something that seems too easy usually means shit is about to hit the fan. Yet I'm sitting here without much worry at all, and I can't decide what that means.

FIVE

An intense pounding in my skull woke me up before my alarm this morning. It's not a daily occurrence, but it happens enough to be a nuisance. Thankfully, by the time I went out for our walk, the meds had started to kick in. I'm not sure if the events of this morning brought on this second bout, but it's unusual for me to need to take something more than once in a single day. I pull out my phone to make a note in my app about it. If it happens again, I'll bring it up at my next appointment. When I open the cupboard, my prescriptions are there, lined up neatly, a reminder of how orderly my life tends to be.

When the neurologist told me I had to stop playing football unless I wanted to donate my brain at a young age for chronic traumatic encephalopathy research, I hadn't taken her seriously. She'd given me a stern look. "Bennett, you cannot afford one more concussion. And this early in your career, I don't see how you could avoid one more." I was twenty-one and experiencing my first professional training camp. I was about to make my grandfather's dreams come true, which meant he'd get off my ass. I'd heard of the condition, of course; every single player knew about it. Hell, most of us had flocked to see that Will Smith movie about it and left the theatre thinking, "Well, that will never be me." And yet there I was in my physical prime, being told to stop doing an activity I enjoyed because of something I *might* develop. She had been very blunt that this was something that could impact every single aspect of my life, and not in a positive way. If I thought the headaches were bad now, just wait and see what else could happen.

I wasn't a dumb jock. I was pre-med with dreams of becoming a surgeon one day. I figured I'd find a way to balance med school and football, and after a few years of playing and making my grandfather happy, I'd retire from football and focus on my own dream. When I'd told him about quitting, he'd called me a coward. He'd called my generation soft. "Where would we be if the boys had avoided fighting the Germans because of a damn headache?" he'd ranted. The fear of disappointing the man who raised me, who had given me absolutely every opportunity to succeed in life, outweighed sense, so I continued. About a month later, during a drill I shouldn't have had an issue with, I had a fairly dramatic lightbulb moment, and that was it. I walked off the field.

I changed my med school status from part-time to full-time and threw myself into my studies. In doing so, I also ensured my grandfather cut all ties with me. Thankfully, my nan supported my decision, and since it was her family fortune we all lived off of, I was able to afford school and an apartment far from the disapproving rants of the old man. I recognized that my worst-case scenario was beyond a lot of people's best case, so I worked to make the most of it.

My first year was hell. The workload was intense, and my brain often felt sluggish. The headaches had increased, and I found myself down more than I was up. With Nan's blessing, I decided to take a leave from school to get my head on straight. "Med school will always be there, Benny," she told me.

My vision starts to clear, and I realize I've been standing in front of an open cupboard lost in thought. Eyes damp, head pounding even more, I go through the motions that have become more frequent again. Twist the top, pop a pill, drink some water, and repeat. I lean back against the counter, allowing myself to drink the rest of the water slowly, and I think about how the morning has gone so far.

The property my home sits on is huge, and the trails around it, while public, are rarely used. There are far better areas to hike around here, and people tend to stick to ones that offer larger parking lots and public washrooms at the trailhead. My trails are less manicured, with a thick bed of ferns and pine needles, often camouflaging roots, rocks, and rodent holes. After an intense rainfall like we had last night, it's no wonder Marley injured herself.

When I heard the dogs lose their minds, I expected to find a wild animal. I certainly wasn't expecting to see a woman who literally took my breath away. She was laughing, her dark brown hair pulled back in a messy bun. When I finally got the dogs to back off, she looked up at me, and I saw a flash of fear cross her face. I know I'm intimidating in a regular situation, but I would imagine that I'm even more so in the eyes of someone lost and injured. But just as quickly as she looked afraid, she'd asked if I'd called a dog Yogurt. I don't even remember what I said because I was trying to ignore the way chills broke out across my skin when she spoke. In my thirty-two years, I've never had that kind of reaction to a voice. Although maybe it was all of her I had reacted to, but her voice was just the cherry on top. It was probably a good thing I liked the sound of her voice because she talked nonstop until we got back to my place. Time will tell if she naturally talks that much, or if it had just been nervous chatter.

I'd done my best to make her feel safe, always making sure to ask before I touched her. My grandfather had tried to drill that into me. Not because he was a chivalrous gentleman, but because he was a rich old bastard who assumed every woman would try and sue me for assault or be in line to bed me, get pregnant, and secure my inheritance. I remember the first time he'd said "bed you" to me before I left for my first university football training camp. It was the most old-timey thing I'd ever heard, and I burst out laughing. He'd threatened to disown me for that. If I had a nickel for every time he'd threatened that, I'd have had a small fortune myself. My nan had been the one to ensure I always made sure whoever I was with was comfortable purely from a place of being a decent person. I'd love to know what she'd think of the situation I found myself in currently. She'd probably laugh and say something like, "Benny, it's not every day you find a beautiful woman with a great laugh in the woods." She'd be over the moon about how my day was going, aside from the headaches.

I fill Marley's glass and consider adding ice. I decide to add ice to my own and then let her pick, but then I feel weird about offering her a glass I'd had my lips on, so I dump the water into a clean one. Then I go in search of an old tensor bandage I know is somewhere in one of the cupboards above the fridge. I can feel the buzz from earlier start to return at the thought of touching her again as I apply the wrap. I roll my eyes at myself as I head back to the living room. Marley has managed to undo me in ways I have never been prepared for, and I don't know if I should run or embrace it.

When I see her staring out the window, looking pensive, I

decide to embrace the feeling. No matter what happens, it's a change, and I've been thinking I've been due for one of those. I just didn't see it coming in the form of a woman with big brown eyes and a smile that makes everything else fade into the background.

SIX

"I didn't know if you'd prefer it with or without ice?" Bennett asks, carrying two glasses of water, one with ice and one without. I don't know why this does funny things to my brain and multiple other body parts, but I point at the glass without. He hands it to me and then puts his own down on a coaster next to where he'd been sitting before turning back to me and pulling something out from under his armpit.

"It's not the newest, but it will help support your ankle until you can see a doctor," he says, holding up what I can now see is a tensor bandage. "May I?"

I've noticed he's very prudent with the permission seeking. I'm not complaining; it's just a very different approach than I'm used to. I gesture for him to go ahead, and he bends to raise my leg off the pillows which he moves aside so he can sit. Then I watch with a mixture of horror and fascination as he sets my ankle in his lap. I can't help but sneak a peek at Yogurt who is sitting next to the ottoman, staring at Bennett and wondering if he's perhaps jealous of my foot. I'm officially the weirdest one in the room.

"Okay, that should be good," Bennett says, looking up from my ankle and no doubt catching me smiling like a moron at him. I try and look away, but when he smiles back, I'm fucked.

I swallow the Disney princess sigh that's been building and blink a few times before looking down at his handiwork. "Thank you," I manage to squeak out, which seems to draw his eyes from mine down to my mouth.

"You're welcome, Marley," he replies, looking back down and running his thumb lightly over the exposed skin above the bandage. The contact alongside the way my name sounds on his tongue does inappropriate things to me, and those things aren't necessarily purely sexual either.

I've only been in Bennett's home for three and a half hours, and in that time he has applied ice to my ankle five times, sat in companionable silence with me, and turned my brain to mush more than anyone has in the last five years. When he's not with me, he's off doing whatever it is he would normally be doing—at least that's what I assume. I assured him that I'd be fine alone and he didn't need to worry about me stealing anything and taking off, which had earned me a tiny smile and bashful nod. He was upstairs for a while—I could hear him walking around directly above me—and when he came down he said he was going to check on the dogs. Meanwhile, I've sat twiddling my thumbs as my body re-enacts the reaction to his touch. All seven times he's attended to my ankle, I've jumped a little the minute his skin makes contact with mine. He, on the other hand, has not reacted once, which makes me think it's all in my head. Bennett did bring me a few books, and I pretended to be excited to read one, but truthfully physically reading is a sure-fire way to put me into a foul mood.

People tend to assume that those with dyslexia can't read at all, which is bonkers. There are countless super successful people who have it. I love stories with all my heart, but fighting with the words ruins them for me, and the more they shift the more frustrated I get. I was never one of those patient kids that could keep at it. I got it or I didn't, and while I eventually got reading, it was a long hard road, and the joy that was supposed to come with being in control never materialized. So I indulge in stories through audiobooks. Reading without the constant battle between my eyes and brain has allowed me to appreciate books in a way I never would have imagined in school.

I've got my thumbs going in a pretty good rhythm, and I'm staring so hard at the book cover that it's blurring when I hear a crash from the kitchen.

"Everything ok?" I call out.

"Yep." His reply comes out somewhat strained. He comes into the room a minute later holding a bag of pasta. "Um, do you have any allergies or anything? Food allergies, I mean, although I guess if you have any other major ones that would be good to know about. I know bees are rare this time of year, but you never know, right? Are you allergic to dogs? I'm going to guess not as you haven't even sniffled once since being—" He stops mid-sentence and finally looks at me. He shakes his head slightly. "Wow, that was a lot, sorry. I just—"

I cut him off before he can apologize again. "You just care about someone else's well-being? Because that's nothing to be sorry about." I've spent a lot of time in places full of people that don't give a shit about anyone else. It's hard to watch someone turn off their humanity in real time; it's scarier than knowing someone wasn't born with any. "I have no allergies that I'm aware of, and I will eat just about anything. I just wish I was able to help out."

"Do you want to come sit in the kitchen? Or you can stay here and keep reading." He points at the book on my lap, and I look down and scowl at it.

"Truth? I'm not a huge fan of paperbacks. I tend to do

audiobooks." He looks genuinely horrified, and I honestly think he's about to throw me out when he tips his head back and groans.

"I should have given you the remote," he says, gesturing at the TV. "I don't use it much so I tend to forget it's there." I'm starting to get the impression that Bennett is too hard on himself.

"It's okay." I shrug. "Circling back to the kitchen, if it's not too much trouble, I don't hate the idea. Although if it is then I can stay here. I've got a pretty nice ass groove developing." I shimmy back and forth to illustrate my point. This at least gets him to smile.

"Not too much trouble at all." He comes over and squats in front of me again, and I awkwardly latch onto his back.

"You know," I ponder out loud once he's standing, "this is far more pleasant when we aren't two halves of a vomit sandwich." This makes him do some sort of laugh-groan hybrid, and I decide I like the sound of that too.

The kitchen isn't nearly the dump I was expecting. "Dump" isn't the right word for it; "dated" would be far more appropriate. The cupboards that remain are pine, and the counters are an off-white material I can only classify as not marble. The appliances, however, look new and definitely not from the bargain aisle. It's a work in progress. Basically the room version of me, just with shinier appliances.

"I'm, ah, doing the work myself," Bennett says, stopping in front of an island stool. "So I have no clue when I'll be done." He drags another stool over and drops the pillow he must have grabbed without me noticing and lifts my ankle on top of it. He makes taking care of me seem effortless.

"I like it," I say, looking around. "It has character."

Bennett glances left and right, his expression letting me know he does not share my view. "If you say so."

He starts filling a pot with water and setting out things he's going to use to cook the pasta. I notice a jar of red sauce on the counter. "Did you make that?" I ask, hoping I don't sound too shocked by the idea.

He grabs it and sets it down in front of me. "My neighbor makes a bunch at the end of every summer and gives me a few jars."

I stare back at him blankly. "You have neighbors?"

"Yeah," he laughs, turning to the pot on the stove. "The Hores live about three kilometres north. We are the only two properties on the road, meaning they're as stuck as we are until the town comes and sorts it out."

"The... whores?" I repeat, needing him to clarify that he means that's their name and not that there are a bunch of whores down the way. Which is fine—you do you and all that—but I still need clarification.

"H-O-R-E." He smiles back at me while opening the bag of pasta. "When we first met, Karl, Mr. Hore"—I snort—"stuck his hand out and said 'We're the Hores. If you ever need to borrow a hoe, we're your people.' And he said it totally straight-faced." I guffaw because that's all I can do. "He then laughed and said when you've got a name like Hore, you've got to just lean into it."

"I respect that," I say, still laughing. "I went to school with a lot of Dicks." I think for a minute. "I mean that in all the possible ways."

"I went to school with Randall Bottum," Bennet says, turning and leaning back against the counter with his arms crossed.

"Oh no!" I say, covering my face with my hands and laughing. "That poor kid."

"I wonder what Randy's up to now."

"I'm sure you could find out on social media."

Bennett shrugs. "Don't have any."

"Excuse me?" I slowly blink at him a couple of times. "You must be around my age, and you don't have social media?"

"Thirty-two, no social media," he replies.

I'm dumbfounded. Flabbergasted. Positively gobsmacked by the notion that someone born after 1990 isn't connected to the world through at least one social platform. Where does he post pictures of dogs and his food and this fucking view? Not the one I'm currently looking at, although deep down I'd be over the moon to be sharing this view with people. *"Look at me, friends and strangers, look at what I get to stare at every day. Oh, quake before me in all this glory."*

"You seem surprised," he says, turning to dump the pasta into the boiling water.

"I honestly don't know if I've met someone my age without it. I mean, sure, I've met a few in areas of the world somewhat cut off from technology, but even then humans find a way to share nonsense on Facebook."

"Never saw much point in it." He shrugs. "I'm pretty private, and my life is all about the dogs these days. Who wants to just see pictures of dogs all the time?"

He cannot be for real. "Have you actually ever been on the internet?" I inquire seriously, because I'm beginning to think he hasn't.

"Obviously." He turns away from me to stir the pasta, and I'm momentarily distracted by his muscles moving below his shirt.

"But like... have you really?" If I'm not mistaken his ears have gone a bit red. It now kind of seems like I'm digging for far less PG information than I intended. I don't care if he has a hundred porn sites bookmarked, although now I'm wondering if he does and what kind he gravitates towards. "I mean, if you had, you'd know pictures of dogs are right up there with cat videos and passive-aggressive memes about everything."

"I have email and pay all my bills electronically. I've got news and weather sites bookmarked. I'm not completely useless in the modern world, Marley." He's smirking at me again, and fuck me, I like it. More of that, please.

SEVEN

Mrs. Nancy Hore makes some damn good marinara sauce. I didn't realize how hungry I was until I could smell dinner and my stomach let the world know. To his credit, Bennett kept his mouth shut. He has excellent table manners. He's holding his fork in his left hand and chewing with his mouth closed. His elbows are nowhere near the table, and he's got a napkin across his lap. Meanwhile, I'm about three seconds away from dropping my fork and just diving face-first into my penne. Thankfully though, after a few mouthfuls, I am feeling more like myself, and the urge to face-plant into the pasta dissipates.

"Do the dogs sleep outside?" I asked, dabbing at my mouth with my napkin.

"No, they'll go into the barn tonight. Usually, they're in here." Bennett replies, his gaze locked on where the napkin had touched.

"Don't make them sleep in the barn because of me."

His eyes meet mine again. "They're fired up about a guest, and I don't want someone jumping on your ankle. If you weren't injured, they'd be inside. Although, if you weren't injured, I guess you wouldn't be here at all." He smiles at me.

I am suddenly overwhelmed with guilt for being a surprise guest and the reason the dogs have to sleep in the barn. "I'm sorry," I say, putting my fork down and leaning back. My ravenous appetite has disappeared, and I'm fighting off very unwanted tears. I'm not a crier. If I was, I wouldn't be able to do my job. My therapist says I disassociate from the trauma I've witnessed, and that's why I'm not a crier. She also says I self-medicate with humour, to which I say, it's better than self-medicating with drugs or alcohol. Dr. Webber grudgingly agrees with that counterargument. Right now, though, I'm struggling to keep the tears at bay.

My swallow rate has increased tenfold, like if I keep swallowing I won't cry. It doesn't work. I feel the first tear breach the surface, and it's game over. I don't hear Bennett slide his stool back or his footsteps as he approaches, and when I feel his arms close around me, I jolt slightly. This is the first time he has touched me without any warning, without asking for permission, and it takes me a second to relax in his arms. I'm now sobbing. I don't know who this person I've suddenly morphed into is. I'm realizing that I've lost track of who I am in the course of forty-eight hours. I don't know if it makes it better or worse that a virtual stranger is witnessing what I assume Dr. Webber would call a breakthrough, but I'm going to settle on calling it a breakdown.

Bennett tightens his arms further without saying a word. He just holds me while I release what is likely years of pent-up emotions.

I don't know how much time has passed since I said I was sorry. The tears have slowed to a trickle, and I've got my breathing back under control. Bennett's arms have loosened but he still has them wrapped around me. I like it here. In Bennett's arms in this house in the middle of nowhere. I like the quiet and the calm of it all, and that shocks me a bit. I've been throwing myself into chaos for so long that I forgot what calmness felt like. I begin to align my breaths with his, and soon I feel myself pulling out of his embrace.

I take a few breaths before I open my eyes. When I do, I immediately deflate. "I've ruined another shirt of yours," I huff, pointing at the Jackson Pollock-esque snot art I've left across half of his shirt.

He doesn't reply right away, too busy studying me. I usually hate feeling like someone is trying to read my mind. When Dr. Webber does it, I physically squirm, which of course she points out. The most bizarre part of this entire experience is that I don't hate this. I have this weird feeling that Bennett isn't trying to read me so much as actually seeing me. That little piece of insight triggers my flight response, and because I can't run away on my own I do the next best thing.

"I really need to pee," I say, almost pleading because holy shit my bladder feels like it's about to explode, and I don't want to add urine to the bodily fluids I've left on or around this man today. I'm suddenly desperate, so much so I don't even care if he has to help me do all the regular things. Which, let's be honest, he won't have to because ankles don't do a lot of work in the bathroom.

Without warning he pulls me into his arms, and within what feels like four strides, is standing in a doorway to a small room. "Do you think you can handle things from here?"

I look behind me and see that the bathroom is small, just a sink and toilet, and I'm definitely capable of hopping from the door to the toilet without assistance. I nod and mutter a quiet "Thanks" before making my way as gracefully as I can to the toilet. When I'm in front of it, Bennett shuts the door and lets me know he'll be in the kitchen. I'm not someone who has any bathroom hold-ups, but the thought of him not hearing what I assume is going to sound like horse piss hitting the toilet bowl does put me at ease.

Years of yoga haven't done much for me; I don't meditate well, I'm not overly flexible, and it doesn't give me a sense of calm. However, what yoga has given me is the ability to balance on one foot, which is proving crucial as I undo the drawstring of my pants and slide them down.

When I'm done, I hop back to the door without a single issue. When I open the door Yogurt is standing there, which for some reason scares the ever-loving shit out of me and causes me to step back onto my right foot. I scream in pain and immediately fall backwards, missing the toilet with my head by about an inch. But I do manage to get my arm into the bowl, which soaks the sleeve of the sweatshirt.

Bennett arrives seconds later to find me breathing like I'm in labour, new tears on my face and my forearm and hand in the toilet bowl. Yogurt seems completely unaware of the issue and is happily licking my face.

"Shit," Bennett says, shooing Yogurt away and bending to help me up. "Are you okay?" He's running his hands over my head, checking for bumps or blood or perhaps to see if it feels hollow.

"Never better," I mutter. When I look at my arm, which I'm now resting on Bennett's, I notice something unexpected. What appears to be a wet piece of toilet paper is stuck to me, and when I looked down I noticed that the toilet had not in fact flushed. I cannot hold in a defeated "Motherfucker!" I have indeed managed to get another bodily fluid on this man today.

Ten minutes later, Bennett's gotten me a new sweatshirt, changed his shirt, rewrapped and reapplied ice to my ankle, put me back into the cozy armchair with a mug of peppermint tea, and went out to settle the dogs in for the night.

I have no idea what a day in the life looks like for Bennett, but I would put money on it not looking like today. When he's back, he joins me with his own mug.

"Dogs good?" I ask, blowing on my tea.

"Yeah." I imagine he wanted to say something like, "Despite having to sleep in a cold dark barn because of an unwanted house guest." The way he looks at me then lets me know he can tell exactly what I'm thinking. "Marley, they are fine, I promise. They've slept out there before. It's a nice change for them, like a sleepaway camp. They've got memory foam beds, water that replenishes itself, and a turf area to do their business should the need arise. It's not a hardship."

They've slept out there before, eh? My brain gets stuck on that point and starts to formulate reasons why that would be, but I decide not to let it get very far.

"You didn't really answer me before, when I asked if this was your job." I realize the minute the words are out of my mouth that my tone made me sound judgemental. "Which is awesome, by the way. They're lucky dogs." I overcorrect and now sound flirty. "I just mean getting to be all together and go on nature walks seems way better than living in those small concrete cages you see at city shelters." He's looking at me like he's enjoying watching me verbally flail about, so I stop.

"It's more of a passion at this point than a job" is all he says.

I want to know more now. How can he afford to run this operation? How many dogs does he rescue a week? Does he accept donations? Can I donate? Did he go to school for this? Can you even go to school for this? Would he take in other animals? Would he take in people on a semi-permanent basis? Is he single? Whoa, nope, we took a sharp left turn onto an unmarked road, and I slam the mental brakes on and reverse quickly out of there.

"My job felt like a passion more than a job for a long time," I say. I don't even know why I say it. Maybe I want him to say he felt like that too at some point but then the passion returned.

"Now it just feels like a job?" he asks as he leans back against the couch, looking truly comfortable for the first time since I met him.

"It's... complicated." I really don't want to talk about work so I redirect the conversation. "So this was your grandparents' house?"

If Bennett knows that I'm avoiding work talk, he doesn't let on. "Yeah. My great-great-grandfather built it as a summer home, and my grandparents moved in after they got married."

"Let me guess, your parents didn't want such a big home."

"My mom actually died a couple days after I was born, and my dad wasn't in the picture. My grandparents raised me."

I feel awful now. "I'm sorry about your mom," I say quietly, desperately wishing I could turn back time and just comment on the weather instead.

He shrugs. "I didn't know any different. I had a great childhood, so no complaints."

"I probably would have committed a crime to live in a place like this as a kid. The proximity to nature seems far more ideal than the concrete jungle I grew up in. And this house seems like it would have been a blast to live in. My childhood home was very sterile. Even my bedroom wasn't kid-friendly."

"I couldn't wait to move away." Bennett laughs. "I had big dreams, and not a single one involved this house." If I'm not mistaken he looks a bit sad, so I don't press him for more. I don't want to talk about my job, and he probably doesn't want to talk about his past, despite what he said about having a great childhood. I force myself to yawn. "I've made the guest room up for you. So when you're ready I'll take you up."

"Oh," I say, surprised. I mean, obviously a house this size is going to have more than one bedroom, but for some reason, I expected to be sleeping down here. "You didn't have to do that."

"What, you thought I was going to leave you down here to sleep in the armchair? I don't think you need to add neck and back pain to your list of symptoms. There are five bedrooms in this house, and four of them don't currently have any occupants."

"That's a relief." I beam at him. "It's exhausting being carried around all day."

"I bet." He stands and takes my empty mug, setting it next to his on the coffee table, and then we repeat the transfer movements. "You know," he says, "I think we're getting pretty good at this."

He's not wrong. After several trips with me on his back, we've become like a well-oiled machine. "We'll be a shoo-in if the sport ever makes it to the Olympics."

"Oh, definitely." He smiles back at me, and I return it before he turns away and heads towards the stairs.

I realize very quickly that I do not love this angle. I have visions of Bennett losing his balance, falling backwards, and using my body as a toboggan. I have absolutely nothing to worry about, of course. Bennett is as sure-footed on the stairs with me on his back as he was with dogs weaving around his legs, which is a relief.

The second floor has a wide hallway with multiple doors, some open and some not, and I catch glimpses of rooms as we pass. Bennett walks towards the open door at the front of the house. The floors throughout are wide knotty planks of wood, and they carry on into the room he walks into. He flicks on the light, and I'm shocked to see what looks like a suite. The bed looks like an antique but also inviting, and it sits across from a fireplace. Bennett's home makes me wish I was all about that paperback life, purely because of the cozy visions of curling up with a book this house gives me. He sets me down and steps back.

"The bathroom is the first door on the right." He points to just inside the room. "I've left a spare toothbrush and some toothpaste in there for you. I'll help you to and from tonight, and if you need to get there in the middle of the night, just shout." It's cute that he thinks I'll be doing that. I'd sooner destroy my bladder than wake the man up. I think he's probably going to be dead to the world after today when he adds, "I'm not a very deep sleeper so I'll hear you." That makes two of us.

I manage to complete all my pre-bed tasks without further incident, and when I come out of the bathroom I see that Bennett has laid out some sleep-appropriate clothes for me. He says goodnight and shuts the door on his way out.

Usually when I'm home I sleep naked, but I am not at home so I opt to at least wear the boxers. I set the folded T-shirt on the bedside table and crawl slowly under the covers. I roll onto my right side because it's the only position that doesn't put pressure on my ankle and close my eyes. I'm so tired that I expect sleep to claim me immediately. Instead, I lie here thinking about what I should have done differently today. What am I going to do if one of my contacts calls me with an assignment tomorrow? How long will this ankle keep me down? Do I *want* this injury to keep me away from work for a while? Is this actually a good thing because it gives me time to think about what I want without the guilt of choosing to take the time? Have I disrupted Bennett's life too much? Is he a breakfast person? Is he not, and now he's going to think he needs to make me breakfast? Does he drink coffee? Is he actually as nice as he seems, or is he just trying to make the best out of a shitty situation?

My last thought before I drift off is of the small smile he gave me when he said goodnight, the glance he tossed my way as the door closed. It wasn't the look of someone disappointed by my presence, and that makes me stupidly happy.

EIGHT

I'm lying in bed trying not to think about the beautiful stranger sleeping down the hall. Nothing about today went according to plan. I think back to how I froze when I first saw her. Normally I'd have called the dogs off immediately, but I just stood there staring like a moron. I'm mentally kicking myself for letting her be scared at all and then for probably coming across like an asshole by not saying anything.

I try to ignore the little voice that keeps reminding me that I'm not exactly upset that the road is out. It's not so bad having someone in this huge house with me. But I squash it down because it makes me feel a bit like Heathcliff, and that's certainly not a character I'd like to emulate.

Rolling over, I close my eyes, willing myself to sleep. But I'm afraid this will be the one time I actually don't wake at the quietest disturbance and miss Marley needing help. I'm still not sure she's real. Her lips are what I noticed first, and then when she bit down on the bottom one, that action did something to me. Even thinking about it now, I'm willing myself not to be turned on.

My damn brain keeps taking me back to moments that drew my attention to those lips or the moment I saw her in my clothes.

"You're a fucking creep." I reprimand myself, reaching over to my night table to grab my book. Maybe if I throw myself back into the space opera I'm reading, I'll be able to think of anything else and fall asleep. But the second paragraph has the captain of a ship engaging in some horizontal diplomacy with an alien, and I end up tossing the book to the end of the bed in frustration.

I kick my blankets off and get up, slipping on a pair of sweatpants and a sweatshirt. I go downstairs to track down the baby monitor I use for new dogs and set the receiver outside Marley's door. Then I head out to the barn.

The dogs seem a bit confused as I walk in and turn on the lights. Yogurt, who has never let a little confusion stop him, immediately jumps up and runs over to me. I like to think Yogurt's enthusiasm for all things is his gratefulness to be out of whatever situation he was in before. I sit down on a dog bed and pull the little dog into my lap, looking around at my family. I laugh to myself thinking about how annoyed my grandfather would be at not only the sheer number of dogs, but the fact I refer to them as my family. He'd probably drop dead of a heart attack if he saw what I spent on the memory foam beds for them, even though the cost didn't scratch the surface of my current wealth.

I close my eyes and lean my body back against the wall. Today I've been puked on, painted with snot, and sprinkled with urine water. Usually those things wouldn't be included in a day you'd consider great, but I can't help but label today as just that. The last thing I think, before sleep finally claims me, is "Please, let her love dogs too."

NINE

Barking dogs drag me out of the best sleep I have had in a while. Upon opening my eyes I'm confused for a split second as the room comes into focus. Bennett's house. A little zing of excitement zips through my stomach. The soft light filtering through the white curtains gives the space an almost ethereal look. More barking erupts, and I close my eyes again.

I sit up slowly, cognizant of my ankle as I swing my legs off the side of the mattress. I look at the bathroom door across the room and wonder if I could make it on my own. I probably could if I had already had a cup of coffee, but I feel like trying without it would be a fool's errand. I don't want to injure myself further or, worse, make Bennett feel bad because I made another dumb decision. I hear a door shut downstairs and then the creak of the stairs as Bennett comes up. There's a soft knock on my door, and I call to come in before I remember I'm not wearing a top. I manage to turn and grab the shirt I'd left on the nightstand before he gets an eyeful.

A quick intake of breath has me turning to see Bennett staring at me. He's not looking at me with lust, though. It's something else—horror, crossed with disgust perhaps. Coffee is my preferred way of waking up, but when an attractive man is looking at you like that, well, trust me, it'll wake you up just as fast. As my ego is in the process of shrivelling up and dying, I realize that he's probably got a full view of the scar across my back. On one hand, his expression is now totally understandable, but on the other, he's probably going to want to know what happened, and I'm more of a set-it-and-forget-it type of girl—or in this case, a heal-it-and-don't-deal-with-it lady.

I keep my body turned and slip on the shirt before turning back to Bennett.

"That's how every woman dreams of being looked at in the morning after spending the night at a man's house," I tell him.

He slowly drags his eyes up to my face. "Are you okay?" he asks, that damn expression so plastered on I'll need a chisel and hammer to crack it off.

"I am now," I say, giving him a big smile, hoping he'll catch on that I don't want to talk about it. I notice then that he's holding the clothes I wore yesterday. "Are those my things?"

He looks down and then back up at me. "Yeah. I washed them. I hope that's okay."

"You washed my clothes, and you're concerned I wouldn't be okay with it?"

"Some people are really private," he replies quietly, his face finally relaxing.

I want to ask what about me makes him think I'm "some people," but truthfully I am when it comes to certain things. Just not with clothes. If someone wants to do my laundry, I'm not about to fight them because they might see the size of my pants.

"Well," I say, holding out my hand, "I appreciate it." I'm trying to act cool, but I know I'm smiling like an idiot because this just all seems too perfect. Bennett returns the smile, the corners of his eyes crinkling slightly. He hands me the clothes and turns to leave when I remember I do have an extra pair of underwear in my bag. "Um, Bennett?" He turns back to me. "Would you mind bringing my bag up?"

"Sure, no problem." He nods and leaves the room.

When he comes back, I've put my bra and top on, and I'm sitting in half my clothes and half his. This time the look on his face is far easier to read.

"I'm just going to finish up here, then maybe you can help me back to the bathroom?" I'm trying to be more open about his help and taking some of the responsibility of asking off his shoulders. I keep acting like I've just got a cramp and I'll be good in five minutes, when in reality I may only be somewhat better in five days and I need to accept the literal helping hand.

I'm honestly not sure how I'm going to keep going like this. If I have another day of sitting around and being taken care of, I may actually cry again. So when Bennett is slowly walking back down the stairs, I ask what he's got planned for the day.

"Not too much going on today," he says, in a tone that tells me he would rather have a lot going on. "I'm sure Karl will want me to come down to look at the road at some point. He'll insist I go with him so we can brainstorm useless solutions together. I was also going to take the dogs for a walk and then maybe do some more work on the kitchen. "

"Are you ever worried when you take them out like that?"

"Like what?"

"Without leashes?"

"I was in the beginning. But since I've got the space and typically don't run into anyone, it's easier to walk them off-leash around here."

He walks right into the kitchen and sets me down on a stool.

"Coffee or tea?"

"Oooh, coffee please," I say, rubbing my hands together like a kid on Christmas morning.

"Take anything in it?" he asks, pulling two mugs down from the cupboard.

"Just black is good." When I was younger my coffee was mostly cream and sugar. But in the field, you learn to drink whatever you can get whenever you can get it, and usually that means black coffee. It shocked my system for the first little while, but I eventually grew fond of the stuff.

Bennett puts the mug in front of me and leans on the counter. "Now, for breakfast I usually have cereal, but I've got some eggs and bread from Nancy in the freezer."

"I'm good with cereal."

Bennett pulls out a couple of bowls and a glass bottle of milk. I've suddenly been transported back in time. Who has bottles of milk anymore? My face must be speaking for me. "The Hores have a dairy farm," he explains. "They also have chickens, so I get some basic ingredients from them. Nancy, Mrs. Hore, claims that her tomatoes are so good because her cows shit gold."

"She thinks they shit gold or that their shit's as precious as gold?" I ask as I take my first sip of coffee. It's smooth and strong, and I am a very happy coffee addict at this moment.

"I think she believes it adds value to her garden."

"Well, if she keeps growing tomatoes like the ones that made last night's sauce, she can think whatever she likes."

"Agreed," Bennett declares, putting two boxes of cereal on the island. "What would you prefer?"

He has set out a box of Raisin Bran, which reminds me of my dad, and a box of Cinnamon Toast Crunch, which happens to be my absolute favorite. Part of me thinks I should pick the Raisin Bran to give the impression of someone who is a mature adult, aware of the benefits of fiber, but the other part of me is screaming for the sugary goodness of CTC. I point to the box of Cinnamon Toast Crunch, and Bennett laughs. "Thank god."

"What? You want all the Raisin Bran to yourself?" I ask, one eyebrow raised in question.

"God, no!" he says. "I wanted the Cinnamon Toast Crunch, but I didn't want you to think I had the taste of a child."

"Well, if you have the taste of a child, then so do I, and I say we embrace that. But why do you have a box of Raisin Bran if you don't want it?"

"It was on sale, and I thought, 'That seems like the kind of cereal I should be liking at my age,' so I bought it, and well...it's been sitting in my cupboard unopened for two months."

"Well, maybe you'll rescue a sixty-year-old hiker one day, and they'll be grateful for all that bran."

"That's very true. Better to be prepared than not." He hands me a bowl and the box of cereal, and I pour myself a decent helping. Bennett pours himself double.

After we finish eating, Bennett heads out to take the dogs for their pack walk. I'm back in the armchair with Bennett's laptop so I can check my email. Sure enough, there is an email from one of the agencies I work with semi-regularly.

Marley,

I hope this email finds you well. We are hoping you'd consider going over to the G7 Summit in London next week. We know that it's not your normal assignment, but there's been word that there will be a heavy protester presence, and we want someone accustomed to chaos on the ground to capture it. Simon Newgate is going to be the journalist we send over, and he asked that we reach out to you first.

Please let us know by October 21.

Best,
   Karen Hilcox

I hate covering protests. Mob mentality is not a fun thing to find yourself in the middle of. My worst injuries have come from being caught up in a crowd of people collectively losing their damn minds. I've never been so happy to be injured.

Karen,

Thank you for thinking of me for this assignment. Unfortunately, I will have to decline as I have suffered an injury and will be out of commission for about three weeks. Please pass along my apologies to Simon.

Cheers,
   Marley

In all honesty, I have no idea if I'm going to be better in three weeks. But when I hit send, I'm struck with an immense feeling of relief. I guess that's something. The only time I've declined opportunities in the past was because I already had something in my schedule. I was convinced I'd feel a sense of guilt or failure saying no to this one.

The next email is from Izzy which she sent late last night.

Marley, I'm going to need an update, friend!

Then another one this morning.

*Marley. I will march through those woods and find you myself
if I don't hear back from you by noon.*

The funny thing about Izzy is that she knows that when I'm in the field I may not get back to her for days, and she won't send me progressively more paranoid emails in between contact from me. Yet here I am an hour away from home, and she's losing her mind. The woman listens to way too many true crime podcasts.

*Izzy, I'm going to need you to calm down. I'm okay. Let's act
like I'm on assignment in the wilds of Ontario.*
Love you.
M.

I'm hopping on one foot towards the bookshelf closest to me when I hear the back door open and a woman's voice call, "Bennett, honey, are you here?"

TEN

I freeze where I am and look over just in time to see a petite blonde woman appear at the door.

"Oh!" She lays a hand on her chest and laughs. "I'm sorry, I didn't know Bennett had company." The way she says it makes me think she's not mad to find me here, so that's good. I'm not exactly in fighting shape at the moment. Not that I'm a fighter.

She walks further into the room, and I get a better look at her. She sounds younger than she looks, and I'd peg her age somewhere in her fifties. She's wearing leggings with a matching jacket, and she's got a pair of those thick thermal socks on. She's not Bennett's mom, clearly, but maybe an aunt?

"Um," I say, frozen where I stand, balancing as gracefully as I can on one foot. "Bennett's out with the dogs."

"Really," she says, sitting in the chair I'd recently vacated. "He's usually back by this hour."

"He got a late start," I say, sitting down at the end of the couch, wishing curiosity hadn't gotten the better of me.

She gives me a knowing look, but I'm not sure what it is that I'm supposed to be knowing, so I just smile back. Then it dawns on me that she thinks I'm the reason for his late start. This is technically true, but she is implying that the start was something a hell of a lot less innocent than coffee and breakfast.

Before I can set the record straight, I hear the door open again quickly followed by Yogurt racing into the room and right up to the woman.

"Yogurt!" she exclaims, scooping him up. "How's my special guy?"

"Hey, Nancy," Bennett greets her. "I wasn't expecting you today." She stands to hug him.

"Well, Karl wanted to check out the damage, and I wanted to get some fresh air so I decided to join him" She tilts her head subtly towards me, her eyes wide. She's as good as I am when it comes to fishing for information, it seems.

"Um," Bennett stutters as he seems to catch on, "Nancy, this is Marley. Marley, Nancy."

Nancy crosses the room with her hand outstretched. "It's lovely to meet you, Marley."

I shake her hand. "Same." And then her name registers. "You're Nancy!" I say, maybe a bit too enthusiastically, and also in a way that makes it sound like I've got the memory of a gold-fish. "I mean, obviously, Bennett just said that, but you're *the* Nancy, the sauce Nancy."

"Wow, I've never felt famous before!" she says, looking extremely flattered.

"Marley and I had your sauce last night," Bennett explains. And now she knows I spent the night. Although the road is out so it's not as if I popped in this morning.

"Oh, last night, eh?" It feels like my face has been set on fire.

I open my mouth to clarify, but Bennett beats me to it. Or at least that's what I think he's doing until he says, "Yeah, we had it over some of that fancy penne you gave me. Maybe my favorite batch yet. Marley looked like she wanted to dive face-first into it." Okay, so that intention, as fleeting as it was, did come across. Good to know.

"He's not wrong." I laugh nervously.

"Well, I did have ulterior motives for joining Karl, but I guess it's silly now," Nancy says, sitting back down and waiting for Bennett to sit before continuing. When he does, it's right next to me. He looks at me quickly, lips thin and eyes wide. If I were a betting girl, I'd say he was communicating *Help me.*

"Sophie is home from school for the week, and I thought maybe you'd want to join us for dinner. But I can see you're otherwise engaged." She peers over at me and smiles. And while she could mean it in a passive-aggressive way, she seems genuinely happy that he's "otherwise engaged."

I'm thinking I should let Bennett know he's absolutely welcome to join them for dinner, but once again he responds before I can even form words. "Thanks for considering me but" —he looks at me with a lovely smile—"I've got my hands full at the minute."

I'm staring at Bennett, who is smiling at me in a way that has me hearing love ballads and wedding bells. I'm losing the battle over the butterflies in my stomach until Nancy pulls me out of my lusty haze. When I look over at her, regrettably breaking eye contact with Bennett, she's pointing at my ankle. "When did you do that?"

"Yesterday morning. Head was in the clouds, and oops."

"Mm-hmm, I bet it was," Nancy replies, side-eyeing Bennett.

I could correct her and say that spraining my ankle had nothing to do with looking up at Bennett or daydreaming about Bennett or anything to do with Bennett at all, but I play along because it's almost too easy to imagine. "Yeah, well, you know how it is." Without even thinking, I drop my hand to rest possessively on his thigh. I feel him tense for a split second before relaxing under my touch. When I look over at him, he looks pleased as punch, and while I don't actually know what pleased punch looks like, I'd say it's whatever the look he has on his face right now.

For the third time in about ten minutes, I hear a door open and someone calling out. This time it's a deep booming voice looking for Nancy. A middle-aged man wearing overalls, a flannel shirt, and a well-worn baseball cap joins us. This must be Karl. When he registers my presence, he looks around quickly as though he may have walked into the wrong house.

"Bennett," he says dramatically, "that road is a fucking mess. And you just know the town is going to take their sweet time doing something about it. This happened eight years ago, and it was two weeks until we could get back to the road. Not sure what our taxes go to these days, but it sure as hell isn't road maintenance. Let's hope we never need any real help, am I right?" Karl shakes his head as he approaches me with a wide smile. "Sorry for my little outburst," he says, sticking his hand out to me. "Karl Hore." I see his mouth start to open again, and I think I know what's coming next so I jump in.

"Oh, I've heard if I need a hoe, you're the man to go to."

He bursts out laughing and looks back at Bennett, who for a split second looks like he wants to throw up. But the look is gone as quickly as it appeared.

"I like this one," he says before looking over at Nancy. "So I guess it's just going to be the three of us for dinner?" Bennett's hand is sliding under mine, palm up, and I automatically curl my fingers around his.

"So it would appear." Nancy's smile grows when she glances down at where our hands are joined. "Oh," she gasps suddenly, "do we still have those crutches from when Sophie tore her ACL? Marley sprained her ankle while she and Bennett were out for a hike yesterday."

Karl thinks for a minute. "I'm not sure, I can look when we get home. Speaking of which, shall we, my dear?"

Nancy stands and starts following Karl out of the room, before turning back to me. "It was so nice to meet you, Marley. I hope we see each other again."

"Absolutely!" I give them a little wave before they leave. Bennett gradually releases my hand so he can walk them out, and I immediately miss the feel of his palm on mine.

"So, what was that about?" I ask when he comes back.

Bennett looks at me like I spoke another language. "What was that about?"

"The whole act? Why didn't you tell Nancy why I'm here?"

He sits and pulls Yogurt into his lap, getting him settled before he responds. "The Hores are the best, don't get me wrong. I'm so lucky to have them as neighbors, and luckier that they're three kilometres away. Nancy seems to have taken it upon herself to find me someone."

"Find you someone? As in she believes you're"—I put on my best English accent—"in want of a wife?"

"How very Austen of you."

"Says the guy with the first name Bennett."

"Well, my mother was obsessed with Jane Austen so that checks out. Although she insisted on adding an extra t"

"Aw. You're lucky she didn't go too obscure with it, or worse, too on the nose."

"Yeah, she definitely could have gone the more traditional route with John or Darcy."

"Oh my god." I throw my head back and laugh. "There are so many Johns."

"As a John, I would have fit in splendidly with the Hores, though."

I point at him, trying to get my giggles under control. "That's still no excuse for letting her think there was anything going on besides an excessive number of piggybacks between adults."

"Had I known they were going to pop by, I would have prepared you, maybe even asked your permission to play along. She thinks I'm too dedicated to the dogs to have a social life, so whenever her daughter, who is very nice, comes home from school, she invites me to dinner or sends her over with ten jars of sauce or more milk than any one man can consume."

"And when you say school..." I trail off.

"She's doing her master's."

"Oh, okay, so she's an adult at least."

"Technically, but I'm not going to be guilted into dating a twenty-three-year-old." I sit back and study him. When he's had enough, he lets out an exasperated sounding "What?"

I roll my lips and squint at him. "Nothing." I'm not exactly annoyed with him even though I feel like I should be, which confuses me if anything. I'm not sure I could ever see myself being annoyed with this man, which is fucking irritating; I can only imagine the things I'd let this man get away with if given the opportunity. So it's probably a good thing I don't plan on giving him any.

ELEVEN

After Nancy and Karl head home, and after I assure Marley I'm not some dirty old man out trawling for teenage girls, I excuse myself to go out to my office in the barn. I've got several emails to answer and a couple of phone calls from counterparts at other rescues in the province. After addressing a few of them, I sit back in my chair and close my eyes. I can still feel where Marley's hand landed on my thigh, her hand in mine for far too short of a time. I'd have loved the Hores to stay a bit longer if it meant more of that. I'm annoyed as I feel a headache coming on, and it erases all the lingering pleasurable sensations. I tip my head back and close my eyes, letting myself sink into the fog that's settled in my head.

Marley is sitting at the island drinking her coffee and laughing at something I said. Her laugh makes me happy, and when she stops she asks why I'm smiling like that at her.

"Like what?"

"Like you want to kiss me, Benny." She's grinning widely at me now, eyes challenging me to give in to what feels right.

"Do you want me to kiss you, Marley?" I ask, leaning back against the counter, setting my own challenge for her.

She bites that perfect bottom lip and stands slowly. I let my eyes drift down her body, nearly laughing at myself for admiring her so blatantly as she walks towards me, all smiles and sparkly brown eyes. The anticipation is visceral. I can already feel her skin beneath my fingertips, her breath against my skin, and her legs wrapped around me. I don't know how I'm holding myself in place as she makes her way around the kitchen island. I don't know why she's not already in my arms, and still I stay where I am and let her choose what's next. I'm a gentleman, after all.

When she's finally standing in front of me, I gaze down at her, taking in the little details of her face. Her eyes are flecked with gold, her high cheekbones are more pronounced when she smiles, and she has a tiny scar below her left eyebrow. I want to know how she got it, but that's a question for another time. She draws my attention to her mouth again as her tongue sneaks out to wet her lips. I'm immediately hit with a vision of her on her knees, that tongue on my body.

She's so close but hasn't touched me yet. I'm convinced when she does I'm going to lose every ounce of control I have. I'm wondering how I managed to find the perfect woman for me lost in the woods when Marley's attention is pulled from me and down to the floor where Yogurt sits whining.

"Aw. What's wrong, Milkdud?" Marley asks, squatting down to Yogurt's level.

"Yogurt," I remind her.

She looks up at me, confused. "What?"

"His name is Yogurt."

"That's what I said. Milkdud." She shakes her head at me like I'm the one getting it wrong.

"You keep saying Milkdud," I say.

She looks annoyed now. "No, I don't. Why would I say that?"

"I don't know." I shrug.

"It's not funny, Bennett." She's mad now, and I'm lost. In one swift movement, she's picked Yogurt up and is walking out the door. I'm left standing there, watching as the kitchen door slams. When I go after her she's gone, and Yogurt is sitting on the porch whining again.

"Yogurt!" I scold, looking around to see where Marley went. Then my conscience seems to catch up, and I realize Marley was walking around on two perfectly unsprained ankles. Yogurt whines again, and that's when I snap forward in my chair and realize Yogurt is indeed whining, but I've been dreaming.

I rub my hands over my face and groan. I've never been one to look for the deeper meaning of a dream, but as I lean down to pick Yogurt up, I wonder what the fuck that was all about.

"You've been alone for too long, you dumbass," I scold myself, trying to remember the last time I've gotten laid or, hell, even just flirted with someone. Too fucking long. I turn off my computer and head up to the house.

I stop halfway there. How the hell am I going to walk into the house and look at Marley without seeing the look dream-Marley had just given me? It almost feels like I've violated her trust in some way. Or maybe it's my subconscious trying to get me to act for a change.

TWELVE

"I hope you're okay with the canned stuff," Bennett says, not making eye contact with me as he sets two bowls of soup on the counter. He's been a bit off since he came back in from whatever he'd been doing outside.

Maybe having a stranger in his house is hitting a bit different post-visit from the neighbors. Trying to break the tension that has seeped into the air I decided to provide him with a bit of a work anecdote. "I once spent an entire week eating dry bags of instant noodles because that was all that there was. This is a gourmet meal compared to that."

"To be fair, that seems like a very low bar. Also, I want to hear more about your work," he says as he pulls down a sleeve of crackers from a cupboard.

Well, that backfired. I'm not ready to share more just yet, so I turn the question back around. "Maybe later. What I do is best discussed long after you've digested a meal. But tell me what you do all day. I mean, clearly you don't spend the entire day on a long walk. And you seem like the type of guy who would have this kitchen done if you didn't have twenty-one dogs occupying your time."

"Most days I'm running around getting stuff, taking a dog to the vet, picking up a new rescue, or organising a foster home for a dog that may need help but isn't necessarily the right fit for here."

"Does that happen often?"

"The external foster?" he asks, finally looking at me. I nod. "Not too frequently, fortunately. There's a rescue based a bit further south that brings loads of dogs up from the US. They stack crates in the back of a truck, and the dogs shit and piss on each other through the trip. Dogs that would probably have been lovely go through that and come out a bit traumatized."

"Who wouldn't be," I mutter, as the cracker I've just taken a bite of turns to ash on my tongue. Maybe this conversation should have been had later too.

"Well, I get a lot of dogs because of that charity. People call and say, this dog seemed okay but now it's guarding its toys or food and has snapped at their kid and they don't have the patience to work with the animal." He takes an angry bite of a cracker, and for maybe the first time since I met him, I'm glad to be nowhere near his mouth. "There's no structure to vet people or dogs. They open the doors and ring the dinner bell." I must look horrified because he quickly amends, "The proverbial dinner bell. I don't think anyone is eating the dogs."

"So," I think out loud, "in theory, someone could be walking by a parking lot and see this van or truck or whatever, and just spur-of-the-moment decide they want a dog?"

Bennett nods.

"And that's allowed?"

"Yep," he says around a mouthful of soup.

"What are the parameters for bringing these dogs here?"

"Well, they need to be vaccinated. You can't bring an

animal across the border without a rabies vaccine. They have to be in relatively good health. Which I'm sure on the surface many of the dogs appear to be. There are also laws about humane transport, but it would seem that I have very different criteria for what humane entails."

"It sounds like it would be emotionally taxing work."

"Says the conflict photographer."

I don't want to tell him that it's not anymore because then I'll have to explain further and I'm not in the mood to talk about it. I'm rarely in the mood to talk about my job these days. Instead we just slowly eat our food like some weird mukbang foreplay. If I'm not mistaken, his eyes occasionally flit to my lips, and when I lick them, I see his Adam's apple bob. When his eyes meet mine again, I'm almost grateful my range of motion is limited so I don't do anything stupid.

Honestly, if I was leaving in an hour, I would consider perhaps making some kind of move. But the thought of doing that and then being rejected sounds worse than throwing up on myself again.

Yogurt, being the little angel he is, chooses that moment to start pawing at my left foot, drawing our attention away from one another.

"Yogurt, down!" Bennett snaps his fingers. Yogurt barely looks at him and keeps stretching up towards my seat.

"He can sit on my lap if he wants," I say, pushing my nearly empty bowl away.

Bennett looks torn between doing the right thing, which is likely leaving Yogurt on the floor, or giving in to the little guy. In the end, he gives in. They don't call them puppy-dog eyes for nothing.

"What's his story?" I ask, scratching behind both of his ears and laughing as his eyes begin to cross.

"He was found in a Yoplait box with his siblings on the side of a highway."

I immediately stop scratching as my head snaps up to make sure he's not joking. "Seriously?" I know people suck, but I'm more accustomed to people sucking towards other people. I tend to forget how people can be cruel to all living things.

"Unfortunately. Thankfully they were all too small to jump out of the box, and someone stopped to check it out before anyone hit them."

"That's so fucked up," I say, looking back down at Yogurt.

"The other puppies were all healthy and found homes really quickly, but this guy"—he reaches out to pet him, his fingers brushing mine—"he wasn't quite, well, let's go with ready. The vet thinks he may have been deprived of oxygen at birth and so his brain didn't develop properly. But he fits in perfectly here, and he's probably the most loving dog I've ever had. So, in that case, I'd say his brain developed perfectly."

If I was physically capable of melting, I would be a puddle on the floor. "He's lucky to have you," I say softly, looking from our hands to his face. Every time I look at Bennett, I notice something different. This time I'm drawn to a small patch of his beard that is slightly lighter than the rest.

This time Bennett breaks eye contact first and stands to clear our dishes.

"Do you want to come out for a bit? I was going to throw some sticks around. I could set you up outside the fence so you're protected." He looks at me, his face full of hope.

I nod enthusiastically because that sounds wonderful.

Bennett runs upstairs and grabs a sweatshirt for me, and then I'm up on his back and leaving the house for the first time in what feels like forever.

It's the ideal fall day; the air is crisp and the sun is out, providing just enough warmth that the sweatshirt is perfect.

There is already a patio chair sitting next to the gate, as though he had been planning this since this morning. The thought has me smiling into his shoulder. If I'm not mistaken, his hands are a bit more grippy than before, his thumbs both gently sliding back and forth along my thigh. Goosebumps erupt across my flesh as my brain zones in on the movement. It doesn't mean anything, I tell myself. It's like when I rock a shopping cart back and forth while I'm waiting in line as if to calm an invisible baby. It's. Not. Intentional.

Yogurt, who followed us out to the field, jumps excitedly at the gate. After carefully setting me in the chair, Bennett scoops him up and pushes his way through the opening. I laugh as the dogs go absolutely apeshit, jumping and licking at the man. He looks back at me and smiles.

Before long the dogs are chasing after sticks and each other. I'm not sure how Bennett is able to keep anything straight. It's absolute chaos in there. I laugh at myself thinking that twenty-one dogs are too chaotic to keep track of. What I do requires me to keep track of a lot too, but it's different. There is a huge distinction between happy chaos and chaos brought on by conflict. I think maybe I could rediscover my passion again if I got to be surrounded by Bennett's brand of chaos. Maybe an actual life away from work wouldn't be the worst thing. Bennett is laughing and running around with his pack, his passion and joy for this life on full display, and I can remember a time when I felt that too. I certainly wasn't running around laughing, but I remember how the passion drove me through the hard days. Now those days blur together as I move from one conflict to the next. When I started my career, I never saw a conflict within myself, and every day that passes I wonder if the passion will triumph over the emotionless shell I've become.

THIRTEEN

I don't know how long I've been watching Bennett and the dogs but I've been so distracted that I didn't notice the sun dip behind the clouds until huge drops of rain began to fall. Bennett looks from me to the dogs, and I yell for him to take care of them first. A little rain never hurt anyone. He nods and whistles, and I watch as he leads the pack down a narrow, fenced pathway towards a barn that looks brand-new. My concern about the dogs having to sleep in some dilapidated structure now seems unfounded. But of course there's no way in hell that Bennett would kick the dogs out of a nice warm house if they didn't have somewhere equally lovely to go.

By the time I see him jogging back towards me, a movement my brain seems to transmit in slow motion, the sky has opened and we are caught in a full-on downpour. I stand as quickly as I can so that I can just jump on his back without him having to squat. I'm trying to be as efficient as possible, and perhaps a little ignorant about the physics of how exactly I'll manage such a move. He doesn't squat, though; instead he grabs me in mid-stride, and I instinctively wrap myself around him. When he's almost at the porch stairs, disaster strikes. I feel him slip, swear, and then feel gravity pull us towards the earth. Before I'm turned into a human crash pad though, Bennett flips us around so that he's the crash pad. The sound we make hitting the ground is a humph from him and some kind of weird squeak-snort from me.

We both seem a bit dazed as we look at each other. His eyes are wide, and he's searching my face, his hands coming up to cradle my head.

"Are you hurt?" he asks in an echo of our first meeting, except this time he seems on the verge of panicking.

I shake my head emphatically. "I'm okay, you?" I sound like I'm the one that was running. Adrenaline sends my heart rate into dangerous territory, and I love it.

"Yeah, yes, I'm good. Shit." He sets his head back on the ground and closes his eyes, his hands still at my neck and in my hair. I watch as the rain lands on his face, catching in his beard and eyelashes, and I lean forward a touch so that my head is blocking it. The small movement has him opening his eyes, and now we're staring at each other as our bodies remain in a very compromising position.

"Hi," I whisper.

"Hi," he whispers back.

If we were together, this would be romantic as hell. If I'm being completely honest with myself, I'm not sure our relationship status makes it less so. I watch him swallow, and something passes across his face. The urge to lean down and press my lips to his is almost overwhelming, and it takes a monumental amount of effort to not give in to it.

I swipe my hand across his forehead and smile. "I'm not sure I can be blamed for today's wardrobe change."

He bursts out laughing, his chest bouncing beneath mine, and it's the very best feeling in the world.

Eventually, Bennett slides himself back from me so that I can keep my right knee on the ground with my ankle lifted. I imagine I look like someone who has only heard the names of yoga positions but has never seen them. Once he's up, he crouches in front of me and offers his hands. Together we manage to get me up on one leg, and while I'm prepared to hop like that to the door, Bennett has other ideas. In one swift motion, he's got me in a bridal carry and up the stairs and through the kitchen door before I can even process it.

He doesn't say a word as he walks up the stairs towards my bedroom, or the guest bedroom, rather. He takes us right into the bathroom and sets me down slowly, making sure I'm steady before pivoting to turn on the tub's faucet.

"I'll grab you another towel," he says, then he's gone before I can reply.

I stare at the tub as the room begins to fill with steam, replaying the past few minutes. Bennett comes back carrying a huge fluffy towel, and he slips it onto the rack beside the tub. Then he's bending in front of me and pulling my leg toward him to remove my sock and the tensor bandage. While he's concentrating on the task, I notice a splatter of mud across the tip of his ear, and I slide my thumb over it, wiping it clean. He stills immediately and leans into my touch a bit more until his forehead is resting against my thigh. We stay like that for a moment, my finger gliding over his ear, his head against my body. After he releases a shaky breath, he stands and carefully guides me to sit on the toilet seat so he can remove my shoe and sock.

"I can't believe I'm letting someone touch my feet," I say quietly, half to myself.

He looks up, the intensity in his eyes catches me off guard, and fuck me, I'm starting to question if I'm safe around this man anymore. When he blinks, his expression clears. But that look will forever be seared into my brain.

"Your ankle is still pretty swollen," he says, standing, his eyes glued to my ankle.

"Mm-hmm." I look down at it briefly.

He winces. "You're not supposed to apply heat to a sprain if it's still swollen."

I'm not sure what his point is here, I'm not not-bathing. "So I'll hang my right ankle over the side. Not the end of the world." He still looks worried so I lay out my plan. "I'll sit on the side of the tub to undress, then using my very strong arms, I'll gently lower myself into the water. If my foot goes in, it goes in. But I'll do my best to avoid leaving it submerged." He still looks ridiculously concerned. If he can't handle this minor thing, he definitely wouldn't be able to handle what I do for my day job. I raise my hand to cup his cheek, drawing his attention back to my face. "I'll be okay, Benny."

His eyes snap to mine, and he scowls. "I fucking hate that name." I'd believe him more if his tone matched the scowl on his face, and he hadn't leaned ever so slightly into my touch.

The fact that he's still holding my hand while my other one rests on his face is no doubt adding to the whole vibe of the moment. I look down at where our hands are joined, and when I look back up, he's tracking my lower lip as it disappears behind my teeth with that predatory gleam back in his eyes. And I kind of love that this man, who has asked for permission to touch me since we met, seems to be fighting with himself. Or it's all in my head and I'm projecting because I really want him to touch me. I release my lip, drop my hand, and nod towards the tub. "Help me over, then you're free to go."

"Yeah, okay," he says as he helps me balance so I can hop over.

When my ass hits the side of the tub, I pull my hands from

his grip and steady myself on it. "Go!" I laugh as he looks like leaving me is painful. "You're covered in mud." He looks down and seems confused for a minute before remembering that he fell on his back.

"I'll be fast so shout if you need anything," he says, backing out of the room, those hazel eyes glued to me until the door shuts. I stare at the door for a bit longer before looking into the tub.

Okay, so my arms aren't nearly as strong as I think, and I am far less graceful getting into the tub than I had imagined. The saving grace is that I'm the only one who needs to know just how much I invoked all the elegance of a seal on dry land.

The water is so warm, and keeping my lower right leg over the side is a special kind of hell. In my head, letting my sore ankle soak makes the most sense. But medically I am aware that it doesn't, and the last thing I want to do is disappoint Bennett. Eventually, I reach the limits of what a tub can do for me so I pull the drain and gingerly stand before turning on the shower. There is a bottle of shampoo sitting on the corner of the tub, a brand I don't recognize but I'm not exactly in a position to be picky. The shampoo is clear, and the only scent I can think to label it as is "clean," yet despite the barely-there odour, I know this is what Bennett uses. I've smelled the man more than I've smelled another human being, and I'd have an impossible time waxing poetic about how he smells. He doesn't smell like sandalwood or mahogany, even though I wouldn't have a fucking clue what mahogany smells like. Bennett smells like a man who has good hygiene and isn't concerned with turning himself into a human candle. I wash my hair as quickly as possible. I hear a soft knock as soon as I turn the shower off and do the reverse of how I got into the tub. I tell myself that I did a better job getting out than in—certainly less seal-like, anyway.

"I'm here when you're decent," Bennett says through the door.

I dry myself off with the smaller of the two towels and then wind it around my hair. I use the new towel he brought to wrap around my body. I do a quick look at myself to make sure nothing is peeking out anywhere and let him know I'm good to go.

When he opens the door, his hair is damp and sticking up in all directions. I smile at that, which seems to make him self-conscious because he rakes both his hands through it. It takes everything in me not to reach up and run my own hands through the wild strands.

"How'd it go?" he asks, offering me his arm. I'm somewhat surprised by the disappointment that blooms in my stomach. I'd expected him to pull me into his arms and carry me to the bed.

I've never been someone who wanted romance. Not witnessing it growing up can probably be blamed for the lack of interest. But right here, right now I want to lean into this new desire and see what all the fuss is about.

"Well," I say, looking up at him, "I don't want to brag, but I nailed it."

"I had a feeling you would."

"Really? You looked about ready to call in reinforcements when I told you how I planned to get into the tub."

"My face doesn't always convey what I'm thinking."

"That's good to know. But just so you know, I'm the opposite. My face usually tells everyone exactly what's on my mind."

"Noted," he says, briefly studying my face before leading me to the bed.

As I'm turning to sit down I feel his touch on my back, just above the towel.

"What happened here?" he asks quietly, his fingers skimming across the twelve-inch dimpled scar that covers most of my upper back. It takes a lot of effort not to give in to the pleasant chill that spreads through me. But just for a moment, I lean back into his touch.

I take a deep breath. "I was with a team of journalists covering some protests in Paris. Things were going okay—I mean, 'okay' is relative, I guess. But it was just a lot of yelling and flag-waving until it wasn't." I stop to collect myself because his touch is distracting me, and what I want more than anything is more of it. "An anarchist group showed up, and things went from being non-violent to violent in about two seconds. They had Molotovs, except they weren't using just alcohol. Someone in their group thought it would be a good idea to mix whatever they could find for maximum impact. You know, cause as much damage as possible, and really get their message across. One hit a van I was standing next to, and the liquid splashed across my back. It ate through my clothes and then my flesh." I feel him move closer. His body heat reaches me before he does, and I continue as his arms wrap around my shoulders, my hands automatically rising to rest on his forearms. "It's probably worse —no, I know it's worse because I didn't go get help right away. I was so caught up in everything I barely noticed it. I was running on pure adrenaline at that point, and the only reason I stopped when I did was because the police fired tear gas into the crowd. When breathing became hard, that's when I noticed the burning."

Bennett is silent behind me. The only sound is our soft breathing, and I relish the stillness of it.

"I'm sorry you had to experience that to do your job," he finally says. I think he's going to let go of me and step away, but he stays exactly where he is.

I shrug, and because I've lost all sense of propriety, I dip my head and run my nose along his forearm. I can practically feel the goosebumps form under my touch. "Without the chaos, my job isn't all that, I don't know, meaningful. And without it I'm not sure I'd have much of a job. It feels wrong to need something like that in order to get a paycheque."

"When are you going to tell me about it?"

"Why do you want to know about it so badly?" I ask, feeling at once defensive that he's prodding and grateful that he cares.

"I want to know why something you were once passionate about is now just a job. I want to know how that happens in your world."

I drop my arms and turn towards him, his arms still around me so we are chest to chest. "I'm not sure you'll like me much after I tell you." And it's true. I don't even like myself much these days because when I evaluate who I've become I don't see much of the person I was.

"Have you killed someone?" he asks, his eyebrows raised.

I shake my head.

"Stolen?"

"No."

"Knowingly taken advantage of someone's generosity?"

"I don't think so."

Now it's his turn to shrug. He releases me and steps back. His hands run down my bare arms, leaving chills in their wake. "Then I don't know how I wouldn't like you much after." He gestures to the bed. "I brought you some fresh clothes. Holler when you're ready."

I watch him leave, and it's not until I hear him on the stairs that I suck in the oxygen I'd apparently been depriving myself of. As I get dressed, I wish I had his confidence that he'll feel the same about me after I've opened up, after I reveal the scars that aren't so visible.

FOURTEEN

I can still feel Marley's touch and breath on my arm as I putter around the living room fluffing pillows that the dogs will only flatten in a matter of hours. I'm being a bit more aggressive with this task than required, but I'm trying to take my anger out on something. The thought of Marley being in the midst of such turmoil is doing unexpected things to me. I was worried about her getting into the bathtub on her own, for Christ's sake. No chance of being blown up, shot, or hit with a fucking Molotov cocktail. Holy shit. I drop onto the couch and let my head fall into my hands. I feel a brief sense of relief that Marley will be long gone before she goes back to work, and I'll forget all about her by then. I don't even understand why I'm feeling so intense about her safety so soon after meeting her. This cannot be normal. I need to get out more.

Thankfully, when she calls to tell me she's ready to come down, I've calmed a bit. However, judging by the joy I feel knowing I'm about to touch her again, I don't know how easy forgetting about her is going to be. She'll forget about me easily enough; her days are a bit more intense than mine are. She's probably bored to tears here. A decade ago, I would never have believed someone if they had told me my life would be spent in the middle of the woods, running a dog rescue all alone. I climb the stairs back up to the first person to share this house with me since I moved back. I've honestly been fine with being alone. I got to do things I wanted, not do things that others wanted me to do. But having Marley here makes me wonder if I can live for myself *and* share my life with someone else.

Twenty minutes later we're lounging on the porch swing. Marley is sitting with her ankles in my lap, head tipped against the high back, eyes closed. I've got my hand resting on her shin, my thumb drawing invisible patterns across it. This could be every afternoon, I think as my other hand holds a book I'm pretending to read open. I'm hyper-aware of her leg beneath my hand, and my eyes keep wandering back to her face.

"Good book?" she asks, one eyebrow quirked when she catches me looking over at her for the tenth time.

I clear my throat and feel my face heat. "It's fine."

"What's it about?"

"Um..." I flip the book over to remind myself. "Aliens and stuff."

"Aliens and stuff?" Her eyebrow arches impossibly higher as she watches me. "Sounds riveting."

"Yeah, well..." I'm very obviously flustered. "Do you want to watch a movie?" I ask, lifting her legs so I can escape. She's smiling at me, and it reminds me a bit of how she was looking at me in my dream. *"Do you want me to kiss you, Marley?"* I think about how she looked down at me in the bathroom. It was a look that would have had me dropping to my knees before her if I hadn't already been on them. Then the way she felt in my arms. The way I'd catch her looking at me and how she never looked away guiltily.

"What movie?" she asks, breaking me out of my reverie.

I shrug. "You pick," I say, bending to lift her even though we both know she can hop on one leg.

Right before we reach the door, both her hands cup my face, stopping me in my tracks. She's looking at me with a bit of wonderment, and I can't think of why.

"What?"

"I am just wondering what would have happened if it had been Nancy who found me."

The thought makes me laugh. "She would have found a way to build a sled and feed you on the trip back."

"Hmm. The trip *would* have been made better with a snack." She laughs, and I join in because it keeps me from doing something inappropriate, like kissing her.

This is all temporary, I remind myself. Her life is not here, no matter how much I wish it were.

FIFTEEN

Bennett asks if I'm interested in popcorn once he's got me set up in the armchair with another ice pack. While he goes off to do that I'm charged with finding something on Netflix. I don't know why, but I'm somewhat surprised he has a streaming service. His only stipulation is that he doesn't love movies with explosions or gun violence, oh and no animals dying, but other than that he's up for anything. I see enough violence in my day-to-day life so I tend to stick with comedies anyway.

I settle on *Dumb and Dumber*, a surefire way to lighten the mood after all the heated looks and our chat upstairs. When Bennett comes back into the living room with a bowl of popcorn and a couple of glasses of water, he informs me that he has never seen the movie.

"How?" I ask, in shock.

"I told you, I don't watch a lot of stuff."

"Yeah, but it's *Dumb and Dumber*. Jim Carrey. Jeff Daniels. 'We got no food! We got no jobs! Our pets' heads are fallin' off!'" I break off as I gesture wildly towards the TV as if that will remind him that he has in fact seen this classic and he just forgot.

Recognition dawns on his face and I think my memory retrieval method actually worked, but then his face goes blank as he looks at me dead in the eye. "Nope, I've never seen it. But," he says as he pops a few kernels into his mouth, "I'm very excited now. All the flailing really sold it."

"You better like it." I wag a finger at him. "Or we can't be friends anymore."

"Friends, eh?"

The things I want to do with this man are not things I do with friends.

To my extreme relief, Bennett laughs a lot, and I end up spending half the movie watching his reactions rather than the screen. I've seen it so many times I can quote it verbatim, but you only get to witness someone watching one of your favourites for the first time once. I want to bottle his laughter and take it with me when I leave. I think of how it would brighten up just about any day when I'm in the thick of it.

I end up thinking about work again and how after the movie is done Bennett is probably going to make dinner and then ask me for a day in my life. I don't realize I'm staring at the empty fireplace until I feel a nudge. I look up at the screen to see Harry, knees high in the air, a pained expression on his face, frozen in mid-shit.

"Where'd you go?" Bennett asks.

"Nowhere," I reply, forcing myself to smile at him.

He can see I'm lying.

What I like about this temporary relationship is that I get a bit of a break from myself and from people who know me. I've really enjoyed being the injured hiker rather than someone who can't feel normal things anymore. Hell, I enjoyed crying yesterday. No, I *loved* crying yesterday, and I'm pretty sure it had more to do with feeling something than being held by Bennett. Although being held by Bennett *was* pretty great. Still, the faster he figures me out, the harder it is for me to stay present in this happy little bubble.

Bennett is still looking at me. "Really, Bennett, I'm fine. This part is great," I say, pointing at the TV and avoiding eye contact with him.

He makes a sound and then hits play, finally looking away from me.

Knowing his eyes aren't on me anymore lets me relax a bit, and I do my best to get back into the movie. But for the rest of the movie, neither of us laughs.

My stomach rumbles as the credits start to roll, and Bennett lets me know he'll go get dinner started. He hands his laptop back to me so I can let Izzy know that I'm still alive.

As I expected, I find a new email from Izzy and, perhaps a bit more surprising, one from my other friend Nellie.

> *Marley, you better still be alive because if you're not and you didn't tell me, I will end you.*

That is all Izzy said. So I do the bare minimum and send her a thumbs-up.

Nellie's is calm, cool, and collected in comparison.

> *Mar,*
>
> *Izzy has informed me that you were gravely injured on some hiking trail in the middle of nowhere, but not to worry because you were rescued by a knight in athletic shorts riding a wave of many dogs. Don't forget to ask him what his favorite dinosaur is.*
>
> *Please make haste and inform me of your well-being.*
> *Your most faithful friend,*

Nell

One of the first things Nellie ever asked me was what my favorite dinosaur was, and I've come to learn that it's what she asks everyone when she first meets them. If they have one, she's willing to put the work into getting to know them. If they don't have one, the chances of her spending time with the person are low.

Nell,

Izzy has once again exaggerated. My knight was in joggers and a long-sleeved T-shirt. I assure you his legs were fully covered. However, he was riding a wave of a whopping 21 dogs.

I'm ok, just a bit sore. Bennett says he expects to have a better idea of when the road will be fixed by tomorrow, and when I know I'll let you and Iz know too. For now, I'm enjoying life being waited on hand and foot and carried absolutely everywhere.

Love ya,

Mar

There are three more emails about work, one from Simon and two from newspaper editors. I open Simon's first and brace myself for a telling-off.

Cunningham, goddammit it. I cannot believe you're faking an injury to get out of going to this damn summit with me. And the whole ignoring my texts on top of it is a new low. If you actually are injured, however, please take care so you are ready for the next assignment. Karen is sending George with me to London, and I don't want this to become a normal thing. Also, Anthony is looking at several photography

programs for college or university. He wants your recommen-
dations.

Take care,
    Simon Newgate
    Staff Reporter – AP

Other than the fact he's more to me than simply a colleague, Simon is hands down one of my favorite journalists to work with. He's old-school and will do just about anything, within the confines of ethics, to get a story. It's the reason we work well together; fear doesn't play a role in how we operate. He also, clearly, hates covering protests and anything to do with politicians. He'd rather be bringing people stories that they need to be aware of.

Newsgate,
    I'm sorry you're having to go into the entitled trenches without me. I bet Anthony is very happy you'll only be away for a short time, though. Give that kid a hug for me. I'll send him a list of schools he should strongly consider.
    As far as my injury I'm hoping to be back up and running, in all the ways, before too long. Hey, maybe Karen will send us off to embed with a rebel group for a bit to make up for the summit assignment.

Can't wait to hear all about the trip.
    Marley

Simon's husband passed away five years ago, and he was left to balance his career and their son. Anthony is showing signs of wanting to follow in his father's footsteps, but he also wants to be a photographer. Part of me thinks he'd be a fantastic journalist; he's the type of person anyone would be comfortable talking to. But he's also such an innocent and kind soul that the thought of him seeing what Simon and I see day in and day out worries me a little. I don't want to see the ugliest part of this world drain him of his innocence and joy.

I've just sent an email with a list of recommendations for Anthony when Bennett announces dinner is ready. Instead of going to the kitchen, however, he carries me into an actual dining room. The table is set for two, and there's even a candle lit.

"Well, this is," I say, pausing because I want to say "romantic" but settle on "fancy."

Bennett sets me down in a chair and then pushes it in. I, ever the lady, tip forward and grab the table, totally unprepared for the movement. "Shit, sorry," he says, letting me get settled before he pushes the chair the rest of the way in.

"I take it you never were a server in a high-end restaurant,"

"What gave it away?" He sits in the chair to my left.

"Something smells good," I say, looking at the covered dishes.

"Unfortunately, I can't take much credit for any of it. Nancy brought it over. I just reheated it and put it in serving dishes."

"Reheating is crucial, and presentation is key."

"You're too kind," he says, lifting the lid of the larger dish. "A venison stew." He sets the lid aside then moves on to the next dish. "Smashed potatoes with garlic." It smells absolutely amazing, and my face must say that because Bennett chuckles. "Definitely better than canned soup or children's cereal."

"Hey, don't cereal-shame us. These are uncertain times. Eat the sugary cereal."

"Yes, ma'am."

"Also," I add as I spoon some potatoes onto my plate, "you cooked that pasta perfectly last night."

Dinner is, for lack of a better term, fucking incredible. If Nancy making Bennett food is a regular occurrence, then I may need to stay a bit longer. *Yeah, right, sure, it's the food, Marley, the food is why you want to stick around longer*, the little voice inside my head chides.

"So, does Nancy bring you fully cooked meals often?" I ask after I swallow the most heavenly forkful of potatoes I've ever tasted.

"About once a week she'll show up with something. I can cook, I just often find myself a bit preoccupied with the dogs. Yesterday afternoon I had been planning a trip to the grocery store but, well, you know."

"The weather and a certain clumsy hiker changed things?"

"I'd happily have lived on grass if it led me to this moment." His expression is serious for a split second before his gaze drops to his food. I can count on one hand how many times a man has said something to me that made my heartbeat quicken. I just never thought a comment about eating grass would be the frontrunner. I don't even know how to carry on a conversation after that. I pull out the only logical follow-up.

"What's your favorite dinosaur?"

He looks back up at me like he's not quite sure he heard me right. "My favorite dinosaur?" I nod. "I honestly don't think I've thought of dinosaurs in years." He takes another bite and chews thoughtfully. "A stegosaurus, but don't ask me why," he says. And I won't ask because he passed Nellie's test and apparently mine by simply answering the question.

After dinner, I insist on helping with dishes, and Bennett agrees without much convincing. He helps get me set up in front of the sink so I can wash while he dries, and it's all wonderfully domestic. I'm happy to feel useful for the first time since I got here.

As he's putting the last dish away, he asks if I want tea. I know that tea is going to lead to talking and talking will lead to work, and I hesitate briefly before accepting that I want him to know. He fills and turns on the electric kettle before heading out to check on the dogs.

As I slowly make my way back to the chair, I decide now would be a good time to do a little bit of snooping. It's not like looking around someone's living room is really an invasion of privacy when everything is out in the open for people to see. It would be different if this was Bennett's bedroom, which, I won't lie, I'd *love* to snoop in. The pictures I'd noticed earlier show an older couple, a stern-looking man and a gentle-looking woman. Bennett looks a lot like his grandfather, although I cannot even imagine the man in the picture ever smiling. Bennett's smile is the same as the woman's. Another picture has the couple again, just younger with a young woman between them. She's wearing a cap and gown and is obviously pregnant. Again his grandfather is not smiling. There are pictures of Bennett at various ages. The only picture that shows his grand-father with a smile is one with Bennett in his football uniform. The two men are beaming at the camera while his grandmother is beaming up at her grandson, pride and adoration painted across her face. I feel a pang of sadness that she's no longer here and a tiny bit of jealousy that no one has ever looked at me like that.

On the bookshelf next to the pictures are various old paper-backs in several genres. There is a pile of medical textbooks on the bottom shelf next to a wooden box. My fingers itch to open it, but I decide that's enough snooping for today. I don't want Bennett to find me still hopping around, so I make my way over to the chair that has unofficially become mine and plop down.

When Bennett comes back in and brings out the tea, I've worked myself up so much for this work talk, I feel a bit ill. But then I look at the man sitting across from me and remind myself that everything is probably going to be fine.

"So," he begins, "you're a conflict photographer."

"I am."

"I can't imagine doing that kind of work. I don't know if I'd have the stomach for it. I can't even handle seeing one of the dogs in pain."

I look down at my tea for a minute and figure out where to start. Once I open up, I can't take my fears and traumas back.

"I always wanted to tell stories, real ones, not fictional ones. I was never the kid who could come up with characters or build worlds out of nothing. My teachers used to get after me because I'd try and hand in short stories that were based on what had happened that week in class." Bennett is listening intently, his face relaxed and open. "I was diagnosed with dyslexia when I was six, and writing down stories, even nonfiction ones, was something I struggled with. I desperately wanted to love it, but I've always had a complicated relationship with my frustration, and my parents just kind of gave up pushing me, so I stopped pushing myself."

"So you take pictures to tell a story."

Not many people have put two and two together like that, and I'm almost giddy that he has.

"So I take pictures," I agree. "I get to share real stories through my lens. My grade ten English teacher was the one who suggested I take up photography. She was the first teacher I ever had who saw my desire to be a storyteller and challenged me to explore that desire in a different way."

"So when did it go from a passion to a job?" he asks.

"To be clear, I still feel some passion for it, it's just waned in recent months. When I realized I was telling the same story over and over again." I take a minute to figure out how to word how I feel about what I do. "My job is ethically... ambiguous. I am a documentarian. I am not there to lend a hand. You have to set your humanity aside at some point to do what I do. When you watch a nature documentary and a pride of lions has a baby zebra surrounded you can't help but think 'Oh my god, help it.' And the reason the videographer doesn't is because that's nature. One must die so the other can live, the circle of life and all that. Meanwhile, a child doesn't have to die in another country due to war, malnutrition, or a disease for anyone else to live. But we as humans need to *see*." I put an emphasis on the word "see" because it's hugely important. "We need to see the toll something is having or someone is inflicting on others to care. And in order to care, people like me need to be on the ground sharing the stories."

I look back up at Bennett, and I'm shocked to see that his eyes are wet. It doesn't go unnoticed that mine are not. I cried because the dogs were sleeping in the barn, but I have no tears for the people I've photographed dying.

I swallow. "I had a passion to share the stories of people who needed help. And when those stories first come out, people rush to do just that. Leaders declare aid and support for humanitarian interests. And then the next story comes out and we forget. Then I get to share that story again the next year and the next. Things don't get better, and so now it's just a paycheque because it can't be anything more. And I come home for two weeks or less at a time, have meals with friends, fill my therapist in on whatever fucked-up thing I witnessed this time, and then I get a call and get back on a plane. It's funny—yesterday morning I was thinking I was going to be mauled to death by your dogs. But I've been shot at more times than I can count and stalked by various wild animals, and never once did I worry about dying. How fucked up is that? I decided to go on this random hike yesterday because I was up all night wondering if I could keep going."

The color has drained from Bennett's face, and I clarify, "I don't mean with life, I mean with the work. It scares me that I'm *not* scared. I can't even pinpoint when that started."

"So, why do you keep going back then?" he asks, sitting forward.

"Why do you keep bringing home unwanted dogs?" I reply.

"Because it's who I am, I guess."

"Exactly. And when did you start bringing home dogs?"

"Three years ago."

"Now add eight years to that number and tell me, in another eight years, is that who you will still be?"

He thinks for a second, then nods.

"I've been doing this job for eleven years. I got my first assignment when I was still in college. It was just covering a student protest in the capital, but it was exciting, a pure adrenaline high. A national newspaper used some of my pictures, and that led to making contacts with editors across news media. When I graduated I spent my first five months living out of a rucksack, and opportunities just kind of fell into my lap. I learned quickly that I loved the travel and the changing landscapes aspect of the job. And most of all I like sharing it all with a larger audience. I was teamed up with some of the best in the business, and I remember being in awe of them. But a lot of people in the industry are also jaded, although they'd tell you that they're just realists. You don't see as much shit as they do and automatically see the best or expect the best from people." I take a sip of my tea and sigh. "I remember very vividly thinking how I would never let myself think that way. How much I pitied them for being like that. So I lived on hope and allowed optimism to be what drove me."

"What changed?"

"I don't know what changed. Or really even when it changed. It's like one day I was going through pictures of a field hospital in Sudan, and fuck, Bennett, when I say the conditions were bad, I mean like unspeakably bad. There were dead and dying people everywhere—some men, but mostly women and children. And I was looking at the pictures like I hadn't seen it all in person, like I had blacked out. You'd think I'd be horrified by what I was looking at then, right?"

I shake my head slowly and look up at him. "I had no feelings about any of it. I wasn't shocked, or disgusted. I wasn't enraged. I looked through those images like I was trying to pick out kitchen tile. I started this job because I wanted to tap into the humanity of casual observers. And in the process, I feel like I lost my own. I woke up one morning last month and realized I'd become jaded. I started to ask myself if I wanted to be like the people I'd pitied. If losing my humanity was worth trying to tap into others."

"I don't know much about it, but have you talked to someone about the possibility that you have PTSD?"

"Oh, yes. That was the diagnosis I received early on when I admitted to my indifference about things. I'm rare, though, because I block things rather than react to stimuli. I numb my emotions and suppress my memories. Which in the moment actually serves me well. In the long run, though..."

"So maybe you aren't jaded," Bennet says, standing up. "Maybe you just need to work on feeling again." He picks up our mugs and leaves the room.

He's right about what I need to do; it's what I've worked on in therapy, albeit not very hard. I'm afraid of what happens if I manage to feel certain things again. I hear the back door close and know it's probably for the best that he walked away.

SIXTEEN

The sound of desperate scratching suddenly erupts from the kitchen, and I have a split second to brace myself before the pack bursts into the living room. The sense of déjà vu I experience is intense, especially when a sharp whistle cuts through my thoughts and the dogs all sit, randomly spaced between the entrance and where I am.

Bennett comes back into the room and walks straight up to me. "Give me your hands." Without thinking, I put both hands into his and let him help me stand. Once I'm up he supports me like he did upstairs and guides me across to the couch. "Sit," he practically commands.

"I'm not a dog, Bennett," I say dryly.

He looks at me in horror and shakes his head. "I'm sorry. I don't know why I said it like that. I clearly need to spend more time around people."

I pat his arm as I lower myself to the couch. "It is the first time since I met you that you've demonstrated evidence of a lack of human companionship, so I'll let it slide this time."

"I appreciate that." He smiles down at me, almost shyly.

Leaning down, he takes hold of my ankle, props it up on a pillow, and looks over at me. It feels like one of those looks that should be a quick glance but then we get stuck just staring at one another. His hand is still on my leg, the place of contact tingling in a way it has no business doing. His eyes dip back to my lips, and when he sees me swallow he glances back up and smirks, then without breaking eye contact says, "Okay!" My split second of confusion evaporates as I become the centre of the universe for twenty-one dogs. I now understand why he placed me the way he did. The dogs aren't fully jumping on the couch, but they all seem to be fighting to get their front paws up. My right ankle is protected from the chaos, as long as no one decides to fully commit to being the first one up. I'm afraid that if one makes that decision I'll be the victim of mob mentality. But before long I'm laughing and wishing I had more hands so I could pet all of the heads that keep popping up.

When the dogs start to tire of me and find other ways to entertain themselves, I look up at Bennett who is sitting in the armchair, legs stretched out and ankles crossed, his head resting on his hand. I have absolutely no problem reading his current expression: cocky serenity.

I know exactly what he just did, but I don't know how to say that to him. "Thank you" seems inadequate. So I just smile stupidly at him, and thankfully he returns it. Here sit two virtual strangers smiling like fools at one another in the soft light of a fall evening, surrounded by dogs. I allow myself to indulge in his attention in a way that feels gluttonous. Not even a little white dog lapping at my arm can pull my attention away.

"Yesterday morning I could have sworn you were afraid of dogs."

"No, not afraid, cautious," I say. "I'm used to, like, one or two dogs at a time. A pack of dogs in my experience is not always a good thing." He tilts his head, his eyes narrowing. "When you have a city that's been bombed into smithereens, people tend to leave everything when they evacuate, including their pets. When once-domesticated animals are left to their own devices in an environment like that... well, let's just say me in the middle of the woods would look absolutely delicious."

Understanding dawns on his face, and then it's replaced by sadness. "I couldn't imagine being in that kind of situation."

"Well, the good thing is you likely never will be." He nods and looks lovingly at his pack. We sit quietly for a bit.

"I'm glad—" I start to say just as he says, "Finding you—" and we both laugh. He gestures for me to continue. I feel like I've lost my nerve so I shake my head. "No, you first."

Bennett does not seem to need to rediscover his courage. "Finding you is the best thing that has happened to me in a while."

I was going to say I was glad it was him who found me but pivot. "You finding me is the best thing that has happened to me in a while too. So I guess I'm glad we're on the same page."

"Agreed. It would be very awkward if we weren't." Pretty soon we're both laughing again. I'm not even sure why, maybe because this entire situation is ridiculous, or we don't know how to move forward.

I collect myself to thank him for letting the dogs in. "I thought I'd upset you and you just were done with me."

"I mean," Bennett says, leaning forward and rubbing his hands over his face, "I was a bit upset. For you more than anything. Figured the dogs could add some levity."

"Well, it worked." I'm petting the head of a dog I'm guessing is a golden retriever, not even minding that he's leaving a pool of drool on my thigh.

"You can push him away if he's becoming too much. But that drool just means he likes you."

"What's his name?"

Bennett shakes his head and zips his mouth shut.

"Bennett. What's the dog's name? Is it something inappropriate?"

He's definitely trying not to laugh. "He was given the name before coming here, remember that."

"O...k?"

"Marley."

"Yes?"

"No, his name is Marley."

I look down at the dog, then back up at him and then back at the dog. Then I throw my head back and laugh. I eventually collect myself and look back down at the dog. "Well, I guess it's nice to meet you, Marley. And may I just say, you have a great name."

"It is a great name. You don't meet many people with it these days, though. Goldens, on the other hand," he says, eyes widening, "all the time."

"Oh," I exclaim, the reasoning dawning on me. "Because of that movie with a dog that dies?"

"'Because of that movie with a dog that dies.' Christ, that's dark." Bennett shakes his head in disbelief at me. "You really are a bit messed up, eh?"

"I told you." I smile at him then direct my attention back to Marley. "Thank you," I say quietly before looking back up. "For, well, everything."

"Thanks for making me feel useful." He says it like he's kidding, but his face makes me think he believes that before me he didn't feel useful.

I look around at the dogs before turning to glare at him. "Bennett... What's your full name?"

"Bennett John..." He pauses and rolls his eyes. "...Edmund Morgan."

"Wow," I breathe out. "Your mother really stayed on theme, eh?" He gives me a tired look.

"Why did you want to know?"

"Oh, I was going to full-name you but the moment passed," I say. "Actually, no, Bennett John Edmund Morgan, don't you for one minute tell me you don't think you weren't useful before me. Look around you." He does. "Where would Marley, Yogurt, or any of the others be without you? On the street? Underground? Ash?" I so badly want to stand up and kneel at his feet, take his face in my hands, and look him in the eye before I say another word. "I'd give anything to feel the kind of usefulness you should feel every single day." He shrugs and turns his attention to a massive dog with bowed back legs. As if the dog is trying to help me prove a point, it pushes its head into Bennett's chest and just stays like that. "See?" I point at him. "Useful."

Over the course of the next hour, we make small talk while the dogs wrestle or cuddle with us. I discover that his passion is in fact a real job with a real registered charity number, and he learns that my middle name is Loretta after the actress who was a main character on my dad's favorite show. So we have that in common, I guess. Both named after pop culture icons, although his is far more blatant than mine.

He's playing a lazy game of tug-of-war with one of the dogs when his phone lights up beside me, drawing my attention to a notification that says "Meds."

"Um, Bennett?" He looks up at me, and I point at the phone.

He looks up at the clock in the corner of the room and stands. "I'll be right back."

Having to take meds at a certain time is normal. Time keeps us consistent, that's it. Meds could literally mean a multi-vitamin. I try not to think too much about it. But of course, I'm a doomsayer so my mind goes to all the dark places as I hear the tap turn on and off. What if he's a psychopath, and those meds are keeping him from murdering me and a house full of dogs? Unlikely. What if he's dying? He seems pretty healthy. A dying man would have a hard time carrying my sad ass around everywhere. He could be diabetic, and meds refers to an injection. That's not so bad—Izzy is diabetic, and she's rocking the socks off of life. It could literally be a magnesium tablet or some other supplement that's just easier to write down as a med. I pull out of the doom spiral just as Bennett comes back.

"I'm going to let the dogs out one more time, then I'll take you to bed." He looks stricken the moment the words are out of his mouth. "As in, I'll carry you up to your room so you can go to sleep."

My immediate thought is to casually suggest he should stick with the first idea, but the mature part of my brain overrides it. "Sounds like a plan." I give the other Marley one more scratch before he chases after the rest of the pack. Yogurt stays curled up on the armchair I'd been occupying, ignoring the call to go out.

When I hear the door close, I close my eyes, letting my mind wander to dark dilapidated places. To buildings once called hotels, reduced to shells but still acting as accommodations. Rough fingers on my skin and the smell of whiskey in the air. All of my sexual encounters in recent memory were hushed and rushed, both parties just looking to scratch an itch or pass the time. If I had a passport for partners, it would have stamps and visas from all over the world. I can't help but wonder what Bennett taking me to bed would be like. I wonder if the little sparks that run through my body do that because it's been a while or if it's because I want him. Probably a bit of column A and B.

When I open my eyes to the sound of the stairs creaking,

either Bennett is carrying me or I've learned how to levitate. My arms are around his neck, and I've got my face buried in his chest. No man who spends as much time around dogs should smell this good. Earlier I thought he just smelled clean, when in reality he smells like a fall forest. It's like he spends so much time in there that his skin has absorbed the scent.

When he reaches the top of the stairs, I tighten my hold and press my face in just a little harder. I'm not ready for him to put me down and walk away. I don't even need more than this. I've been held more in the past forty-eight hours than forty-eight months, and until this moment I didn't know what I'd been missing.

Bennett passes through my bedroom door and approaches the bed. I wait for him to bend and set me down, but he just stands there, holding me. At the point I expect his arms to loosen they tighten. I can't be sure what's happening in his head right now, but I have a feeling it's similar to what's going on in mine. So I say the thing I have a hard time following through on myself: "Stay."

It's one thing to watch someone fight an inner battle, but it's a whole new experience feeling it. His muscles contract and then relax over and over again, and his breathing bounces all over the place. Just when I think I've made him uncomfortable, I feel him nod.

He pulls back the blankets before finally putting me down. I then watch as he rounds the bed and climbs in on the other side. On his back, he reaches his right arm out, and I roll into him, my head resting on his chest and my arm wrapping around. Eventually, I feel his hand begin tracing patterns on my shoulder. I'm just thinking about how this may be the most intimate moment of my life when his lips make contact with the top of my head. He lingers there, breathing me in before slowly rolling and wrapping both arms tightly around me.

"Is this okay?" he asks, his breath teasing the top of my ear, causing a shiver to inadvertently spread through my body. When I nod and hum a sound of approval, he squeezes me tighter, and one of his legs slots in between mine.

Getting physical with someone I barely know has never been an issue for me before. And it's not until this moment that I realize physical relations are very different from intimate ones. I know I want more; everything in me is screaming for more. But I'm also incredibly content with doing just this. It's the first experience in a long time that ignites something posi-tive inside me. The wildest thing about this moment is that I'm allowing myself to feel it, and that fucking terrifies me. Bombs? Shrug. Being held by someone I may be developing feelings for? Run, Marley, run.

It has been a while since I found myself just cuddling with a woman. And I've never done this with someone I barely know. Yet, somehow, everything with Marley has felt right. I'm trying not to question it and trying to keep myself present. I've had more on my plate since her arrival, but I've felt better than I have in years. She hasn't felt like a stranger since the first time she smiled at me. During one of my last conversations with my nan, she reached out to pat my chest and said, "Find someone who relaxes your heart, Benny." Then she laughed softly and raised her hands to my forehead, running her fingers lightly across the frown lines I'd had since childhood. "And this forehead of yours."

I feel the last bit of tension leave Marley's body as sleep takes hold of her, and I resist the urge to let myself follow. I start making lists of things that I need to get done. The vet is scheduled for next week, so I should probably reach out about the road. While it will likely be fixed by the time the appointment rolls around, I'll give him a heads-up. I've also got to follow up with the company I've hired to fence in one of the larger fields. I had hoped to have it done before winter, but at this rate it may be a spring project.

Marley sighs in her sleep, and I'm pulled away from my checklist. She smells like my shampoo, and there is something incredibly hot that I've claimed her with my hygiene products. I pull back a little bit to look down at her and take in how peaceful she looks. Most of the time she looks like she's on high alert. Not so much like she's about to run away, but she definitely is aware of what's happening around her at all times. I can't imagine having to be on guard constantly like that. I can feel my anxiety start to ramp up as I imagine how one wrong step could change everything. I have the sudden urge to hold her tighter and refuse to let go. But I do manage to slide myself away from her and walk as silently as I can from the room, allowing myself one more long glance at her sleeping form before I close the door.

I head to the living room to spend a bit of time with the dogs before heading to bed. My plan backfires, however, as I sit there and think about how she responded when I let them in the house. Her smile and then the way she looked up at me. I stared back at her, soaking in her attention, knowing it could fade just as fast. But we'd ended up locked in some dream-like staring sequence. I'd half expected some symphonic music to build the longer our gazes met. Now I'm flipping through my memory and trying to remember someone else smiling at me like that. Trying to remember *wanting* someone to smile at me like that.

Yogurt stands from where he was curled up on the armchair and stretches and makes his way over to me. Part of me wishes that the dogs didn't respond to Marley the way they did. If they didn't like her, this would be so much easier. Yogurt in particular seems to be taken with her, and he's usually not quite as enthusiastic about new people as some of the other dogs are. But if someone asked me what I liked about Marley, I know the dogs liking her wouldn't even make the list.

I sit there listening to the sleepy grunts and snores and think about what she said about her job. Learning about medicine was a passion for me, though I don't know if practicing it would have been. Running a dog shelter had never been in the cards, and yet here I was living a dream I had never considered. Knowing my grandfather would be pissed was only a tiny piece of what made me love it so much. Marley was right, though, that I hadn't really allowed myself to think about my usefulness. She made me see the nonverbal cues the dogs have been giving me for years. As I head up to bed, I wonder if she would ever see her own usefulness beyond her viewfinder again or figure out how to tap back into her humanity. Although, from where I've been sitting, it's there, shining through. Maybe she just turns it off when she gets on a plane for work.

EIGHTEEN

Rolling over to find I'm alone in bed brings with it a sense of disappointment I wasn't expecting. I lay there for a while listening to the soft murmur of voices coming from somewhere in the house. Laughter erupts, and I hear a shushing sound followed by quieter laughter. It's a big house, but it's old and sound definitely carries.

I'm still wearing the clothes from yesterday, and it's not until I've got myself balanced on my uninjured foot that I notice my clothes folded at the end of the bed. And crutches as well? I'm torn about them. I guess this means no more piggy-back rides? Time to get back to reality.

I get dressed, use the washroom with the help of the crutches, and then start to make my way towards the stairs. Before I can take the first step, though, Bennett is taking two at a time on his way up to me. The smile he gives me has my face burning.

"Sorry, I didn't hear you until you were already in the hall." He turns and bends a bit so I can climb on, then reaches to the side and takes each crutch. I think he's going to stop at the bottom, but he continues to the kitchen where I discover the source of the laughter. The Hores are both leaning against the island, smiling at us. Nancy looks between Bennett and me like a plan she concocted is coming together.

"What are you doing, Bennett? The woman's got crutches now. Give her her independence," Karl says as Nancy elbows him hard in the gut.

"You look well rested, Marley," she says, beaming.

"I feel well rested." I hope I don't look as uncomfortable as I feel right now. I can sense Bennett's eyes on me, and I do my best to keep my eyes on the Hores. "I assume I have you to thank for the crutches?"

"It took a while to dig them out, but I knew we still had them." Nancy gives her husband a look.

"Well, I really appreciate you doing that and bringing them over." Bennett slides a mug of coffee over to me as I slip onto a stool.

He's busy making coffee for everyone else so I have a minute to just stare at his back like a total weirdo. When I look away, I realize I have an audience. "I was just checking to see if there was a Marley-shaped indent on Bennett's back," I laugh, trying to brush off being caught staring.

Nancy leans forward to look around Karl at Bennett. "Not that I can see, but you've definitely left an impression." She winks at me, honest-to-god *winks*, and I kind of want to evaporate. "Oh!" she suddenly shouts, making me jump. "Bennett told us you're a photographer."

I nod. "I am." I have no idea if Bennett told them exactly what kind of photographer I am, and after last night, I don't want to dive into it again.

"This feels meant to be." She clasps her hands, looking like she's plotting something evil. "We are showing two of our girls at a big farm fair, and we need new pictures for both of them."

"Show two of your girls at a farm fair?" I ask slowly, very confused. Bennett only mentioned them having one daughter, and I'm a bit horrified that they actually have two and they are "showing" them at a farm fair. I know country people do things a bit differently, but I always expected something more along the lines of taking their time or not being big fans of road rage. What exactly does this entail? Is it like some kind of Miss Universe thing? Do they wear coveralls and straw hats? Are talents...farm-y?

"They are both competing in the heifer category," Karl says matter-of-factly, as if any of those words put together make a lick of sense to me.

I must look as troubled as I feel because when I glance over at Bennett he's mouthing something. I blink slowly at him, trying to focus. "COWS."

"Oh, right, heifers. Beautiful animals." I have no idea if I've saved myself from the kind of humiliation that follows a person around at every gathering. *"Oh my god, this one time we were talking about cows, and city girl Marley here thought we were talking about the Hore girls."* But a girl can hope.

"They really are and so sweet. Anyway since you're a photographer, maybe you could come by and take some pictures. We've got a cute little—" Nancy mimes what I think is a point-and-shoot camera. "What is it, Karl?" He shrugs in response while I resist the urge to give into a full-body shudder. "Regardless, you can use that, and we'd pay you of course."

"No, I couldn't accept money. Maybe some help holding something, or getting the, um, cow's attention, but consider it a thank-you for giving me some of my freedom back. Oh, and I have a camera with me, so no worries." I've taken lots of pictures of cows, but usually they're part of the bigger picture, herders in some middle-of-nowhere place for a story on nomads or people in a busy city living peacefully with bovines wandering the streets. But I've never taken glamour shots of cows.

"How about Bennett bringing you by later today? Sophie can help me get them all cleaned up, and we'll find the perfect spot before you get there." Nancy sounds like I've made her entire year, and I can't help but feel good about agreeing to do this.

"Yeah, I can do that," Bennett says. "It'll be fun," he says with wide eyes and a smirk.

Nancy and Karl stick around long enough to finish their coffee and give me the recipe for the raspberry muffins Nancy baked at four a.m. I'll be passing it along to Izzy or Nellie because unless I'm possessed by some kind of baking demon, I won't be putting it to good use. She also double-checks that I'm okay with photographing "the girls" about five more times. After they leave, I wait until I see them on the path before throwing my head back and letting out a frustrated sigh.

Bennett sits on the stool beside me. "You know, you didn't have to say yes if you didn't want to do it."

I look over at him. "It's not that I don't want to, it's just like..." I take a deep breath. "When I was first getting started. I was constantly traveling to these incredible places. I mean, a lot of them were also kind of horrible, but when I'd get home people would act like every kind of photographer was the same. And I'm not saying that any one kind is better, but we are not the same. I, for instance, would not have the patience for wedding photography or those stiff family pictures. I capture moments, lots of movement." I realize I'm rambling. "Anyway, it was a lot of 'Oh, don't worry Marley will just bring her camera,' like when I got home from three weeks of sneaking from one bombed-out building to the next what I really wanted to do was take pictures at Tiffany's fucking baby shower."

Bennett is staring at me. "But," I quickly say, "maybe cows will be a nice change," I give him a big fake smile to really sell it.

I don't think Bennett believes me, but I never claimed to be a good salesperson. I do convince him to go get the dogs ready for a walk while I wash the dishes though so I'm not completely hopeless. When I open the cupboard to put the mugs away, I notice several bottles of prescription meds. The "Meds" notification now makes sense. I slip the mugs next to the others and close the door. As curious as I am, it's none of my business, and I'm not about to betray the trust of a man who's been so accommodating. Still, I desperately want to know what they're all for because supplements definitely don't come in orange bottles like that.

NINETEEN

When Bennett comes back in, I'm leaning against the counter on my phone, Vance Joy singing softly about looking at him like that in the background. The Hores, aka my new favourite people, brought a charger for me too, since apparently Bennett had mentioned that my phone was dying. Sophie, bless her, sent her parents with one of hers.

His cheeks and the tip of his nose are a bit pink, and I have the sudden urge to ask if he needs me to help warm him up. I don't move or say anything, though; I just stare at him. When he looks up from taking off his boots, he gives me a questioning smile. "What?"

I don't miss the way his eyes find my mouth, lower lip trapped between my teeth. When his eyes meet mine again, I see the same look from yesterday in the bathroom. Where last night felt vulnerable, this morning has felt charged. Like if I touched him right now, I'd ignite. So I stay exactly where I am because if I'm being honest with myself, I'm really enjoying this nonverbal conversation we have going.

After a few seconds—or minutes, who can tell—of staring at each other, I mumble "Nothing," and turn my attention back to my phone. I was in the middle of texting Izzy and Nellie that I was still going strong. I hit send before putting it down and turning back to Bennett. I'm surprised to find him standing right next to me and step back automatically. He reaches out to keep me from putting any weight on my right ankle. I let my eyes travel down my arm to where his hand is wrapped around my right bicep. He lets go almost as quickly as he'd grabbed me and clears his throat.

"How are the dogs?" I ask, trying to break the tension.

"Good." His voice is more gravelly than normal. "Actually..." He clears his throat again, almost sounding nervous. "I was wondering if you'd like to join us on the pack walk today?"

I look to the crutches leaning behind me and then back at Bennett. "I'd actually really like that." I smiled at him. "Although I feel like I'll slow everyone down, and I'm not sure how far I can get before I collapse from exhaustion." Exhaustion may be a stretch. Tender underarms and me turning into a whiny baby seem more likely.

"They slow themselves down, don't worry about it." Bennett laughs. "Lots to smell and roll in out there. And if you get tired, I can think of a pretty great way of getting you off your feet." He means a piggyback, but all I heard was "getting you off," and then I'm pretty sure my brain fully short-circuited because he's still talking, about what I cannot for the life of me figure out. Before we head out, Bennett slides a toque over my head, his hands adjusting for far longer than necessary but I'm not one to complain about such things.

Bennett was right about the dogs. At some points we are the ones waiting for them to catch up. When one finds a good smell, they all need to go investigate. There's no barking, so it seems like a certain amount of time spent by one dog indicates they've found something really good. It's also fun to see them all together but clearly in their own little sub-groups. Yogurt seems to gravitate towards a couple of the larger dogs. They look like something you'd see in a Disney movie. Marley is partnered up with a medium-sized, three-legged black-and-white dog called Chance. They bop around smelling and playing and smelling again.

"You'd think they'd get bored of smelling each other's butts after a while," I say as Marley goes in for another long sniff.

Bennett laughs along with me. "I don't know, I think when you like someone, you never get tired of their smell." My heart gives a little twirl as I remember the sound of him breathing me in last night. When I look up at him he's looking at me with an expression I haven't seen from him before. Longing.

"Are all the dogs adoptable?" I ask, forcing myself to look back out at the dogs.

"Most are," he says. "Yogurt, as I mentioned, is never leaving. Clarence, the English bulldog will likely be here forever too. He's got a lot of health issues so it would take a special applicant. Let's see." He looks around. "Penny, the greyhound, needs someone really specific, so I'm not holding my breath."

"Specific how?"

"Someone with a fenced-in yard and time to spend with her. Preferably someone with one other dog. She's got some anxiety issues, and managing them can be hard."

I had never really thought about dogs having similar mental health issues to humans. "Are there a lot of dogs with mental health struggles?"

"A lot of these dogs come from shitty situations. They may have had something up to begin with and their family didn't know how to deal with it, or they developed something because of how they were treated. Penny ate through a door. Someone found her running down a busy road. She had escaped and when they called the number on her tag the owner said to keep her. I honestly don't even know how they managed to catch her. She was a retired racing dog, and she's still fast as fuck." He nods towards a grey dog that looks like it came from a kid's imagination. "Thunder..." He looks down at me. "For the record, I haven't named a single one of these dogs."

"Noted."

"Thunder doesn't trust men in general. It took a solid week for him to stop growling at me and even longer for him to come over to me willingly."

"Do you know why?"

"I suspect that he was abused by a man. Sophie was helping out when he came in, and he was totally fine around her."

"But now he's okay?"

"He seems to be. After he seemed to be doing better with me, I had Karl and a couple of other friends meet him, and while he was timid he did eventually approach them without any signs of aggression."

"So would he need to be adopted by a woman?" I can imagine being on Bennett's side of things would be somewhat stressful.

"My hope is that he's at a place where anyone could adopt him, but honestly I don't know if that will ever happen. One of the most stressful parts of this whole operation is pairing people up with a suitable dog and vice versa. I don't want a dog to end up in another terrible situation, and I don't want someone who means well to end up being afraid or turning their back on adoption. The balancing act is almost the whole battle." He sighs and tips his head back. "That's why I have twenty-one dogs right now. I'm picky."

"You say that like it's a bad thing. Have all the dogs come from bad situations?"

He shakes his head. "No. Marley was surrendered because his owner's son got really sick, and they just didn't have the time to dedicate to him anymore."

"That's sad," I say, watching Marley rolling in something next to a log.

"It is," Bennett agrees, "but I respect that they did right by him. Some people would still hang on because of what the dog brought to their lives and wouldn't consider the type of life they were providing for the dog."

That makes me stop. "I don't know if I would have ever seen it that way."

"Did you ever have pets growing up?"

"Nope. Well, no, that's not entirely true. One year for Valentine's Day, my grandparents gave me a hamster."

"Hamsters are pets, Marley."

"Oh, I know, but I only had it for two days."

"Two days?"

"I learned about death that week."

"Yikes."

"So what are all the others named?" I want to know even though chances are I'll never remember them and even if I do, I'm not going to be here for much longer. A little fact I keep forgetting as I allow myself to sink further into the comfort of this place.

Bennett starts pointing and listing off names. Bart, Mortimer, Spike, Sparky, Poppy, Rover, Thor, Bella, Daisy, Milo, Max, Buddy, Buster, Farley, Ella and Clyde.

"Then we have the geo crew." He points behind at five dogs that are very happy to take their time. "Dallas, Paris, London, Brooklin, and Dakota."

"How convenient that they like to hang out together."

"They all came together. Hoarding situation."

"Oh." I wince. "Were there more?"

Bennett nods but doesn't elaborate.

After thirty minutes, my arms are on fire from the crutches, but I don't want to say anything. I'm caught between wanting to continue because almost everything about this moment is ideal and wanting to just fall over because my arms are burning.

"How are you holding up?" Bennett asks because he's a bloody mind reader.

"I'm fine." The look on his face tells me he knows I'm full of shit. "Okay, my noodle arms are perhaps getting a bit too noodly." He looks at me for a minute then bursts out laughing. All the dogs surround us barking as if Bennett's laugh was a call to action. He breaks mid-laugh as a pained look crosses his face and then says something that has the dogs all shutting up.

The look on his face is one I've seen before, and I have a feeling it has everything to do with the pills in the cupboard.

"We should head back." He smiles, but it's not his usual one. It's tight-lipped and thin, and it doesn't come close to reaching his eyes. He also doesn't offer to carry me, which is a huge red flag.

I do my best to keep up, but the speed is just making every-thing harder, so I tell him I want to take my time and enjoy being outside. He hesitates until I assure him I'll be okay on my own. I can tell that he doesn't want to go back without me with him, but it's also obvious he is in pain, and this is the best I can offer in terms of taking care of him for once.

To my surprise, Yogurt sticks with me. The entire time I've been here, the little dog has been glued to Bennett's side. I'm not at all bummed to have a companion on my walk back, and Yogurt seems just as pleased.

Instead of heading straight back, I decide to rest for a bit on a large boulder near the end of the trail. I stretch my back and arms and let my neck lull side to side before looking up at the canopy. The sun is out, and there's a light breeze that makes the falling leaves look like they're taking the scenic route down to the forest floor. A lot of assignments seem to pop up between October and November, so I haven't been home during this time of year for a few years. I'm trying to soak this view in as much as possible. I have no idea when I'll get a chance to enjoy it again.

Yogurt starts to whine after a few minutes, and I do one more quick set of stretches before standing up and beginning the trek back.

The dogs are all in the field when I arrive at the house, and I wonder if I should let Yogurt out there or bring him in the house with me. He seems to have no interest in going out with the other dogs so I open the door and watch him run in. Before I close the door I hear a vehicle coming down the driveway and turn to see Nancy on an ATV, waving at me.

I stand and wait for her to reach the porch and hope she's not here to take me to her place.

"I'm your ride to the farm," she says cheerfully as she starts walking up the stairs. Shit. I had been hoping to collapse in the armchair for an hour or four.

"Oh, okay," I stammer. "I'll just grab my camera."

"Grab Yogurt too. He loves the cows."

"A dog named after a dairy product loves cows, go figure."

The house is silent except for the sound of Yogurt drinking. I glance at the pill cupboard as I'm heading to find my bag. I've had bad headaches before, but I've never reacted like Bennett had. He's clearly not okay, and it turns out I care about his well-being. I do a quick search of the kitchen and find a half-torn envelope and a pen.

I'm over at the Hores'. I hope you feel better. M

It takes more energy than it should to not add an "xo" before signing my name, which catches me off guard. I've never been an "xo" kind of person.

When I join Nancy back outside she picks the dog up and gestures for me to follow her back out to the ATV.

"I think Bennett is taking a nap," I say after I manage to get myself situated on the back of the vehicle.

Nancy only nods and then fires up the ATV, yelling back for me to hang on tight.

Bennett and the Hores—which sounds a bit like a band name, now that I think about it—share a long gravel road. Dirt and stone fly in all directions as Nancy speeds down it. I'm amazed at how the landscape changes between Bennett's and the Hores'. While Bennett's home feels like it's in the middle of a forest, the Hores farm is surrounded by lush rolling hills and a structured treeline. The smell also becomes noticeably different.

We pull up to a big white farmhouse, and Nancy dismounts, setting Yogurt down just as the front door opens and a massive German shepherd comes running out. I panic for a split second as the two dogs run at each other and wonder how I'm going to explain to Bennett that I let his precious probiotic baby get ripped apart. But it becomes clear quickly that if there is going to be a dog being ripped apart today, it won't be Yogurt. The minute the shepherd hits the grass, it drops and rolls, exposing its belly. Never in a million years would I guess that Yogurt was the dominant dog in any kind of scenario.

"That's Tank," Nancy says, gesturing at the shepherd. "He was one of the first dogs Bennett rescued."

"He's lovely," I say, watching the two dogs start to play.

"He's something alright." Nancy laughs and leads me into

the house. "We decided to adopt him because we figured he'd provide extra security."

I look around, wondering who's coming out to the middle of nowhere to rob them.

"We were having some issues with coyotes and foxes. Lots of chickens were going missing."

"Oh."

"Turns out he's afraid of chickens. The bastard won't go near the coop."

I look back out the door and watch the two dogs rolling around. "I bet that came as a surprise."

"Well, we went from no dogs to two in the span of a month because Bennett brought home a Great Pyrenees who lives to protect livestock and Tank had already made himself at home, so here we are."

I'm only half listening as I follow Nancy through the house. If you asked me to imagine a farmhouse, this would be it. Family pictures hang on the walls, and everything is done in warm tones. She leads me into the kitchen where there's a pot bubbling on the stove and a rustic loaf of bread sitting on the counter.

"I figured we could have lunch before we head out?" The room smells incredible, and I nod excitedly.

"Mom, have you seen my—oh!" A young woman, who I assume is Sophie, walks into the kitchen and stops when she sees me. I'm about to introduce myself, but she beats me to it. "You must be Marley," she exclaims, sticking her hand out. "I'm Sophie."

"It's nice to meet you," I say, shaking her hand. Sophie is stunning, and if Bennett hadn't been so against the idea of dating her I'd be riddled with jealousy.

"What are you looking for, Soph?" Nancy asks, stirring the contents of the pot.

"Have you seen my grey ballet flats? I swear I brought them home, but now I can't find them."

Nancy thinks for a minute then shakes her head. "Sorry. Maybe ask your father?"

Sophie gives her mom a deadpan look. "You want me to ask Dad if he has seen my grey ballet flats?"

Nancy rolls her eyes. "Well don't ask him exactly like that. Leave off 'ballet' and 'flats' and call them grey shoes. And while you're at it, let him know lunch is ready."

"Sure thing," she says, whirling around and leaving the kitchen.

"Honestly," Nancy says, giving me a look, "the girl is doing her master's, and I'm amazed she can find the building she has classes in sometimes."

Nancy sets me up at the end of the long island with a bowl and a side plate. "Bennett said you ate anything, so I hope that applies to tomato soup and fresh bread." I make a noise of approval that sounds a bit X-rated. "I'll take that as a resounding yes."

Karl and Sophie join us as Nancy is ladling some definitely-not-from-a-can soup into my bowl. Karl is giving Sophie shit but in a joking way. "Can you believe our daughter didn't think I'd know what ballet flats were? Honestly, I raised a girl and paid attention to things. I even know what butterfly clips are."

Nancy squints at her husband before setting a bowl in front of him.

"Well, I'll have you know," Sophie says, "Mom didn't think you'd know either."

Nancy tosses her hands in the air trying to look innocent. "It's not like we go around throwing out terms like 'ballet flats.'"

Sophie levels her mother with a look. "I literally asked if he knew where my grey shoes were, and he said, 'Oh, the ballet flats?' and then he goes 'They're in the front hall under the bench.'"

Nancy is looking at her husband like he's grown a second head. And I'll freely admit, I'm enjoying the show as much as the meal.

"You asked me where your boots were yesterday. The ones you wear every single day."

He shrugs. "They weren't where I left them."

"They were exactly where you left them. They were just under a coat that had slipped off the hook. All you had to do was pick the coat up."

Sophie looks like she's enjoying her parents' little tiff too as she rips up a piece of bread.

Karl turns his attention to me. "Marley, welcome to our home. Can I get you a drink?"

"Water would be great, thanks."

He nods. "Hore women, what would you like?"

I'm sure when your last name is Hore you get used to it, but I am definitely not used to it and I have to push down the urge to burst out laughing.

Sophie seems to recognize my issue because she leans towards me and whispers, "When it comes to our last name, my father is still fifteen. He loves to mess with people."

I'm enjoying the banter of the Hore family. I didn't have this kind of upbringing. My parents were both incredibly busy, and at least one of them usually wouldn't be home for dinner. I could probably count on one hand how many meals we ate together that weren't for a holiday. Including my birthday. My parents weren't a great example of what a desirable romantic relationship was. They carried on like they were business partners and my brother and I were necessary in order for the business to be successful. These three are having lunch together in the middle of the week. It's breaking my brain a little bit.

"So." Sophie turns her attention back to me. "What kind of photographer are you, Marley?"

I'm surprised by the question. I'm accustomed to people just assuming that a photographer is a photographer, and that's that. "I'm a conflict photographer."

"Oh wow." Sophie leans in further. "Like you take pictures in war zones and at those big protests that get out of hand?"

I nod. "Yeah, pretty much."

Sophie looks at her mom. "When you said she was a photographer, I thought you meant she did, like, weddings or something."

Nancy looks confused. "Honestly I hadn't really considered that there were different," She stops, clearly in thought. "What would you call them, tiers? Levels? Genres? I hadn't thought beyond the taking pictures part."

"It's ok, people don't realize there are different fields."

"Are you sure you're okay with taking pictures of the girls?" Sophie asks.

"Absolutely. It'll be a nice break from my usual subject manner."

"What's the most dangerous thing you've photographed?" Karl asks, his mouth full of bread.

"Karl, let the girl eat."

"No, it's okay," I assure her. "I got caught up in a bombing raid eight years ago in Syria. We were trapped in rebel territory for a few days and weren't sure if we would be able to get out. Wearing a press badge doesn't always make it safer, and we weren't sure how we'd be treated if we were discovered."

"What happened?" Sophie asks, wide-eyed.

"Clearly they weren't found, Soph." Karl nudges her.

"Actually, we were. We were technically taken prisoner but then released soon after to a United Nations envoy. We were treated well, all things considered, but it was..." I don't remember how I felt at the time. I've taken pieces of what other people who were with me have said and turned it into my own narrative. It took another two years before I admitted to anyone that there were certain things I couldn't fully recall. I can't say that to these people, though. "Scary, I guess."

"You guess." Karl's eyes are wide. "It was scary, you *guess*? I would have been shitting liquid for a solid week if that had happened to me."

"Ugh, Dad, really?" Sophie says, gesturing at her soup with a pained look.

"Well, it's the truth."

"How about the best thing you've witnessed?" Nancy asks, glaring at her family.

This one is easy. "Photographing survivors being found after a 7.8-magnitude earthquake in Pakistan. You're surrounded by this unbelievable destruction that isn't man-made, and yet there were these incredible moments of how enduring the human spirit can be. Grown men weeping at the sight of another survivor. People who had been trapped for a week in the rubble smiling despite being hurt and starving. Even the dogs. The dogs' reactions when they pulled someone out were magical. The sense of relief and joy that washes over the entire crowd in those moments is..." I try to come up with the right word. "Well, it's hard to describe, but I do my best to capture it in pictures. At least I hope that comes through. I spend a lot of time showing people the worst things imaginable. It's nice when I can share some good moments, despite the reason I'm there."

"So you're kind of a photojournalist?" Sophie says.

"Yeah, but I don't document the natural disaster stuff too often. I just happened to be covering a story in India when the quake hit, and my editor redirected me and the journalist I was working with to Pakistan. It was faster and cheaper to get us there than fly out others." I shrug, before taking another spoonful of soup. I probably should have told Bennett there were still good moments for me behind the camera instead of implying it was doom and gloom all the time. I find myself wishing he was here.

TWENTY

The sun has dipped behind the clouds, and the lighting is about as perfect as I could hope for as the Hores line up their cows. We opt to place the girls one at a time at the entrance to the barn so the light hits their front but their backends disappear into the darkness behind. I have a surprisingly good time working with the girls and the Hores. Maybe when conflict has thoroughly kicked every trace of passion out of me, I'll make the switch. Marley Cunningham, acclaimed conflict photographer turned livestock photographer. It would be a weird transition, but I think one I'd consider, although I'm not sure how much work there would actually be in this field, or quite literally, any field. I've never really thought about what I'd do if I quit conflicts. I had gotten stuck on the question of "Can I keep doing this job?" and hadn't gotten to "What would I do instead?"

I let the Hores know that I'll edit and send the photos when I get home, and they assure me I don't need to rush. But the fair is in a week and a half, and from what Karl said about the town and road management, it may take that long just for them to come to deal with it. I could actually be better by then and end up just walking back to where my car is parked, assuming no one has stolen it by now. There is a piece of me that secretly hopes the road stays as is for the foreseeable future. I'm enjoying the pace of life at Bennett's.

After the girls are let back into the field, Sophie and I sit and chat on the porch. She tells me about school and how she'd felt a bit guilty for wanting to pursue something other than taking over the farm. About how Karl cried when she got into the master of social work program and she had thought it was because he was upset.

"I remember thinking, so this is what it looks like to break someone's heart in real-time. And then he whooped."

I don't need to have been there to imagine what that looked like. Watching the three of them together has been entertaining, and Karl seems like an incredibly proud dad.

I'm about to ask Sophie why she picked social work when she cuts in.

"Sooo..." I know exactly what kind of "so" that is; it's the type that starts an intrusive question. "My mom mentioned that you and Bennett have gotten close." I look over at her, half expecting her to be angry, but she's blushing and looking hopeful.

"Um... I mean I guess we've had to get to know each other really quickly. He spent two days carrying me around, after all."

"What I wouldn't give to be carried around by Bennett Morgan," she whispers dreamily.

"I bet if you sprain your ankle around him you could find out." Sophie laughs. "Seriously, he will absolutely refuse to let you walk or hop or slide around on your butt." I think about how he has let me hop. "Okay, so he will let you hop, but not for more than about ten steps. It's like a three-legged race, and he's two of the legs."

She throws her head back and laughs harder. "Oh, I believe it. About...hmmm..." She thinks for a minute. "I was like thirteen, so ten-ish years ago, he would come home from school to help take care of his grandmother. I mean, how many other med school people are going to use their weekends and breaks to drive five hours home to spoon-feed someone?" I try not to look shocked because I don't want her to stop talking.

"Yeah." I pretend to be in the know. "Certainly not what the average person is going to do."

"Nope. Add to that how his grandfather treated him for giving up football and the fact he was dealing with his own health issues, I'm not convinced he's not an actual resurrected saint."

I knew he and his grandfather hadn't been on good terms, but I didn't know the rest of it, and I technically don't know much about that. Now I want to know all of it.

"Shit, you didn't know about any of that, did you?" There my face goes giving me away again. "Crap, please don't mention anything. I had no right to tell you any of that." Sophie sounds like she's spiralling so I put my hand on her arm and give it a little squeeze.

"I knew about some of it, and the rest I was probably going to get out of him tonight. Now I just know how to approach it." She doesn't look quite as freaked out so I let go and sit back. "And I won't let on that I know more than I already did, don't worry."

"Thanks," she breathes out.

I change the subject back to her life and goals and learn that she's seeing someone but hasn't told her parents because they likely wouldn't approve. Before I can dig more into why, Nancy appears carrying a giant blue Ikea bag and tells me she'll give me a ride back home. Even though I know she means Bennett's home and not mine, I feel a tiny zing of excitement to have it referred to that way. I thank Sophie for the chat and climb back on the ATV, Yogurt wrapped in my arms. The drive back feels twice as long, and I assume it's because I'm anxious to make sure Bennett is okay.

I have nothing to worry about, though. When we pull up to the house, he's out throwing sticks for the dogs. He waves and heads our way as Nancy cuts the engine. Before I can swing off, he's there holding the crutches and offering me his hand. I take it and instantly feel the anxiety drain away. Who knew someone's touch could be as powerful as a drug? Once I'm off and I've got the crutches back, Nancy hands Bennett the bag. He takes it from her, but his eyes stay on me, probably watching the blush creep across my face.

"You've got a bottle of milk, a carton of eggs, a loaf of bread, a pumpkin loaf, tomato soup, and a couple of onions since I noticed yours have sprouted. And I tossed some feta in as well. Sophie is texting you a recipe for eggs in purgatory. You've still got some jars of tomatoes to use up before I bring the next batch." Then Nancy looks at me and smiles. "I put some of Sophie's clothes in here for you so you don't have to rotate between various loungewear of Bennett's." She smirks at me. "We really enjoyed having you over today, Marley." Then she pulls me in for a gentle hug. When she backs away, she points at Bennett, who has finally looked at her. "If that road isn't fixed by Sunday, you two better come by for dinner."

I look over at Bennett in time to see him give a quick nod. "Yes, ma'am."

Then Nancy is back on the ATV and flying down the laneway.

"How was—" comes out of his mouth as "How are you—"

comes out of mine. This time he tells me to carry on so I do. "How are you feeling?"

"Better, thanks. How was your day?"

"Good. Felt really good to be a bit busy again." It's weird to call having lunch with people and taking some pictures of cows busy, but compared to my last week, it has been.

We start walking up the path to the house, Yogurt practically attached to Bennett's left leg, and things feel like they had before our walk ended so abruptly. Almost. There's a new tension now, like being apart for a few hours has us both on edge. Bennett opens the door, and just before I cross the threshold he stops me. I watch as his hand reaches for my hair and feel his touch in a way that seems to cause every cell in my body to tighten. When he pulls his hand back, there's a ladybug on the tip of his finger.

"A stowaway," he says before blowing gently towards the tiny red and black insect, and then watching it fly away.

The house smells amazing, and even though I'm not hungry yet I want whatever that smell is.

"Figured we could have chili for dinner," Bennett says as he starts putting away the food Nancy sent. "My god, that woman must think I can't cook or grocery shop," he mutters.

"I haven't had chili in eons," I say, leaning against the counter and watching as he moves around the space. I was going to wait until after dinner to chat, but now feels right. As he's walking past me, I reach out and wrap my hand around his forearm, stopping him mid-stride. He looks down at me, his brow furrowed, and I'm reminded of how I thought about licking it when he did that the other day. That same urge is not quite there, but I wouldn't mind kissing those frown lines away. So I tug, and he moves a bit closer. When he's finally close enough, I release his arm and raise my hands to his face. I watch the lines deepen even more, and so I use each of my thumbs and run them from the middle of his forehead to his temples, applying just a little bit of pressure. I keep doing it until his hands are bracing him on either side of my body and he's tipped his head forward so that it's nearly touching mine. I can feel him relax under my touch, and when his eyes are no longer squeezed shut, when I see his eyelids relax slightly, I lean forward and press my lips to where the deepest line lives. I feel his warm breath caress my neck and shiver.

"Marley." It comes out even more gravely than his voice was earlier, and a split second later I feel his hands closing around my waist and lifting me up onto the island. Every look we have shared before now feels like an appetizer that has only fueled my appetite. His eyes are searching mine, a mixture of confusion and need swimming in their depths. I want to say something flirty, something that lets him know I'm totally on board with whatever he wants to do to me, with me. To hell with boundaries—future Marley can re-establish those later. Bennett's hands are still on my waist, branding me, his eyes are now pleading with me, and I'm not sure I've ever seen anything as beautiful as the want he's conveying. It's almost too much for me to comprehend that this man, this too-good-for-this-world man, wants someone like me. I don't think I can even form words right now so I give a small, desperate nod, hoping he's not going to tell me that he needs a verbal confirmation. Thankfully, whatever he reads on my face has him pulling me to the edge of the counter, our bodies and lips finally meeting.

Air? Who needs it? Equilibrium? Overrated. Any sense of decorum? Hell no. We both seem to have one goal and one goal only, and that is to make up for what feels like years of lost time. Three days have felt like years in the best and worst ways imaginable. Somehow Bennett is touching me too much but not enough. Every cell in my body is being suffocated while new life is being breathed into me. Can kissing someone completely remake a person? I try to turn my brain off, try not to analyze the way his left hand trails down to my neck and pulls me closer. Try to ignore the way his right is gripping my thigh, pulling my leg higher around his waist. His other tangles in my hair and tips my head back just so. I'm overwhelmed in the most delicious way as his tongue slides along my own and he somehow pulls me even closer.

I've experienced rushed, desperate kisses before, but never like this. I've never once thought I'd never get enough. But right now that's how it feels, that we've crashed through some invisible barrier, and I'll be cursed to keep wanting this, needing it.

I manage to slow our pace, our grips easing slightly but still strong where we are connected. I snag his bottom lip between my teeth and gently pull away, letting them slide over and off of it. We are both breathing hard, and it takes a minute for our gazes to meet again. I don't know what I expected to see in Bennett's eyes, but it wasn't fear. He seems to come back to himself all at once, and in one fluid movement, he puts my leg down and loosens his grip on me.

"What?" I pull back to look at him.

He blinks a couple of times and then wrinkles his nose. "You smell like you were around cows all day."

Mortified, I immediately try to pull out of his grip, but he doesn't let me. "Sophie said I smelled fine."

"Sophie has gone completely nose-blind to farm smells. Her nose cannot be trusted."

I groan and drop my head to his shoulder. "Will you carry my smelly ass upstairs so I can take a shower?"

"With pleasure," he laughs as he turns his back to me so I can climb on before he practically runs up the stairs.

TWENTY-ONE

While Marley is in the shower I pace between the door to her bedroom and mine. Today has possibly been more bizarre than the day I found Marley sitting on that log. No, *definitely* more bizarre because she kissed me and I kissed her back and even though I've wanted to kiss her since she first smiled at me, I acted like there was something wrong with it, like maybe she felt like she had to thank me with some kind of sexual favor. I don't truly think that, but self-doubt is a powerful thing. Her lips on mine were better than any dream I'd had since she'd arrived. Realizing she was attracted to me in the same way I was to her was overwhelming, and in that moment I doubted it. Then I went and acted like the reason I pulled back was because she smelled like cows—which she absolutely did, but I didn't actually care. Hell, I'd take Marley any way she'd let me if it meant getting to kiss her again.

And then there's the fact that she still kissed me after I practically abandoned her today. I'd blame it on her just needing some kind of release, but the way she touched me didn't feel like that's what she was after. Maybe we both just needed this to break the tension which I had clearly not been imagining. My attraction to Marley is all-consuming and terrifying in a way that feels almost too good.

I stop pacing and stand staring at her door with my hands on my hips, replaying every look, smile and touch that just happened downstairs. I can still feel her hands applying gentle pressure to my forehead and her warm breath as it caresses my skin. The surge of need that coursed through me was something I'd never experienced before. I've wanted before, but what I felt downstairs overwhelmed every one of my senses. The little sounds she made while we kissed. The feeling of her hair between my fingers as I pulled it free from her elastic. I want to burst through that door and kiss her again. Burst right into the shower, fully clothed and pull her to me. *She's leaving,* that little omnipresent voice says from somewhere in the depths of my mind. I know, I tell it, and yet I don't think I fucking care anymore.

TWENTY-TWO

"Stupid Sophie," I mutter as I'm washing the cow out of my hair. I finally worked up the nerve to kiss the man, only to have that very man point out that I smell like cows, which basically means like shit. Bennett went from kissing me back to proclaiming that I smelled like shit. I don't think I've ever been so mortified.

I came back with a plan to talk to Bennett about what was up with him, and somehow I ended up... I don't know, seducing him, simply by grabbing his arm. I can still feel his fingers pressed into my skin. Eventually, I let a long groan out into my palms before turning the water off.

I'm so lost in thought as I make my way back into the bedroom that I don't realize the right crutch has slipped backwards under my arm. The minute I put weight on it, I slip forward, right off the pad, and go down hard. The sound of me hitting the floor and then the clatter of the crutches sends Bennett bursting through the door within seconds. The towel I had wrapped around me is now wrapped around one crutch, and I'm in the process of yelling "Wait!" when I hear a sharp intake of breath. I am a serious person other serious people send into war zones, I silently remind myself as I feel Bennett's presence move over me.

"Just leave me here to die of embarrassment," I say dramatically, throwing my arm across my face, because apparently that's less awkward than using it to cover up my very exposed chest.

"You know," he says, helping me back to my good foot, "if you were that serious downstairs, all you had to do was ask."

I whip my head back towards him and glare. "Excuse me? You're the one who backed off." I jam my finger into his very solid chest.

I have to give him credit because he at least has the decency to look embarrassed. "I didn't know if you meant it or if you were just being, I don't know"—he shrugs—"grateful."

"Grateful? Is making out with someone a new way to show them gratitude? If so, I have not adequately thanked the Hores. Did it feel like I didn't mean it? Fuck." I throw my hands up in frustration, and my towel slips off me again. And now I'm standing here balancing on one crutch, angry, likely red-faced, and very naked. I bend down to grab the towel, but Bennett's faster. He wraps it around me and then scoops me up in one seamless motion. I barely hear the sound of a crutch hitting the floor for a third time as he carries me towards the bed. He sets me down gently, my back against the headboard, and then sits just beyond my feet.

"It did feel like you meant it," Bennett says quietly.

"Okay, so did you not mean it then? Was that all me forcing myself on you, because if so I am really sorry. Clearly I read it all wrong."

"I can't remember the last time I meant something more," he begins. "Not with another person, anyway."

I have no idea what to say.

"It kind of freaks me out, you know."

"What does?"

"I've known you for three days, and I'm already dreading the road being fixed."

"Why?" I ask, my voice barely audible.

"Because it's the thing that's going to take you away. It doesn't matter if you've only been here for three days or three months, it won't be long enough."

If a friend told me that a man said that to her after three days of knowing him, I'd instruct her to run and never look back. But being the one hearing it makes me realize that he's not wrong. A lot of my decisions since coming here have been based on leaving soon. And yet I haven't once thought about the leaving part. I've never been great at thinking of the future. Being surrounded by unpredictability has trained me to think about the here and now, not tomorrow. I'm out of my element here, and as much as I've resisted admitting it, I am starting to wonder if I like it a little bit.

I try to make light of the situation. "Maybe you just need to get out more."

"I get out plenty." I hate what he's implying, which I clearly convey with my face because he shakes his head. "It's ridiculously hot that you're jealous right now."

"I'm not jealous," I say, sitting up straighter and crossing my arms.

"Yes, you are," he teases.

"How do you know?"

"Because I feel the same way."

"You're jealous of you getting out?"

"I'm jealous of you getting out... and I'm jealous of everyone you've gotten out with." My mouth drops open, and I pinch myself to make sure I'm still solid.

I snap my mouth shut and swallow. "You can't just say stuff

like that to a woman while she's in nothing but a towel, Bennett."

"Oh?" His right eyebrow lifts along with that side of his mouth.

"And stop smirking at me, it's not fair."

"Me smirking is unfair?"

"Yes. It does things to me."

"Things?" I should just stop talking because his smirk is getting more aggressive and more suggestive, and I may actually be about to lose my mind. "While we're on the topic of being unfair, I'm going to need you to stop nodding at me."

"Nodding?"

"Yes, it's irresistible."

"Jackass." I roll my eyes.

"And that, stop rolling your eyes."

"I'm afraid that's a default setting that came with this model." I gesture down my body, his eyes following my hand and then traveling back up to my mouth where I've once again pulled my lip between my teeth.

He points at me. "And that. I'm really going to fucking need you to stop biting your lip."

I am buzzing now and fully in on discovering what the endgame here is. "And what if I don't, Bennett? What are you going to do if I don't fucking stop?"

One minute he's sitting at my feet, and the next he's hovering over me. I'd be slightly disturbed by his speed if I wasn't so damn turned on. "Do you really want to know, Marley?"

I lick my lips and nod.

He slowly lowers his head to mine, but he passes my lips. I feel his breath brush my ear before he whispers, "I'll show you later." Then he's up and across the room, leaving me on the edge of throwing a full-fledged tantrum. "I'm going to run down and grab the clothes Nancy packed for you." He fucking smirks again and walks out, and if I'm not mistaken he's added in a bit of a strut.

When I'm fully clothed, relishing the black tights and long knit sweater Nancy sent, Bennett carries me back down the stairs. I decide to play a little game halfway down that's both cruel and possibly dangerous. I take my index finger and run it down the back of his right ear. He stops so fast that I yelp and grip him tighter. I can hear him collecting himself—yes, hear him, and that is a hill I will die on. He practically speed-walks back to the kitchen.

"You seem tense," I say once I'm perched on a stool.

"I'm fine," he grumbles as he pulls down a couple of bowls. It does not go unnoticed that he's taking slow, deep breaths while he very slowly plates dinner.

"You are that," I say, putting my elbows on the counter and resting my chin in my hands. When he turns back to give me a quick look, I make sure he sees my eyes drift down his body, my lip firmly between my teeth. His very audible swallow tells me I'm currently winning this game.

It feels like floodgates have been opened, and we're both taking turns trying to pile up sandbags while the other one is removing them. I'm really enjoying the process at the moment.

While we eat, he asks me about my ankle and about how the day went. I tell him about everything other than the chat Sophie and I had. Throughout the evening I find myself watching his hands and remembering how they felt on me. I catch his eyes going to my mouth more frequently than usual, and it takes all the willpower I have not to lean into him. After dinner, I dry while he washes the dishes, and he tells me about growing up in this house.

"I was so convinced it was haunted," he says, handing me a couple of spoons. "My grandfather was notoriously cheap about house stuff so things would go unfixed for a while, and it seemed like everything that needed fixing made weird noises at night."

"Noises like what?"

He smiles and then makes a creaking sound followed by a whooping noise.

I look at him skeptically. "Maybe you just had an overactive imagination as a kid?"

He shrugs. "Maybe. But my nan would insist that it was probably just her great-aunt banging into stuff."

"What, like walking around with her eyes closed?"

"Apparently, she was a heavy drinker and would spend a few nights a week here," he whispers.

"Oh, well, that's... not what I expected you to say. And why are we whispering?"

"I don't want to offend her." He smiles at me. "Apparently she was dealing with undiagnosed depression after her husband was killed in the war."

"Well, then I guess that's understandable. I wonder if she was like that at her own house."

"I don't know." He shakes his head and pulls the drain. "We didn't really talk about her beyond that."

"So you lived here with your nan and grandfather?"

"Yep. Until I was seventeen when I got into university. I did spend some of the summer here, but that was mainly to spend time with my nan. Otherwise, I was training."

"What kind of training?" I finish drying the last bowl and lean my hip against the counter.

"Oh, I played football throughout university."

"Were you any good?"

"I was alright." He shrugs, color darkening his cheeks.

I tilt my head and lean in slightly. "I have a feeling you were better than alright."

"I guess I was better than alright," he relents.

"What did you study?"

He cups his neck with his right hand, looking uncomfortable, "Um, biology."

"Ah." I nod. "A science nerd, eh?"

"Shocked?"

I study him for a minute then shake my head. "No, not really. More surprised you could carry that kind of course load and play football."

"I played for my grandfather. I studied for me."

Fuck, that's hot. When I see Bennett's eyebrows go up, I realize I said that out loud.

"You think so?" I nod, maintaining eye contact, and I know instantly I've officially won the game. I see his control snap in real time, and it's the hottest fucking thing I've ever witnessed.

His hands cup my face as mine go to steady myself at his waist. "Tell me you want this, Marley." I nod, and he shakes his head. "I need a verbal yes, sweetheart." Somehow I get the yes out, but I don't know how because I'm pretty sure I've swallowed my tongue. I just went from someone who thought "Ew, pet names" to someone who enthusiastically thinks "Call me sweetheart again."

My verbal confirmation has me leaving the ground as he pulls me up his body and into his arms, my legs immediately wrapping around his hips. I love being plastered to Bennett's back, but I thoroughly enjoy being plastered to Bennett's front even more.

I lose myself so much in his kisses that I totally miss the journey from the kitchen back to my bedroom. We could have teleported, for all I know. He lays me down, and his lips leave mine as they trail down my neck, hands slipping beneath my shirt and pushing it up and then off. I hate the brief lack of his mouth on me, and a whine slips out. "Greedy," he murmurs as his lips find mine again.

Damn straight I'm greedy, buddy. Has he met himself? Living with him for three days, being lightly touched, carried, and taken care of has me turned on like a live wire. And that's not even taking into account the way he openly looks at me or that he's all ridiculously tall and broad and hot in a way he doesn't even seem to know.

We are ravenous, and yet Bennett still seems aware of my body and exactly where my injured ankle is at all times. While his touch is almost desperate and enjoyably rough, it lightens the minute he's near my ankle.

When he suddenly breaks away from me and stands up, I feel dread spread within me. He shakes his head and I think he's about to back off again, but he just tells me not to move and then races from the room.

I'm propped up on my elbows in only my bra and leggings when he returns, flashing a packet at me. Excellent, yes, smart man.

"I don't want to stop anymore," he says, tossing his shirt off to the side, giving me an eyeful of softly defined muscle and a light dusting of hair.

"Good," I say. "No more interruptions."

TWENTY-THREE

This is not the first time I've seen all of Marley. But it's the first time I've allowed myself to really look. The first time she's very enthusiastically allowed me to touch. I'm not going to waste a single second letting myself think about what any of this means. The minute the last article of clothing leaves her body, I slam the door shut on that annoying little voice asking about tomorrow. She's watching me intently, and I hope this isn't something she blocks later. I hope she remembers it always. I know I'm not going to be forgetting a single second of this.

"Look at you," I murmur appreciatively, reaching out to touch her and watching in awe as a flush spreads across her skin.

Her skin is so soft, and I wonder if she likes the feel of my rough hands as I trail them down the gentle curves of her body. By the way she's responding, I think she's fine with them. I'm lost in her, only finding my way by using the little noises she's making. I'm doing my best to hold it together. My body is absolutely ready to go, but I'm trying to figure out how best to make us both feel good without causing her pain. While I work out the logistics, I nip at the skin just above her collarbone at the same time as I tweak her right nipple. She practically levitates as she claws at my back, and I add a line to the mental note I have on things Marley likes. A list of the things Marley responds a certain way to, things I very much would like to revisit in the future. So far the only thing she doesn't seem to like is the skin just below her ass touched. When I caress her lightly there, she giggles and tries to roll away from me. As much as I enjoy the sound of her giggle, the getaway attempt is not something I want a repeat of.

When she reaches between us and squeezes me, I see stars. When she moans, "Please, Bennett!" I nearly lose it completely. Pulling back, I try to collect myself. The way she's touching me isn't helping, so I grab both of her wrists and drag them above her head, holding them with one hand. Marley's eyes go wide.

I want to take my time with her and draw this out, but between how she's reacting and what that's doing to me, I may have to take my time later. Right now it seems like an impossible task, but still, I grin down at her. "Have a little patience, sweetheart." I kiss her deeply, my tongue sliding along hers as my free hand snakes down her body, her back arching, a gasp meeting my lips as my fingers reach their destination. I really like making Marley smile and laugh, but it turns out I like dragging this reaction from her the most.

When she's on the edge, I pull away, let go of her hands, and try not to come completely undone when she releases a desperate little sound and reaches for me again. So much for patience. She watches intently as I get ready for her and smiles wickedly when I crawl back over her body, pulling me down to her lips, crying out against my mouth as I slide into her as slowly as I can manage. When I'm all the way in, I allow myself to look down at those golden-brown eyes meeting mine. There's an expression on her face that I can't quite read. She said everyone always knows what she's thinking, but she can't possibly be thinking what it looks like. Right now she's looking at me like I'm the only person she ever wants to see again, like I'm home after a long absence. It's too much, and I have to drop my lips to her neck to avoid her gaze.

I want to last as long as possible and drag her little noises out all night, but I'm a human pop can that has been shaken for three days straight. The only saving grace is that she seems to be in the same situation. When she starts whispering little demands, I don't have it in me to deny every single one that passes through those lips. Harder? Yes, ma'am. Faster? Hold on, sweetheart. Just like that? Even if it kills me. Three fucking days in, and I'd do absolutely anything this woman asks of me, without question.

TWENTY-FOUR

I wake up in a cocoon of warmth, and I snuggle in deeper. The cocoon wraps tighter around me, and I sigh contentedly. Then my eyes snap open. The cocoon is Bennett. The fact that I can feel that he's not wearing any clothes is a reminder that I'm not either.

I slowly pull back and look at him. His eyes are closed, and the only thing he's wearing is a soft smile, like he's having the most pleasant dream.

"Where are you going?" he asks, one eye opening slowly.

"Nowhere." It's the truth; I just needed to make sure I wasn't having some kind of extremely vivid hallucination.

"You're not about to freak out, are you?" he asks sleepily, pulling me back into his body.

I give my head a small shake. "That was not my plan, no." I really was just making sure this was real. That *he* was real.

In the distance, I hear a dog bark and then the beep of the coffee maker. "You were already up?" I murmur into his chest.

"Mm-hmm."

"Why didn't you wake me?"

"Because then I wouldn't be able to come back and do this." His rough hand runs down my back, lighting my skin on fire before he squeezes my ass. "Definitely worth coming back to bed for."

"Did you even put clothes on to let the dogs out?"

"I'm not insane, Marley. It's minus one." He shivers dramatically.

"Then you took them back off?"

"Well, I didn't think it was very fair to have you naked and me fully dressed. I'm a big fan of equality and fairness." Thank god for that.

We lay there together in companionable silence, just enjoying the feel of each other. That is, until my stomach rumbles.

Bennett laughs softly and begins to unwind his body from mine. "I'll run down and grab some coffee." I admire him as he disappears from view and make a mental note to ask how many squats one would have to do to get an ass that nice. Bennett has a body you can tell was all hard edges and definition ten years earlier. There's still definition, but it's just a bit softer, although no less intimidating.

While he is downstairs I do some quick morning maintenance. I don't want to knock the guy out with my morning breath. Stopping mid-brush, I stare at my reflection. My hair looks a bit like I gave a monkey a comb and said, "Knock yourself out," and I've definitely got a bit of dried drool at the corner of my mouth. But what I'm expecting to see in my reflection is nowhere to be found. I have never spent the entire night with a man. I've spent parts of nights, but I've never gone to sleep and woken up beside one. I feel like I should be freaking out more. I blink at my reflection a few more times before splashing my face with some cold water, rubbing around my mouth and eyes, then heading back to the bed. I don't even bother brushing my hair; it's a nice reminder of last night. So is the slight soreness in my body that has nothing to do with my ankle or hauling myself around on crutches all day.

I'm halfway to the bed when Bennett comes back into the room, carrying an honest-to-god tray. I halt my progress and let my eyes do a lazy sweep of his body, appreciating it from a whole new angle.

"If I looked like you. I'm not sure I'd ever wear clothes," I say, crawling back into bed and pulling the duvet up to my neck.

He puts the mugs of coffee and a single plate with the pumpkin loaf from Nancy on the side table. "Marley?"

"Yes?"

"Would you be more comfortable if you had some clothes on?" I bite my lip and nod, which earns me a look that is somewhere between pleading and a warning.

"I wouldn't say no to a shirt," I say. He picks up his T-shirt and sweats, then walks to my side of the bed and slips the shirt over my head. I hold in a moan because Bennett putting clothes *on* me should not be turning me on. Once I've got it on, he leans in to give me a kiss. And wouldn't you know, the man also had a date with his toothbrush this morning. Before he gets back into bed, he pulls on his pants, and I'm torn, because goddamn, grey sweatpants should come with a warning, but I was really appreciating the view. Although I may currently be the most spoiled person in the world and shouldn't complain.

Once he's settled beside me he hands me my coffee before putting the loaf between us, two forks hanging off the edge of the plate.

"Have something against slices?" I ask, wondering how this is going to go.

He leans back against the headboard and rolls his head towards me. "I don't know about you, Marley, but the appetite I worked up last night will require more than a slice to satiate. Especially if I plan to be very hungry again in a bit." Then he takes a long sip of his coffee like he didn't just say that to me.

The man has made me blush more in the past twelve hours than anyone has in my entire life. He has left me absolutely discombobulated in a way I could happily get used to. After round one, we snuggled on the couch talking about random things, all the dogs spread out in the living room. I had allowed myself a split second to imagine that scenario becoming my nightly routine. Dog cuddles followed by Bennett cuddles. When the little voice telling me it was all temporary tried to cut in, I banished it to the back of my mind. I was fine living in this fantasy for a bit longer. Although ideally my fantasy involved no sprain and me being able to run around with Bennett and the pack. Piggybacks would still be welcome, however.

"So," I say, leaning back and sighing, "what made you stay in this house and not sell it?"

"Well, for one, no mortgage," he replies, breaking off a corner of the loaf with his fork.

"Oh yes, I can see how that leads the list of pros."

"I like the quiet, the space is great for the dogs, and no one drops by unannounced. Well, almost no one." He peers over at me. "I technically brought you here so you don't count. And the Hores are basically family at this point."

I smile as I pop a piece of the loaf into my mouth. "Oh my god," I moan around the bite. "How does she do this? How does everything she makes taste like unicorn shit?" I hear a snort and then a sort of wheezing from next to me and look over to see coffee dripping from Bennett's nose, which makes me laugh and then promptly inhale some crumbs directly into my windpipe.

Bennett puts his coffee down and thumps me on the back a few times until the crumbs clear my airway. I look up at him, tears in my eyes, and burst out laughing. Partly because of the coffee still clinging to his beard, but also because even in his current state, I still totally would.

"What?" He moves his head around. "Do I have something on my face?" I put my coffee on the side table then turn back to him and in a spur-of-the-moment decision whip my shirt off and use it to clean the coffee snaking down his beard. When I drop the shirt, he looks shocked to find me sitting there topless, this time not giving into my modesty.

His shock disappears quickly, and he reaches for me.

There are so many things I want to do with this man that physically I can't right now. Luckily, whatever hint of frustration I begin to feel is wiped out by how Bennett manages to manipulate our bodies. I hate to be that person who claims this is the best I've ever had, but holy fuck, it is. I'm not even sorry about leaning into that cliché. Part of me wants to do one of those annoying family newsletters people send out during the holidays but instead of talking about my professional accolades and how I took up needlepoint, I'd simply title it "How Spraining My Ankle Led to the Best Sex of My Life" and then just list adjectives like "mind-blowing" and "stupendous." I wouldn't even send it in an envelope; I'd turn it into labels and ship it on jars of Nancy's sauce. Mouthgasms for all, Happy Holidays. If it's this good and I don't have full range of movement, I can't help letting my imagination run away with the concept of a future here.

I'm pulled out of my thoughts when Bennett says, "Get on your knees, sweetheart." Despite a flash of worry about pain, I follow his instructions. He murmurs "Good girl" against my back, causing a little thrill to dance through my body. I've heard Bennett say that before, but the way he says it to me is definitely different and definitely not unwelcome. When I'm at the edge, understanding dawns as my ankles slide off the mattress. I reprimand myself for worrying at all because of course Bennett wouldn't do anything that would hurt me. He, no doubt, had worked out which positions would be best by using his big, brilliant, biology brain.

He runs his hands down my sides and then back up. I feel his lips just above my ass as he begins planting kisses along my spine, his lips lingering a little longer where they connect with my scar. When he stops touching me, I glance back and watch as he covers himself. He looks up and catches me admiring him, bottom lip trapped between my teeth.

"That fucking lip," he groans as he lines himself up with me. "I fucking love what it does to me." He pushes in slowly, one hand gripping my hip and the other in my hair, gently pulling my head to the side as his teeth make contact with my neck.

When his pace quickens and his hand moves down my body, I think, to hell with the adjectives, I'm just going to mash my hand against the keyboard—they'll get it.

TWENTY-FIVE

Around ten, we decide to be the kind of adults that exist outside of the bedroom. We shower in Bennett's room because the shower is huge and I don't have to step over the side of a tub.

"I should have had you shower in here before. I wasn't even thinking." He looks so remorseful my heart sinks a little.

Reaching up I use my thumbs to smooth those deep lines on his forehead. "Do you know how long it has been since I got to soak in a bathtub? It was a gift I didn't know I needed." His face relaxes slightly, and he leans down to press his lips to mine.

The absolute best part of showering together—okay, second-best because naked Bennett is the clear winner here—is that I get to use him for balance. There isn't an ounce of fear that I'm about to slip and crack my skull open. He is the sexiest and most stable handrail I could ask for. I find this a little funny since his presence in general has me a little off balance.

We manage to get ourselves showered with only some relatively innocent kissing, and out for a walk with the pack before noon.

"I love how they are pure chaos and somehow not," I say, slowly trailing behind the dogs. Marley the dog has decided that today he'll keep pace with me. Bennett doesn't respond so I look over at him. He's watching the dogs with the most serene look on his face, as if life could not get more perfect than it is right now. I wish I'd brought my camera along, but my memory will have to do for now. "You seem content," I say to him.

He finally looks over at me and stops dead, worry splashed across his face. "Did I dream this morning and last night?"

"Oh, that explains it." I roll my eyes, earning a warning look and laugh. Then the dogs go absolutely bananas, and Bennett is running after the sound, disappearing from view, around a bend in the trail. The barking stops abruptly and I hear Bennett yell "Move!" before he comes flying back around the corner, followed by a very angry-looking cow. Before I can even register what's happening, Bennett's got me in his arms and is jumping into a thicket of thorny shrubs as the cow runs by, the dogs close behind.

Bennett slowly slides me back down his body, his eyes tracking the cow as it bursts out of the forest. Then his hands are running over my face and body. "Are you hurt anywhere?"

I shake my head and run my fingers across his face. "You're cut." It's not very long, but it does look somewhat deep.

He lets me wipe the blood away, but it pools again and drips down his cheek. "Fucking wild roses," he huffs, glaring at the bush we crashed through before looking back down at me.

"I'm going to go out on a limb and assume that has never happened before."

"You'd be correct. Seems like I should expect the unexpected in these woods when you're involved." He hauls me back up against his body and back the way we came. He sets me back down and hands me my crutches, then pulls out his phone. After he taps the screen a couple of times, he raises it to his ear, his eyes looking toward where the cow disappeared.

"Hey, Karl. No, road's still out from what I could see." He looks over at me, rolls his eyes, and mimes talking with his hand. It's probably a good thing there are only three Hores; I'm shocked anyone ever gets a word in during a single conversation with any of them. "No, I'm actually calling about your bull. Yeah, Jason nearly took us out on the Creekside trail." Another break, more eye rolling. "We are fine, dogs are fine. He ran towards the house with the dogs hot on his hooves." I burst out laughing and slap my hands over my mouth. "Yes, by we, I was referring to Marley and I." Oh, I think, such a missed opportunity for a pop-culture reference there. "I'll tell her... Sounds good. See you soon." He hangs up and looks at me with the same exasperated face I first saw him with. I reach out and grab onto the front of his sweatshirt then pull him into me. I move my hand to the back of his head and pull him down so I can kiss him right between his eyebrows. "What was that for?" he asks when he stands straight.

"Just because." I smile at him, silently commending myself for yet again not giving into my day-one desire to lick that deep frown line away. I shall leave the licking to canine Marley and stick with using my lips on every inch of this man. "Is Karl coming to get his cow? Or would it be a bull since it's a he?"

"A bull. He's gotten out before but never made it this far."

"How the hell do they catch him in such an open space?" I ask as we begin to walk back.

"With lots of grain, determination, and above all, patience." Bennett sighs. "This is not how I wanted to be spending my day." He looks down at me suggestively.

"Stop that." I point at him. "We are adults, and we need to do adult things. Like care for dogs and catch an escaped bovine."

"To be fair, what I wanted to spend my day doing are adult things. Can I at least give you a ride back? If I can't have you under me in the next fifteen minutes, I'd at least like you pressed against me in some capacity."

"Now that is a solid pickup line, sir."

"It's one of those double-duty ones to boot." He squats, taking my crutches as I climb on.

We can hear the dogs barking, two in particular as we leave the trees. Daisy and Buster, both border collie crosses, have the poor bull running in a circle. "This may be easier than I had anticipated," Bennett says, just as the Hores pull into the yard. Karl maneuvers the truck and trailer in a way that looks strategic, but I can't for the life of me figure out how this is all going to work.

All three Hores jump out, and Karl throws the end of a rope to Sophie, who opens the trailer and ties it to the handle before going to tie the other end to a fence post, while Nancy does the same thing on the other side. I'm impressed watching them operate so efficiently, though clearly they've had practice. Karl grabs a bucket from the trailer and begins shaking it.

Sophie greets us and gives me a knowing look. Why do I feel like the Hores are the most insightful people I've ever met? Like they just know things, when to show up, when to not, when to give a little nudge. The all-knowing, all-seeing Hores.

"He jumped his fence this time," Sophie says, hands on her hips as we watch Jason turn on the dogs. "You'd think he'd want to stick around all the ladies, but lately he's been kind of a loner."

"We can all use a bit of alone time occasionally," Bennett says, his head moving with the movement of the animals as they race back and forth.

"It's almost hypnotic," I say. "Like a metronome that keeps time with anarchy."

Bennett harrumphs. "I'll take Marley to the house then be right back out," he says, starting to walk away from Sophie.

"But I can't watch from the house." I pout.

"You also can't get run over by that tank of an animal in the house."

"Bennett, I have managed to not get run over by literal tanks. I think I'll be okay."

"Marley," he replies, using the exact same tone. "Those tanks didn't have four legs and a brain. And I bet you had the ability to run away."

"True, but they did have rocket launchers and drivers who didn't like the press much." I feel him sigh and know I've won. "If you could just set me down on the porch, that would be lovely. Oh, and can you run in and grab my camera? I have a feeling this is going to be something I want to remember forever."

Bennett does as I ask, and before long he's running back out to the others. The first picture I take is of that beautiful backside running away from me.

I was not wrong about this being something I'd want to remember. The ground is slick, and the humans are not faring nearly as well as Jason. For such a large animal, he's surprisingly agile. I manage to capture Sophie in mid-fall, arms flailing and a look of panic on her face. She jumps up fast, seemingly uninjured, so I didn't feel bad about laughing. Bennett is clearly using his football skills, his stance low before he bursts into a sprint towards the bull. He too slips and goes down, smacking the ground in frustration before he's up again. He's going to need another shower. The man has gone through so many clothes since I've been here. I doubt he has to change as often in a normal week. At least no one can blame the current situation on me.

Eventually using another long rope and a whole lot of

strange noises, they're able to guide Jason towards the trailer. Granted, the poor guy is breathing awfully hard so this may be a case of him just giving up more than the humans winning. Before too long, he's safely in the trailer and Bennett is helping the Hores untie the guide ropes before waving them off. As he walks towards me, I keep shooting, and just as he comes through the gate he notices what I'm doing. I capture his knowing smirk perfectly.

As tempting as it is to jump in the shower with him again, I decline the offer so that I can call Izzy.

"It has been nearly twenty-four hours, Marley!" is how she answers the phone.

"I'm sorry! I've been busy."

"Oh my god, you slept with him."

"What? How did you come to that conclusion?"

"What else would busy mean?"

"Literally anything else. I'll have you know that I was at his neighbor's place taking pictures of their cows for some online profile."

"Oh," Izzy says, almost sounding disappointed.

"It wasn't until after I got back that I slept with him."

I have to pull the phone away from my ear as Izzy squeals. It's amazing how she can go from sounding accusatory to celebratory about the exact same thing seconds apart. I hear her apologize to someone and pull the phone back in.

"Okay, overreaction, my friend."

"Mar, I've been married for twelve years and have three children, and all extracurricular activities with my husband are scheduled right down to the orgasm. Let me live through you, okay?"

"You would orgasm like clockwork." I laugh, leaning back in the chair and flipping through the images on the back of my camera. When I get to the one of Bennett smirking at me, I zone out and miss whatever Izzy says next.

"Sorry, what did you say?"

"I asked if you're together now. Are you a thang?"

"Ew, don't say it like that, please. And, um, I don't think so. We haven't really had that talk. Besides, I'm really only here until the road is fixed. Assuming that happens before my ankle is good enough for me to drive."

"Hmm. How do you feel about the leaving part?"

"Don't therapize me, Iz."

"I did nothing of the sort," she replies, sounding offended. Izzy had been a therapist but walked away from her practice after having her second child. Kate required more care than any daycare could offer so Izzy learned as much as she could to offer the best environment for her middle child. "I just know you. You don't do relationships, you don't even spend the night with a man, and you are literally living in this guy's house."

"It's been a day, Izzy. I'm not going to analyze what it is or isn't right now. Right now it just is, and I'm fine with that. You know I prefer living in the moment anyway."

"Yeah, that's what I'm afraid of—for him, not so much for you."

"Do you want to see a picture of him?" I ask, changing the subject.

"Why the hell was that not the first thing you offered?" I quickly connect the camera Wi-Fi to my phone and then do a quick crop before forwarding it to her.

There is a moment of silence, and then I hear a very quiet "Well, fuck me."

"That's what I said. And it worked."

I hear Bennett coming down the stairs and glance up to offer him a smile. He's all freshly showered and dewy, and I want to throw my phone across the room and then throw my body at him. By his expression, I can tell he knows exactly what I'm thinking, and he makes his way over.

"Hey, Iz?" I say, eyes locked with his.

"Ugh, go have fun. Don't make me wait another twenty-four hours to hear from you, though."

"Right. Bye." I barely get it out before I end the call and watch as Bennett drops to his knees beside the chair.

"Hi." He leans in and captures my mouth, using his hand to hold me against him, although it really is unnecessary. Good lord, he smells good. My hands go to his still-damp hair, and I pull him in and somehow manage to deepen the kiss more. A car door slamming has him jumping back, our hands pulling away from each other and he's on his feet in seconds.

"Um, Bennett?" I say as he starts to walk towards the kitchen.

"Yeah?" He turns back to me.

"You may want to let me go to the door." I gesture at his body.

He looks down and blushes. "Right, good idea. I'll be out there in a minute." He helps me up and gets me situated with the crutches. If I brushed by him when I was leaving, it was purely by accident and was absolutely not worth hearing his response.

Karl is standing on the other side of the door. I'm surprised that he knows how to do that.

"Back so soon?" I ask, opening the door.

"Yeah, I tried calling but there was no answer," Karl says, stepping into the kitchen.

"Oh, Bennett was showering so that's probably why." I notice Karl's gaze flick to my very dry hair.

"Right." He's blushing a bit, and I have a feeling Nancy may be responsible for him not barging in this time.

"Karl," Bennett says, walking into the kitchen, coming to

stand next to me. "To what do we owe the pleasure?" Referring to us as a "we" should freak me out, but instead I'm actively keeping myself from breaking into a little happy dance.

"Just came to let you know that the town called me back, finally. They're sending someone over now to take a look. Some overpaid structural engineer or something. Thought maybe you'd want to go down. Nancy suggested that if they actually saw that the damage was impacting real people, they may be more inclined to get this done."

Disappointment blooms on Bennett's face, but he quickly covers it. "Yeah, sounds good. Marley, do you want to come?" What I want to say is *yes, I'd like to come with you everywhere and have you come with me everywhere else.* But instead, I shake my head, hoping I'm masking the panic that is settling in my bones. Time is running out.

TWENTY-SIX

When I get back, I grudgingly tell Marley that the guy doesn't think it's going to take long to fix the road, maybe a couple of days. Her response is...complicated. Her voice is thrilled but her smile is forced, and I can't decide if I love or hate that she doesn't seem to be in love with the idea of leaving so soon.

We don't talk much through dinner. I take a pill before we decided to put on a movie and cuddle on the couch.

At some point during the movie, I fall asleep, and when I wake up, I'm alone. I sit up and follow the sound of Marley talking softly. The kitchen door is open and she's sitting on the porch swing, chatting with Yogurt like they were old friends. The other dogs are spread around the yard and near her, and I lean against the doorframe to quietly appreciate the whole scene.

When a dog brings a stick, she throws it. When they do something silly, she laughs. When they nudge her, she scratches behind their ears and kisses their noses. The whole scene is like something taken from my wildest dreams.

Yogurt notices me first and trots happily to the door,

distracting Marley from Clarence who'd waddled up the stairs to flop down in front of her.

"Hey!" she says, smiling up at me.

"Sorry I fell asleep," I apologize, pushing through the door and joining her.

"I've been known to fall asleep during a movie occasionally too. It's not a crime." She leans into me, and we sit there quietly for a while watching the dogs play, her head resting on my shoulder.

"I have something important to ask you," she says quietly.

"Shoot."

I feel her take a deep breath and prepare myself. "How many squats would one have to do to get an ass like yours?"

It takes my brain a second, and when it clicks, I can't help but laugh.

"I'm serious," she says, poking me in the ribs. "I mean, all of you is toned and muscly, but your ass looks like it was carved by Michelangelo. Looks like it should be on display in the Louvre. I bet it would be a top draw too."

I wipe the tears from my eyes and look down at her. "I can't really tell you. I don't actively do them."

"I think you're full of shit. I think when you say you're 'going to work on the kitchen', it's code for going to work on your glutes."

I throw my hands up in surrender. "You've figured it all out, Marley. I'll also have you know that when I go out to feed the dogs, I'm actually doing chin-ups the entire time."

"I knew it," she says triumphantly before snuggling back into my side. "Can I ask you something else?"

"Anything."

"I've noticed you seem to get headaches a lot. Are you okay?"

I've never wanted anyone to know me like I want Marley to. "Remember how I said I played football in university?"

"Mm-hmm,"

"Well, I was drafted, and during my first training camp I was hit hard—harder than normal, I guess. Anyway, I had a concussion from the hit. I went through all the concussion protocol stuff, which at the time wasn't very robust, not like it is now. So when I was cleared I returned to training, except I was getting headaches pretty regularly. I'd get them while working out, reading, watching TV. It didn't seem to matter what I was doing, although noise and light were major triggers. Specifically, sudden loud noises." My eyes wander to where creatures known for sudden loud noises are sprawled around the yard. "One day we were doing fairly easy drills, and I just fell to my knees and vomited. The headache was so intense it felt like the only way to relieve the pain. I was sent for tests, and eventually a sports neurologist was called in for a consult. I was basically told that one more concussion would be devastating. I'd had a few in university and a couple playing other sports growing up, but since I'd never had any long-term effects, I just never really thought much of it."

"I mean, why would you? If the people around us don't seem worried, why would we be?"

"Exactly. So long story short, I made the decision to leave the sport, which my grandfather did not approve of at all. Thankfully my grandmother was supportive, so I had at least one person on my side. My girlfriend broke up with me shortly after, saying I was no fun anymore. And the few good friends I had just kind of disappeared, which wasn't entirely their fault. I definitely isolated myself as a form of self-preservation."

"I'm sorry, your girlfriend left because a medical condition meant you weren't"—she raises her fingers in air quotes—"'fun anymore'? I'm guessing what she meant was you're not going to be a pro and there go all those sweet dollar bills?"

"To be fair to her, it wasn't about the money, not for her or for me."

"Oh, just the passion of the game, then?"

"Honestly, she just liked the party lifestyle, and that was hard to be around when I stopped playing. I didn't like it that much when I was playing, come to think of it. But football for me was about making my grandfather proud. I had my heart set on med school. He had his set on his grandson doing something different with our name."

"Something different than what?"

"Um..." I hesitate.

"What? Is there a history of bank robbing in your family? Generations of reliable insurance agents? Car sales?"

"Have you heard of Morgan Kelly Inc.?"

"I'm guessing it's a company?"

"A company started by my great-great-grandfather eons ago, although it was just Kelly then. My grandfather added his name when he took over. I'm not involved with it now. My grandfather sold his share in the company when I was in high school because he wanted to buy a football team. That was honestly his main goal in life, which is weird to me, but I guess that's just one of the reasons we didn't exactly get along. We did not understand each other at all. He wanted glory that could be easily bought, or so he thought anyway. Turns out people are not just out there selling pro football teams, even if you offer a ton of money. Anyway, I wanted to do something more than run around a field. I wanted to help people."

"By becoming a doctor?" she asks.

"I came home and told my grandparents that I planned to enroll full-time in med school instead of staying part-time, and he went off the deep end. Told me I wasn't a real man because a real man could handle the odd headache. I ended up leaving that night and didn't come back until Nan was moved into the hospital. I'd come home and keep her company there on my weekends. But I didn't come back here, to this house, until Nan's funeral. The old bastard didn't even talk to me then. Sophie was actually the one who called to tell me she had died."

"I'm sorry, Bennett." Marley wraps her arms around me, and I melt into her hold.

"It was what it was. My nan was warm and supportive of whatever I did, and at the end of the day my grandfather hated everyone else more than me so there is some vindication that I was the only one he could leave his stuff to. Sometimes I think she stopped fighting cancer just to get away from him."

"I doubt it," she says, sitting back and shaking her head. "There's no way she would have chosen to leave you alone with him. What happened with med school?"

"Nan was sick throughout, and between that and managing my own health, I just couldn't keep up. I went down to half-time again, which made everything feel more impossible. After she died, I dealt with some depression. That's actually why I got my first dog. She gave me something to focus on other than death, pain, and feeling like a failure."

She laces our fingers together and squeezes, and I am relishing how she is initiating every touch tonight. "You're not a failure, Bennett," she says quietly. "And you're still taking care of people." She points to her ankle then sweeps her arms around gesturing at the dogs. "Not people, I know, but it's the same in a way."

I squeeze her hand back. "I know that now. It may have taken years of hard lessons, therapy, and nailing down the right medication, but I do recognize that I'm not a failure."

A moment passes before she speaks. "The bottles in the cupboard."

"Saw those, eh?"

She shrugs. "Kind of hard not to."

"Yeah. My doctor suspects I may have CTE—um, chronic traumatic encephalopathy," I clarify.

"Oh." She sits up straighter. "So the headaches?"

I nod. "CTE is fucking terrifying, but the neurologist I see yearly has said it's promising that my symptoms haven't gotten worse. The headaches are about as frequent as before, and I haven't considered myself depressed in years, so that diagnosis may not have had anything to do with the CTE. The most promising thing is that I haven't developed any new symptoms. Granted, they can't truly see the extent of damage in a living patient."

I hear the intake of air from beside me followed by a slow exhale. "You say that so calmly, it's unnerving."

"I've had years to come to terms with it."

"How do you do all this alone? The other day you kind of disappeared when you had a headache. What happens if there's no one around? Why not hire someone?"

"I've thought about hiring, but it's a lot of work, and that someone has to be the right fit. I also don't want to have to rely on someone." I don't add that I've become comfortable in this bubble of isolation; it's not purely a decision based on the reliability of others.

"Bennett," she says disapprovingly. "That sounds like your grandfather's influence. Relying on others is part of being human."

"Oh, because you were so welcome to the idea at first."

"That's different."

"How?"

She huffs. "It just is."

As the swing sways slowly, it's getting harder for me to live in the moment. The movement reminds me of a clock, each back and forth another minute ticking by. Marley lives for the here and now, and I envy her for it. Instead of just enjoying this, her and me swinging peacefully on my porch, my mind is already showing me visions of next week and beyond. And in them, I'm alone again, and for the first time in a very long time, it hits me that maybe I don't want to be.

TWENTY-SEVEN

What sounds like an explosion wakes us abruptly the next morning. In fact, it sounds so much like an explosion that I'm flat on the floor before I really know what's going on. Incredibly, I've managed to take cover and not do further damage to my ankle.

Bennett, who is still in bed, leans over the edge to look down at me, eyebrows nearly touching his hairline. "You alright?"

I look up after I've collected myself. "What the hell was that?"

"My best guess is that they're here to work on the road. Do you always hide on the floor when there's a loud noise?"

I stand gingerly. "Sometimes if you don't do that, you can be crushed by rubble or falling bodies." I say it so absentmindedly that at first I don't know why Bennett is looking at me like I just casually said that I regularly feed children to lions at the zoo. "What?"

"Rubble or falling bodies?"

"I mean, it's not exactly an everyday thing, more like a

once-in-a-blue-moon thing, but I have seen a blue moon, so best to be prepared." I bury myself under the covers again and wrap myself as best I can around Bennett's body. "I guess this really does mean the countdown is on."

"Countdowns are usually for things I look forward to. Let's not call it that," he says, brushing the hair from my face. He leaves his hand on my cheek and just looks at me. I like the way he looks at me when we're in bed. I like the way he looks at me while we're eating breakfast or walking with the dogs. I like the way he looks at me while we're catching our breaths after an impromptu make-out session on the porch swing. But mostly, I love the way he looks at me and just smiles. I can only hope he likes the way I look at him too. "You know you don't have to go straight away, right?"

I know that. Every single look he gives me tells me that. "Careful, I may decide to never leave." Deep down I know there is part of me that loves the idea of never leaving. The part that wants to stay here and frolic every single day with Bennett and his pack. I want to be part of it. But I've also realized now that I'm not done doing what I do. I'm not done sharing stories for the people who can't share them on their own. I'm not done chasing that one image that may actually put an end to the suffering of an entire country of people. I'm simply not done, and until I am, there is no way I can be the kind of person Bennett needs. I am not someone a single person can rely on to be there when they cannot be. Not yet anyway. I've got some more things to figure out. Some more questions I'd never considered asking until a few days ago.

When Bennett kisses me it's all-consuming, and when he makes love to me it's slow and passionate, and in a way it feels like the start of a goodbye.

Two hours later I'm wrapped around Bennett's back, standing at the fence of a cow pasture. About ten minutes after

Bennett had called Karl to tell him they were fixing the road, Nancy called back and invited us over for breakfast. I could almost hear her telling Karl off for not thinking of it himself. We had still been in bed, but the thought of not having to listen to the noise all morning outweighed being naked together. I know there are two meanings behind the invite. One, the noise could trigger Bennett's headaches, and two, the sound of digging and dumping would turn into the ticking of a clock. I managed to make it halfway to the Hores' on my own before Bennett insisted that I, in his words, "ride him the rest of the way."

After we arrived he let me down, and I leaned against the top rail of the fence. He takes this opportunity to wrap himself around me from behind and rests his chin lightly on top of my head. Bennett has done his best to stay in physical contact with me since we heard the road work begin, and I am soaking up every touch he's offering me. I'm usually not so open to being the focus of someone's attention. I spend so much of my life trying to be invisible, and yet that has been impossible with him. And I'm giddy at the thought of not being invisible to him. The girls are near the fence and I point at them, introducing them to Bennett.

"The one with the black around her eye is Clarice, and the other one is Glenda."

"We meet again, Clarice," Bennett says, doing his best Hannibal Lecter impression, which is truly terrible but makes me laugh. When I look up at Bennett, he's looking down at me, and for a minute we just stand there like that. Sophie calls us from the porch announcing that breakfast is ready, and Bennett lets me make my way to the house slowly as he does one last check on the dogs. Not that he has to worry about them much; after a three-kilometre walk, they're pretty happy to sprawl out around the lawn.

I sent Izzy and Nellie a text before we left, asking if they'd be able to come get me tomorrow. I insisted I'd need two people so someone could also drive my car back to my place. Izzy had asked if I really wanted to be picked up or if I was doing it for her sake. Apparently, she thinks I want to get back to the real world just so she stops worrying about me. Go-with-the-flow Nellie just said sure, whatever I needed.

"So," Karl says, cutting into a sausage, "Marley, I bet your family and friends will be happy to have you home." I nod back and pretend I don't notice the daggers both Nancy and Sophie are sending his way.

"My friends will be for sure."

"Oh? No family?"

I would probably be annoyed by the intrusive question if I wasn't so humoured by the looks the man's family is giving him. Either he's used to them and doesn't care anymore, or he's completely oblivious.

"Well," I say, putting my fork down and glancing quickly at Bennett. I feel like he's told me everything about his family or lack thereof and all he's gotten out of me is that I'm not sure I love my job anymore. "No, I have a family. We just aren't that close."

"Falling out?" Karl asks.

Nancy grinds out an irritated "Karl!"

"No, not really. We've never really been a close group."

"Hmmm," I hear Sophie say.

"What?" I ask, a tad more defensively than I mean to.

"Nothing, it's just you referred to your family as a group and not a family. It's interesting, that's all." Then she looks a bit embarrassed. "Sorry. Sociology nerd."

"It's okay. I mean, we... When I was younger..." I look over at Bennett again and he frowns at me.

"You don't owe anyone an explanation, Mar," he says,

shortening my name for the first time and making my stupid heart do the stupid cancan.

"It's okay, I just don't really talk about them. Not because there's some deep dark secret or trauma or anything. We just aren't close, and that's basically the beginning and the end of it. I didn't grow up with parents who wanted to know how my day was or who I had a crush on. My parents had kids because they felt like they had to." I pick my fork up again and begin absently playing with my scrambled eggs. "I think it took until I was about twenty-three to see true love, and it was in the form of grief. This mother, wailing beside the body of her dead adult son." I look up at Bennett and hold his gaze. "I remember thinking that my mom would probably feel relieved at that moment. Free from one of the two kids, grateful to have one less burden."

Everyone at the table is silent. Sophie's mug is frozen on the way to her mouth, and she's staring at me like I'm the saddest person she's ever encountered. "I'm okay, though. Honestly, you can all stop looking at me like that."

Bennett's eyes slide over to Sophie, and I see him swallow. "Soph, are you showing the girls this year, or is your cousin?"

Sophie is still looking at me, but she does at least go along with the change in subject. "We both are actually. I'll take Glenda, and she'll show Clarice."

"And when are you showing again?" Bennett asks.

"November fifteenth, and then if we finish in the top three, we do an exhibition thing on the night of the seventeenth. They think a bunch of horse snobs want to watch cows walk around a show ring for some reason, but I'd rather be in there than not."

"Sorry," I cut in, "I should have asked the other day, what exactly is it you do with them?"

"The cows are judged on a number of factors. Confirmation, so, how they're built, how they move, their mammary system." That gets my attention.

"So essentially they are judged on the size of their boobs?"

"Udder quality is pretty essential in dairy cows," Karl says matter-of-factly.

"I guess that makes sense."

"In fact," Sophie jumps in, "things that are deemed less attractive in humans tend to be more desirable in cows."

I squint at her. "How so?"

"For instance, veining. The veining isn't necessarily a desirable trait in human breasts but in cows..." She mimes a chef's kiss, and I laugh.

"No offence, but this all sounds absolutely ridiculous."

"When you think about it," Sophie continues, "human beauty contests are ridiculous. They set impossible standards for millions, leading to numerous mental and physical disorders while pitting people against one another. These shows help people produce animals that meet the ideal standards for a multitude of reasons. Unlike with humans, there is a purpose beyond vanity and capitalism."

"I'm not sure vegans would agree with you about that," I say, opting to take a sip of coffee instead of a bite of sausage.

"I'm not sure vegans would agree with me about a lot of stuff, but I'm always willing to hear them out."

"And just for the record, I think human beauty contests are just as ridiculous. More so, actually."

"Well, we can agree on that at least." Sophie toasts me with her coffee.

"So Marley, how's the ankle?" Nancy asks.

"It's doing a lot better. Thank goodness for Bennett. He's far more diligent with icing it and wrapping it than I am."

"She very well could have undone all that diligent icing this morning. You should have seen her jump out of be—" He stops abruptly, seeming to remember he's talking to other people, and very nosy other people to boot.

Nancy smacks the table and holds her hand out to Karl. "That'll be twenty bucks, Mr. Hore."

"Goddammit, woman," he grumbles, leaning back to reach into his pocket for his wallet. He pulls out a twenty and smacks it into her hand.

Sophie has gone red, and she's staring at her plate while my gaze is bouncing around the table before finally landing on Bennett who looks like he's about to puke. His eyes slide to mine, and he winces before mouthing, "I'm so sorry."

"Why?" I say aloud. "I'm not." I go back to eating like nothing happened.

The rest of breakfast is full of laughter, and I keep having to remind myself that this is not going to be a regular occurrence. I kind of hate the little voice of reason that keeps popping up, but I can't let myself get too comfortable with everything, or maybe with the *idea* of everything. Because frankly I've never been more comfortable in my life than I have been this week, with a sprained ankle, surrounded by strangers.

"Marley, can I send you home with some sauce?" Nancy asks as she gets up to start clearing the table.

"Sit down, dearest," Karl says, jumping up and pulling the plates from her hand. "We've had this she-cooks-I-clean routine for nearly twenty-five years, and she always manages to forget about it when we've got company. Makes me look like a lazy husband."

I love them. "I bet a lot of people wish they had that kind of arrangement."

"Well, there's a lot that people aren't good at," Karl says gruffly. "But wishing for things is not one of them."

"I say you don't give her any sauce, Mom," Sophie says,

helping her dad by grabbing the serving dishes. "That way if she wants some, she has to come back for a visit."

"That's bribery," I gasp.

"Some say bribery." She shrugs. "Some would call it strategy." I do not miss the wink she gives Bennett as she walks out of the room.

I swing my head in his direction, but he ignores me and takes a sip of his coffee.

"Don't worry, Marley," Nancy says, patting my hand, "I'll give you enough to tide you over until you have time to come back to see us." She looks at Bennett when she says "us" and I feel like they're all in cahoots. "Just for the sake of curiosity, when do you think that might be?"

I laugh nervously because when I leave here I don't actually plan on coming back. When I leave, I need to walk away and not look back.

"Oh," I say, dabbing my mouth with the corner of my napkin. "I don't know. Between recovering and then getting back out there, it could be a whole year." The look on Nancy's face doesn't hold a candle to the one on Bennett's. "It's not that I don't want to," I lie, or I think I lie. At this point, I'm not sure if it's them or me I'm lying to. "My job is sporadic. I could end up embedded for weeks at a time with a group somewhere. And then there could be something else that pops up, and I've got to go cover that." I feel a bit frantic at the moment. Like I'm trying to tell them that it's not them, it's me, but it all just sounds like I'm making excuses. "I'm nomadic by nature, I guess."

"She's got a very important *job*, Nancy," Bennett says, and he makes it clear that it is my job and not my passion with the way he says the word. Then he stands and takes his mug to the kitchen, leaving Nancy and me alone at the table.

We sit there silently for a minute before she speaks. "He

knows you can't stay. Deep down he knows that. But I think part of him wishes you would."

"Part of me wishes the same, it's just—"

"Not who you are," Nancy finishes my sentence for me, and I nod.

"No... not yet anyway. He's such a good man," I say quietly because for some reason I don't want him to hear me. "If I could change who I was instantly for one person, it would be him. Which is insane to say after, what, four days?"

Nancy is shaking her head. "One of the very best things about Bennett Morgan is that he never expects anyone to change for him. Don't let him know you would because that would break his heart. If he likes you, it's for who you are right now and not for who you could be."

"I've never had a relationship. Honestly, life with him is as close as I've ever gotten to one."

"So you just threw yourself into the deep end, eh?"

"I mean, it wasn't intentional. Everything just kind of happened."

"And besides never having had a relationship, and your job taking you away from the people you care about for indeterminate amounts of time, what's holding you back from attempting one?"

"I have never really wanted one before. I didn't see the point and... what I do is dangerous," I begin, admitting out loud what I have never said before. "Where I go could be where I stay. Every kiss, text, photograph, wave, it could be my last. I'm not afraid in the field. And the thought of people I leave behind being afraid when I don't feels wrong. Like I'm leaving them to worry about me. When in reality, when I'm working I don't think of anyone else. I barely even think about myself."

Nancy takes my hand between hers. "Marley, I hate to tell you this, but you never coming back here won't keep us from worrying about you. And for the record, you don't need to be going into the middle of a war zone in order for something to be your last. That's why we need to hold onto the things that make us happy while we can. Hell, Karl could drop dead of a heart attack standing in the kitchen, and our last interaction would be about the dishes. That's life, kiddo. No matter what you do for a living, life is un-fucking-predictable."

Have I mentioned how much I love Nancy Hore? But at this moment when she's making all the sense in the world, I absolutely despise her.

TWENTY-EIGHT

The long walk back from the Hores is mostly quiet. I'm replaying what Nancy said, and I'm sure Bennett is as irritated with me as I feel. At some point he steps in front of me and squats down, not bothering to ask if I'm tired. As much as I have enjoyed all the piggyback rides, I find myself resenting this one. I'm used to walking for hours while carrying heavy cameras, without needing a ride or to rest. I hate that I even need or accept help when so many others would and do power through their perceived limitations. And I hate that Bennett can so easily see when I've reached my limit. I hate that he has seen everything I don't say so easily since day one. I have spent years buttoning up my life, only letting people see what I want them to, and this guy drops into my life and has me figured out in no time. But perhaps what I hate most is that I don't fucking hate it at all.

When we get back to the house, Bennett says he's going to head out to his office to get some work done. In this whole time, I've never thought about what he did beyond the physical action of rescuing dogs. Of course, he has an office and charity things to do. I don't even know what this operation is called. I shake my head at myself and grab my phone off the charger in the kitchen before I head to the living room. I practically fall into the armchair, exhausted. I'm sore from the crutches and from, well, other things, and I'm annoyed at myself for being such a child.

Izzy has texted me to let me know that she, Nellie, and Tom will be coming so that Tom can drive my car back and I can fill them in on everything. Because that's exactly what I'm going to want to do the minute I leave here, relive it all. I do, however, want to take some pictures of the dogs before I leave, if only to offer to Bennett for adoption purposes. Assuming he doesn't already have great pictures of them, which he probably does. I just don't know how else to say thank you. So I slip my phone into my hoodie pocket, grab my camera, and make my way back outside.

Most of the dogs are running around the field, and when they see me they fly to the gate. I think what I love most about dogs is that no matter how often they see you, they react like you are the sun after days of rain. Every. Single. Time. I manage to squeeze my way into the space and make my way over to the little bench Bennett put out here for potential adopters to sit on while they get to know a dog. My instincts make me want to get right on the ground with them, really put myself in the midst of the action, but I also know that I'd probably regret that immediately.

A lot of the first images I get are of the chaos around me, blurs of dog fur and tongues hanging out of the sides of mouths. They won't bring anyone up here to adopt, but they do represent a certain kind of whimsy of being surrounded by dogs. Eventually they calm down, and I'm able to get some great shots of different dogs in various states of being. Playing, sleeping, sitting and just staring at me, rolling around, and carrying around sticks and balls just because they can. At some point, I make the decision to sit on the ground, and before long I've flopped onto my back. This seems to act like an invitation, and soon I'm at the bottom of a massive dog pile, which is why I hadn't sat on the ground in the first place. Soon enough, though, everyone seems to be on the same page, and various body parts are turned into dog pillows. Yogurt has his head cradled between my neck and shoulder, Daisy and Milo have each taken a thigh, Marley has somehow wedged his entire body between Milo and Yogurt to claim my left boob. Someone's tail is softly batting my upper arm, and I cannot remember the last time I felt this calm. I pull my phone out of my hoodie and hold it above my head for a selfie, something I never do, but I feel almost panicked about not capturing this for myself. One day when I go back to my normal world, this will all seem like a dream, and I don't want to be Dorothy trying to convince others that what I experienced was real.

At some point I must fall asleep because when I open my eyes Bennett is crouched over me, smiling. My stomach does its little flip thing, and I realize I was terrified of not seeing that smile again before I left.

"Enjoying yourself?" he asks.

I smile up at him and nod. "What's the rescue called?"

He sits next to me, Yogurt immediately leaving me to go jump at his face, tail going like a propellor. "It's kind of boring."

"Too cool for a punny name?" I squint up at him as the sun slips back out from behind a cloud.

"Would you believe those were all taken?"

"Come on, what is it?"

"Morgan Estate Rescue." He winces as though he's embarrassed.

"As in your last name and this property?" I gesture with both hands in a circle.

"Sort of. Remember how I said my grandfather hated dogs and that he desperately wanted me to make it in football so we'd have our family name on something else?"

"Unfortunately yes," I scoff, grateful I never had the displeasure of meeting the man.

"Well, I figured with the property and then all his money technically being his estate, I'd call the rescue Morgan Estate. Then his name was on something, and his death represented something else."

"That's diabolical." I sit up. "So, is this it, or do you have plans to expand?"

"Expand how?"

"I don't know." I look around at the property. "More dogs, more animals in general?"

"I don't really plan on running an animal sanctuary, but I don't think I have it in me to turn away an animal if it's in need." We're both looking at my ankle. "I can see this place being the in-between for most animals rather than a permanent home." He's still staring at my ankle, and I can't help but wonder if that's how he sees this little blip in time for me.

"If you take on more, you'll definitely need help." I say, looking around.

"Yes," he agrees, finally looking up at me. "Maybe even someone who can do stuff for social media. Someone told me people like videos of dogs." His smile is teasing now, and I want to kiss it off his face, but I hold myself back.

"Can I see your office?"

"It's nothing special."

"But it's yours," I say, almost embarrassed.

"Really, Marley, it's nothing. It's a desk and a computer with a filing cabinet and some baskets of dog supplies." He sounds frustrated and a bit like he had at the Hores' table so I don't push him on it. Knowing Bennett, he has his reasons, and I respect them without needing to know what they are.

We sit there together, the tension I felt earlier returning. Then Bennett flops back and closes his eyes. So I do the same. After a bit, my fingers find their way to his, those little sparks returning.

I'm about to ask what he has planned for the rest of the day, but the sound of a truck has us both sitting up and looking out at the driveway. A man with a hard hat and safety vest steps out, and Bennett is up and striding to the gate as it dawns on me that the man being here means one thing. The road is passable, and I will officially be home this time tomorrow. I flop back down, trying to keep the real world at bay for just a little longer.

TWENTY-NINE

The morning started so well but then took an unexpected turn at breakfast. I'm frustrated with how I'm feeling, and I'm not entirely sure how to deal with that. I am not a passive-aggressive or possessive person, but something about the way she so easily talked about leaving made something inside me snap. Karl and Sophie both assured me that I hadn't lost it, that they can see we aren't just two people sharing a house for a few days.

"It takes some people years to admit how they feel about another person," Karl had said, his hands deep in soapy dishwater. "Meanwhile, others see one another across a room and know instantly. That's half the fun about human connection—there are absolutely no rules."

"Well, there are norms," Sophie had piped in then. "Let's use you and Marley as an example."

"Must we?" I'd huffed, crossing my arms and leaning against the island.

"It seems the most relevant to the situation. Now, you

found each other in less-than-ideal circumstances. You became her caretaker immediately, and she depended on you. That could very well build a false sense of comfort and attraction." She thought for a minute. "Like, hero worship. Then there's you. This guy who lives his life to rescue dogs and provide a better life for them."

"Are you saying our attraction is based on a hero-worship dynamic?"

"In a way, but hear me out. I don't actually think that's what's happening here. I know you. You're just a good, helpful guy. You don't get off on helping."

"That's true," Karl said while drying his hands. "I've never thought, 'He's enjoying this a bit too much' when you've helped out, if you know what I mean."

Sophie rolled her eyes at her dad and continued. "And Marley definitely doesn't strike me as someone who enjoys being rescued or even taken care of. She's fiercely independent, and I'd actually wager that admitting she needed help was a big deal for her."

She'd make a killing on that wager. "What's your point, Soph?"

"My point is, I think you two would have ended up feeling the exact same way if you'd run into each other at the grocery store, or made eye contact across a room."

"You're talking about fate," I'd replied, letting my skepticism really shine.

"Fate, or more like a natural compatibility. If you'd met at a party, you'd eventually get to the point you are now, sharing looks and oozing sexual tension. You just got there faster because you've spent 24/7 with each other."

Karl had nodded sagely throughout the entire conversation and eventually voiced his agreement with his "brilliant and favourite daughter."

"She's your only daughter, Karl."

"That we know of," he replied, earning a sigh from the daughter in question.

I'd spent the walk back replaying the conversation over in my mind and trying to decide if it was something worth bringing up to Marley. Four days felt like a lifetime somehow and yet too short. I wasn't ready for her to leave, but I also wasn't about to insist that she stay. I didn't want to tie her down or make her think that staying was the only way we could try to make a go of it. No matter how we felt, there would always be that voice saying everything happened too fast, and I had a feeling that would eat away at both of us.

I'M ALSO MATURE ENOUGH to admit that I'm worried that what I feel is one-sided. Not that she's done anything to make me think that. I can't even decide if it would be better if she didn't feel the same or did but was unwilling to stick it out. What I do know is that having Marley here has reminded me what it's like to not be alone all the time. And as much as I hate being left behind, I'm starting to realize it's perhaps better to have something for a short time than never at all. I pull my phone out to text Sophie.

> I think I need to hire some help.

Her reply comes almost instantly.

> SOPHIE
>
> YES! How much help?
>
> Full-time? Part-time?
>
> Qualifications? Wage?

Her questions keep coming, and I do my best to come up with things that will hopefully bring in some decent applicants.

Once she's given me the thumbs-up, I deal with a request for help with a litter of Dalmatian cross puppies that I make arrangements to pick up tomorrow evening. Marley will be long gone by then, and it'll give me something else to focus on, some other rescue mission. Maybe I just get attached to the living things I bring home, and maybe I should talk to someone about that. In the middle of updating my calendar, it hits me that I only have a bit more guaranteed time with Marley, and I'm spending it locked in my office sulking. I roll my neck, power down my computer, and march myself outside, hoping she's easy to find.

As it turns out, finding her takes absolutely no effort on my part. She's lying in the field, surrounded by the dogs. I instantly feel some of the tension leave my body. Compared to the first time I found her surrounded by them, this is a total 180. Everyone is asleep, including Marley, under the perfect October sky. I feel kind of bad waking her up, but then we get talking and I'm glad I had. I want to soak up every moment I can before she walks out of my life. When she asks if she can see my office, I can't tell her that it's the one place I don't have a memory of her in. I don't think I can tell her I need to have that space stay a Marley-free zone because it's where I need to focus on other things. But I don't, and of course after the words are out of my mouth I feel like I've moved us back ten steps.

I end up lying back and closing my eyes. I hear her follow suit shortly after, and then I feel her fingertips brush my hand. I've always thought the spark people talk about was bullshit, but I've felt it since the day I found her. The fact she nearly jumped out of her skin makes me think she felt it too. It's probably some kind of sensory anticipation thing, completely explained by science, but I hold onto hope that our upcoming goodbye is more of a "see you soon." I find myself hoping she treats my hope the same way she gives to those she photographs.

THIRTY

Bennett makes pasta with Nancy's sauce again for dinner, and I savour every single bite. I have to wonder if it will taste as good when I use it at home without this man sitting beside me. Does the company make the food better? I kind of hate that I'll be able to answer that question soon enough.

By the time we're doing the dishes, we have mastered small talk.

"So can your place accommodate the crutches?" he asks, looking at the plate he's scrubbing instead of at me.

"We'll move some stuff around, but that won't take long. I'll be zipping around there in no time." I don't tell him the truth, which is that I'm actually only stopping at my apartment to grab some necessities and then going to stay with Nellie for a few days. Tom also has me booked in at the hospital where he's an anesthesiologist, for an X-ray to make sure it is just a sprain, but again, I don't tell Bennett that. I'm closing him off more by the minute, and even though I know it's not fair, I feel like I need to do it in order to protect myself.

"Are you going to go to the hospital?"

"Probably. Bennett?" I put the towel down and move towards him. In my head, I'm doing this very gracefully and somewhat seductively, but it's impossible for me to do with the crutches.

"What?" He's watching the water swirl down the drain and doesn't turn my way until I'm right next to him.

"If I was the type of person to stay in one place..." I swallow and collect my courage before continuing, "this is the only place I'd want to stay. This is the only place I've ever felt like I could stay." And fucking hell, his eyes actually fill with tears. I want to drop dead for making him sad. But I don't have much time to think about it because his soapy hands are pulling my face to his before a single tear falls.

He's got me in his arms seconds later, and then my ass hits the island and he's laying me back and kissing down my body. It's kind of fitting that this was where everything started, me on the counter, Bennett taking charge and not asking permission.

Before I really register what's happening, he's got my leggings and underwear pulled off my left leg and dangling around my right ankle, then he's on his knees between my legs. I'm not really an oral kind of girl and I'm about to say as much when I feel his lips drag up my inner thigh, his beard causing interesting sensations to spread across my skin, and the words die on my lips. There are a lot of labels I'd never apply to myself, and yet with Bennett, I'm ready to invest in a label maker and cover myself with them.

When I'm close, I reach down and grip his hair, tugging gently so he stops.

"Did I hurt you?" he asks, looking up at me.

"God no." I shake my head. "I just, I want you... but..." I'm turning into some bashful virgin apparently because I have no idea how to form the words I'm trying to say. But because it's Bennett, he nods in understanding. He kisses his way back up my body and runs his tongue from my collarbone to my chin, sending shivers to the very tips of everything on my body.

I sit up and wrap my arms around his neck, keeping his mouth fused with mine as I scoot my ass to the edge of the counter. And that's when I stop and pull away.

"Oh my god," I say.

"What?" Bennett asks, his breath coming out heavy.

"This is not sanitary." I'm bare-assed on his counter, and to put it plainly, I'm horrified.

Bennett looks down and grins wickedly, then captures my mouth again as he slides one finger inside me, causing my eyes to roll back. The last thing I think before he takes me back to the edge of oblivion is this is why they invented Lysol.

Later, when Bennett catches me looking at the counter and biting my lip, he assures me that it's going to be gone soon anyway. He's got new butcher block counters ordered, and besides, we were the only two who ever sat there.

"Literally, you mean?" I grin at him as I hand him a plate to put away.

He shrugs. "On, at, both."

The dogs are all inside again and settled in for the night, and we both seem to be drawing out the nighttime routine. It's taken us way too long to put a few dishes away, and then I have him stop in front of his bookshelf on our way upstairs. Asking him to tell me which ones he loved most or is looking forward to reading. I give him my phone and have him make a list of his favorites so I can download the audio versions to listen to when I'm gone.

We shower for so long that the hot water begins to cool, and even then we seem to be fine with using our own body heat to stay warm. This morning felt like a quick goodbye kiss in comparison to this drawn-out affair, the physical version of "You hang up first." The entire time I'm being pulled in two different directions by two sides of myself. The side that is struggling to get me to stay is weak from disuse, but it's surprisingly tenacious.

"Imagine this every night," it pleads as I moan into Bennett's mouth, his hips pressed between my thighs. But a stronger voice is insisting that it's only this good because it's desperate. That an end date makes everything more intense, and without it, complacency takes over and things will just hurt more in the end. Best to enjoy it at this level while I can. Don't think about tomorrow.

Hours later as we're tangled together under the duvet, Bennett pulls me tighter and says what I need him to say.

"I don't want you to leave, Mar, but I know why you have to." I honestly don't know if he actually knows or if he just thinks he does. Hell, he could just be saying it for my benefit, but I love him at this moment for saying it. "But for the record, I'm not going anywhere." Translation: I'm here when you want to come back. Not *if* you want to come back, but *when*.

"Have I told you how happy I am that you found me, Bennett?" I murmur into his chest.

"You may have mentioned it once before."

"I should probably have told you every day while I've been here."

"You have, in different ways," he says, kissing my head. "I need you to do something for me."

"Anything."

"Tell me something good about what you do."

I take a deep breath, and I tell him about the earthquake survivors in Pakistan and then about the brothers in Ukraine, and once I've started, I can't seem to stop telling him about all the good I've seen in the midst of death and destruction. How even when I think about how nothing can make me smile again, someone manages to do that.

"I tend to forget how regular people on the ground respond. Seeing us there brings them hope in a way not much else does. Even when our governments move on to the next conflict, seeing us covering something gives people that extra push to keep going. Seeing the resilience of humans can be... inspirational."

"Maybe you need to focus on that more?" Bennett says quietly.

"On the hope?"

"In the hope you help give to people. I can't imagine how exhausting it is to maybe feel like you're the only one, or at least one of very few, who cares. But also focus on showing the resiliency of people who have been put through unimaginable hardships."

"It's just hard. Sometimes it takes days of shooting things to finally get to someone. And then it's hard knowing that people see bombed-out or burned buildings and don't seem to care so it takes a body or evidence of suffering. Hope is so buried sometimes."

"So give it up and open a livestock glamour photography studio. I know a few heifers that would just love you to *moooove* into that field." The way he committed to that pun has me laughing so hard my laugh morphs into snorts.

"Yeah, the pigs would probably love it too." And now he's laughing with me.

"I'll probably be able to make a few *bawks* with the chickens too."

"Yeah, doesn't seem like a *baaaad* way to make a living."

"It would be *udderly* ridiculous," I manage to get out despite the fact I can barely catch my breath.

"Don't be such a *neighsayer*." The emphasis he puts on "neigh" has me snorting again, and we spend the next five minutes laughing.

When we finally pull ourselves together, I bury myself as far as I can into his arms and just focus on matching my breathing with his. My eyes are heavy, but I don't want to give in to sleep yet. I let my thoughts wander to the day Bennett found me. I'm having a hard time understanding how that was only five days earlier. It's an escape from reality, I tell myself. This isn't real life, this can't be real life. Still, I'm not ready to go back to my reality just yet, and every passing minute I'm in Bennett's arms I'm having a harder and harder time reminding myself why I have to. A tear slips from my eye, and I press my face harder into Bennett's chest and inhale. I feel his arms tighten ever so slightly, keeping me close, even in sleep.

THIRTY-ONE

Sleep has the audacity to come, and then morning light taunts us cruelly through the blinds. I wake on my side with Bennett spooning me. I can tell it's still early because the house is silent. The dogs haven't begun to stir yet so I let myself relax into Bennett's hold and stare at the wall.

"I can hear that brain of yours working, sweetheart," Bennett whispers as his hand winds its way up my body. He gently grips my chin and turns my head until he can easily kiss me. I don't focus on my morning breath or that this is the last early morning kiss I'm going to get from him. Instead, I melt back into his body and roll my ass along his length, earning a sharp intake of breath and a noise that rumbles from deep within his chest. I want to bottle that sound and take it with me everywhere.

I tell him with my body how I feel because I'm afraid my words will betray me. We hover somewhere between feral and reverent until we can no longer ignore life.

Bennett is out with the dogs while I pack up the clothes Nancy had given me. Bennett had washed them and left them for me to fold because I had insisted on doing some of the work. At ten, Izzy texts to say they are about twenty minutes away, and I start preparing myself to walk away from Bennett Morgan and his pack.

There's a bag full of stuff from Nancy for me to eat, and while I love that she did this I'm not looking forward to the reminder. I'm convinced eating that sauce while not in Bennett's presence will feel like I'm cheating on him. I watch him from the porch, running around with the dogs and laughing, and I think of the cupboard full of pills. I decided at some point last night that I needed to push him to hire some help. I don't know if he's purposely isolated himself or if it has just happened, but it makes me sad. I hate the idea of him here in pain and pushing through it instead of taking care of himself.

He sees me standing there, throws a couple of balls, and then uses the distraction to sneak out of the gate before jogging over to me.

"What's that look on your face?" he asks, stopping at the bottom of the stairs.

"I need you to promise me something," I say, sitting on the top step.

He joins me, leaning on his knees before looking at me. "If it's that I forget this ever happened, I'm afraid I can't," he says wryly.

"Oh please, I'm unforgettable. I won't set you up for failure."

"What can I promise you, Marley?" he asks so sincerely that I take a second longer than I should to respond.

"I need you to hire some help, Bennett."

"Why? Do I seem like I'm not managing things?"

"No, I think you're doing well, but I'm afraid you won't always be doing well." I don't know if that's the right thing to say. It's what I meant, but when it came out it sounded insulting, like I don't believe in him.

He looks away from me. "Is this about what I told you about the depression? Because I've got that under control. I have a whole team who help me keep that under control." He definitely sounds a bit miffed.

"I'm not talking about the depression, I'm talking about the headaches. I know you have a team of doctors, but they aren't here, Bennett. They aren't going to go out and feed the dogs so you can deal with the pain in your head. They aren't going to head out to pick up a dog in need when you can't see straight because the pain is so bad." I take a deep breath. "I think you love to have people and dogs to take care of so you don't have to focus on yourself. I think it's easier for you to be everyone else's support than allow anyone to support you."

"You say that like it's a bad thing."

"It is if you're so busy worrying about everyone else being okay that you don't make sure that you are. How can you help anyone else if you're locked in the dark? You need help here, but it seems like you don't want to accept that."

He stands and walks away from me, and I let him. But he doesn't get far before he turns and comes to stand in front of me again. I look up at him and wait.

"Everyone who I thought would support me left. They walked away or died. So even though some days it feels like literal torture to get up and do my job, I do it because I know I can count on myself. And I know that those dogs can count on me too." I know he's talking about his ex and his friends and his family, but I can't help but feel like he's grouping me amongst them.

I stand so we're chest-to-chest then raise my hands and run my thumbs across his brow. "That's not true, Bennett. You've got incredible neighbors who would walk through fire for you.

Seriously, we should all be so lucky to have a group of Hores down the street." He humours me with a one-note laugh. "And employees aren't friends or family. You pay them to support your operation. It's totally different, and you cannot look at it like you look at things in your personal life. You'd be an amazing boss, Bennett. Add to that working daily with that lot" —I point behind him at the dogs—"dream come true for the right people." His arms wrap around my waist, and he pulls me in for a hug. "There also isn't anything wrong with just having someone else around. Not to knock the dogs or anything, but having someone who can talk back isn't the worst thing. I need to know you're going to be okay so I don't worry about you."

"Says the one who works in literal warzones," he says into my neck.

"Yeah, well, that's why I need to be focused on the task at hand and not worried about your sexy ass."

"You think I'm sexy?"

I pull back to look at him. "Have I not made that clear this week? My god, I'm bad at this." He kisses me, and I feel gravity trying to keep me there. Holding me in place, trying to tell me that this is where I should be staying. Somehow leaving feels like I'm breaking the rules of physics.

The sound of wheels on gravel has him pulling back. When he looks down at me, I can practically see thoughts swirling. "I..." he begins, then he looks over at the car pulling in. When his eyes return to mine, I can tell that whatever he was going to say is gone. "I don't want you to go," he finally says, his forehead resting against mine.

"I know." I know he wants me to say that I wish I didn't have to, but I don't. Because despite my revelation that giving someone hope is something that brings me joy about my job, I can't bring myself to give him any. And it makes me feel like a shitty person.

Izzy jumps out of the car before Nellie even puts it in park and races over to me.

"You're alive!" she says, grabbing onto me so tightly that I'm struggling to breathe. Izzy is 5'1" but has the hug of a man three times her size. Tom and Nellie follow behind, both giving me hugs that are far more normal.

I gesture back to Bennett, who I notice didn't leave the bottom of the stairs. "This is Bennett. Bennett, Izzy, Tom, and Nellie." I point at each one in turn.

Bennett finally steps forward and shakes each of their hands. Izzy is studying him carefully while Nellie is already distracted by the field of dogs.

"Nell, you should go meet the dogs."

"Am I allowed to meet the dogs?" Tom says, looking longingly at the field.

"Just *look*, Thomas," Izzy says. "And that applies to you too, young lady." She points at Nellie.

"Come on, I'll introduce you." Bennett tips his head towards the field.

Izzy grabs my bag and throws it in the car then comes back to stand beside me, watching as everyone is swarmed by the pack.

"The picture did not do that man justice," she says nonchalantly.

"No," I agree, trying but failing to look away from him.

"Are you okay?" she asks, turning her attention to me.

"Yes and no." I smile sadly. "I just wish he wasn't so..." I shrug. "And that I wasn't so..."

"Ah yes, the timeless conundrum of two people destined for one another being so..." She shrugs, and I laugh.

"Come on, you know what I mean."

"I don't actually. Care to elaborate?"

I hate it when she does this to me. She never lets me get away with being vague; she always needs to dig.

"I don't do relationships, Izzy."

"Yeah, but why is that exactly?"

"I... I don't know how, and I'm not going to try and figure one out while I put someone through the worry of me not coming home. I can't do what I do and be afraid of breaking their heart."

"You do know that every time you go away, Nellie and I are losing our minds, right? That if anything were to happen to you, our hearts would break?"

"That's different," I say sullenly.

"How? We love you. How is that different from someone you're romantically involved with loving you?"

I give her a look.

"Oh, so this is about sex. Are you afraid that if you break some guy's heart, he'll never be able to have sex again and that would be on you for not being incredible in bed but because they'll never get over you?"

"What? No!" I cry out, causing everyone, including the dogs to look over at me. "No, this has nothing to do with sex," I hiss.

"I'm sorry, but it feels like you don't actually have a good reason. It seems like you're scared just because you've never had a proper relationship before and you don't want to fuck it up. You don't want to be your parents. Who, newsflash, you're not like at all."

"Iz, all week you've been bugging me about this guy helping me for the wrong reasons, and now you're standing here trying to tell me to just start a relationship with him? None of this was real. He took care of me because I was hurt and he's a good guy. We slept together because we both wanted it. That's it. None of this means more than that." Even as I say it, I know it's bullshit. I also know I'm making excuses, but I'm stubborn and apparently I've decided this is a hill I will die on. A hill I'll die on alone with no one waiting at the bottom.

Izzy doesn't say anything back to me, so I know she thinks I'm lying. That's usually how she handles falsehoods, with stoic judgemental silence. Nellie is sitting on the ground with Clyde between her legs. He's on his back with all four legs sticking straight up. She's in her element, and I feel a twinge of jealousy that if she had been the one Bennett found, we wouldn't be here to pick her up but to attend her wedding. But Bennett is not looking at Nellie or Tom. He's zeroed in on me.

"This was a mistake," Izzy says, shaking her head.

"What was?"

"Bringing Tom to a place with dogs. He's like a kid asking weekly if we can get one. But we all know who's going to end up taking care of it." She tilts her head towards me and mouths "me" as she points at her chest.

"Yeah, but imagine the Christmas cards with a Daisy or a Farley in the family picture." I nudge her with my elbow.

"Oh, I am, and I'm the only one in the picture that looks exhausted. I've told him when the kids are older we can revisit it. Nellie, on the other hand, came here and found the love of her life too."

My head whips back towards the field, and I see Bennett crouched next to Nellie, chatting and rubbing Clyde's belly. The twinge of jealousy I had felt earlier grows, and I swallow and look at the ground.

"Hmm," Izzy says quietly. "Very interesting." I look at her, and she leans in and whispers, "For the record, I was talking about the dog."

Eventually, Izzy is able to pull Tom and Nellie out of dog heaven and back to the car. They say goodbye to Bennett, thanking him for taking care of me and then leave us alone.

There's a foot between us, and I desperately want to erase it but I also have a feeling that if I do, it will make things harder on both of us.

"So," Bennett starts, "this has been fun."

"By far the best-sprained ankle experience a girl could ask for. Five stars, would recommend." We laugh awkwardly.

He holds out his hand. "Give me your phone, Mar." I unlock the screen and hand it over. "I'm giving you my number and email. That way if you want to stay in touch, it's on your terms." I bite my lip, mainly to keep myself from bursting into tears, and nod. His eyes darken slightly. "Sweetheart, I don't think you want to do that so close to other people." I let my lip slip free. "Good girl." A week ago, I hated pet names and I certainly didn't have a praise kink, and now I want him to tell me what to do, call me sweetheart, and then praise the hell out of me.

I make a split-second decision to erase the space between us, wrap my arms around his waist, and bury my face into his sweater. "I will miss you and this place," I mumble.

"You'll be too busy to miss it," he says, pulling me in tighter. He doesn't say it, but the way his hold tightens makes me think he knew I was lying earlier. His hold feels like a last attempt at keeping me in his orbit. Finally, we break apart and make our way to the car. He opens the door and helps me in, and when I tell him to give the crutches back to the Hores, he shakes his head and slides them in at my feet.

"Karl said that you're to return them yourself when you come to get your sauce fix."

"Well, that sounds suspect," Nellie says from the driver's seat.

Bennett smiles that smile, although it doesn't meet his eyes. "Take care, sweetheart," he says, and then he closes the door.

As Nellie drives away I fight the urge to turn around and

watch him out the back window. Everyone is silent until we get to the main road, then Tom turns back to Izzy sitting beside me.

"Did you see the one with—"

"No," she cuts him off, making Nellie laugh.

"But Iz, she was so fluffy and—"

"Thomas Andrew Hawthorn, if the next words out of your mouth aren't 'perfect for another family,' I do not want to hear them."

Tom turns back to face the front without another word, and Nellie and I burst out laughing. I can't think of a better group to take my mind off the best man I've ever met.

THIRTY-TWO

Turns out getting to the lot I had parked in was a lot farther than the eight kilometres I'd hiked, but at least my car is still there.

The minute Tom is out of the car, both of my friends turn to me expectantly. "What?" I feign ignorance.

"You know exactly what. Tell us everything, and don't leave out a single detail," Nellie says.

Izzy glances over at her. "You can leave out all the bits without the hot hero." My friends are ridiculous.

"Don't roll your eyes, Mar. We both have very boring lives and rely on you for these things."

"When have you ever relied on me for these things before?"

"You've had some pretty fun hookup stories from your trips," Nellie says, like the trips are nothing more than jaunts to all-inclusive resorts. "Remember the one with the interpreter?" She nudges Izzy.

"Oh, right!" Izzy fans her face. "That one was pretty hot."

I'm looking at them like they've both lost their minds because, in all honesty, I don't remember these stories. That could be because I embellish. I tell them about the hookups but then make them sound like more than two people trying to forget about the shit they saw that day. It's much easier to focus on something that feels good so you don't succumb to the stuff that doesn't. Avoidance as a survival technique is how Dr. Webber describes it. She doesn't agree with me that if survival is the ultimate goal, getting there by any means necessary, as long as you aren't hurting anyone along the way, is just fine. Apparently, I'm hurting myself and that's something I shouldn't be so cavalier about.

I end up giving them a glimpse of my week with Bennett. Some things are ours, and I don't feel like letting the girls into that space. They don't need to know that he's the only person I've ever felt truly free with because that will hurt them. They don't need to know I've felt somewhat invisible until Bennett looked at me. And I don't mean physically invisible, I mean that he saw the real me despite years of hiding from others and from myself. I do veer off course and tell them about the Hores because they played a pivotal role in my week. I tell them how Bennett doesn't think he really has anyone in his life, and how he seems to be a bit unaware of just how much his neighbors love him.

It takes around two hours to get to my place because of road work, and when we get there, Izzy insists on grabbing stuff for me because she doesn't want to risk me falling up or down the stairs. Considering I haven't tested proper stairs out since the sprain, I'm grateful. We have an hour to kill before my appointment so we go to Nellie's to get me settled in her guest room.

Tom is waiting in the driveway, and he has several grocery bags at his feet.

"Tom's going to take you to your appointment, and Nellie and I will make dinner. Hopefully, it's a celebratory one."

"Sounds good," I say, slowly getting out of the car.

"He better have found the good shit," Nellie says mostly to herself as she slides out of the car and walks straight up to the bags at Tom's feet.

Izzy rolls her eyes at me before grabbing my stuff. "Remember when she didn't care about what she ate? Now she's so particular."

I shrug. "Sometimes it's good to know what you want."

Izzy looks at me, one eyebrow raised, one hand on her hip. "Oh? And acting on what you want, is that good too?"

"Shut up, Iz," I say quietly as I hobble towards my car.

Nellie had moved into an older neighborhood last year, and while the homes aren't all on top of one another and the street is lined with large mature trees, I find myself instantly missing the openness of Bennett's land. There is a major renovation happening down the street, and the noise of hammers and drills drowns out any chance of birdsong. It's for the best, I remind myself, and this too is temporary anyway. Soon I'll replace all other noise with sounds people in this country can't even fathom. I've become a pro at drowning out with the sound of my shutter.

My appointment is quick, and I leave with a prescription for a powerful anti-inflammatory and a mild painkiller. I'll fill out the anti-inflammatory script but not the painkiller. After I was burned, I learned that I liked how a good painkiller numbed more than just the pain a little too much. I can numb things just fine without narcotics.

Nellie and Izzy have made tacos for dinner, and as we all sit around Nellie's dining table debating whether hard or soft tacos are better, I try to remain present. But my mind wanders to Bennett's kitchen. Is he having dinner at the island, or does he usually eat in the living room? Are the dogs with him? Or is he eating with his own thoughts as company? I'm restless, and can't stop my left foot from tapping under the table, but I try my best to refocus on the taco debate.

"Hard tacos are an abomination," Izzy says, as she perfectly layers toppings into her soft shell without looking because she's too busy glaring across the table at her husband. "Had I known your true feelings, I probably would have never married you."

Tom shrugs and takes a giant bite of his taco, and pieces of shell rain down onto his plate.

"See?" I point at him. "That right there is why I can't get on board with the hard shells. They are way too messy. You lose half the thing the minute you bite it. And what's the point of not getting to eat half the thing you're trying to eat?"

"Listen," Nellie cuts in, "the best thing to do is to wrap"—she puts a flour tortilla onto her plate then grabs a hard shell and places it on top—"the hard shell inside the soft shell and then you get the crunch without the mess."

Tom points at her while taking another bite. "Brilliant," he says around a mouthful of taco.

"That's what the lettuce is for," Izzy exclaims. "And there's less sodium."

"To be fair, Iz," I say, copying what Nellie just did, "I don't know how many people are concerned about their sodium levels on taco night." I add my fillings and take a bite. Once I've swallowed, I put the taco down and sigh. "I hate to admit it, Izzy, but this combination is fucking perfect."

She frowns at me then looks at the plate of shells, seeming to consider giving in. "I'll take your word for it," she finally says before taking a bite of her perfectly composed soft shell taco.

Izzy has been the same since we met in college. She was four years older and had decided to get a diploma in fine arts between getting her undergraduate and postgraduate degrees. We met in a composition class, and despite the fact she was already married with a kid and we didn't seem to have much in common, we hit it off. Nellie and I met when I was researching for a project at the college library she worked at. At some point, we just kind of morphed into a trio that occasionally let Tom and whichever person Nellie happened to be dating join in. Tonight was a pretty accurate depiction of our dynamic.

After we've eaten and cleaned up, Izzy and Tom hug us before heading out to pick their kids up from Tom's parents' place.

"Want to watch some *Schitt's Creek*?" Nellie asks after she locks the door.

"Um, would you hate me if I called it a night? I'm kind of drained."

"Wanna talk about it?" she asks, heading into the kitchen to turn off the lights.

"Maybe some other time." I give her a sad smile, and she nods.

"Well, no pressure, but you know where to find me."

"Thanks." I hug her and then make my way to the bedroom.

When I go to grab my change of clothes, I find a hoodie folded on top of my bag. It's not mine. It's the sweatshirt Bennett had changed into after the rain incident. I pick it up and hold it to my nose. I expect it to smell like laundry detergent, so I'm surprised that it smells like him. And then I laugh because during one of our dinner chats he'd told me how when a dog is adopted, he includes a blanket that smells like his place in the care package. It helps the dogs adjust to their new environments. This is his way of helping me adjust to my Bennett-less existence. I'm gone, but he's still caring for me.

I set it aside and pull out a ratty T-shirt and shorts. After I change and brush my teeth, I plug my phone in and climb into bed. I stare at it for a bit wondering if I should text him and say thank you for everything. But I don't want him to know I'm already thinking about him, that I haven't stopped thinking about him. So I roll over and close my eyes. I lie there for a while, chasing sleep before I swing my legs out of bed and grab the crutches. I make my way back to my bag and grab the sweatshirt. Then I head back to bed and curl up around it. I fall asleep almost immediately and don't wake up until Nellie knocks to let me know breakfast is ready. No dogs barking or coffee in bed today. No strong arms wrapped around my body or beard tickling my ear. I know there are things that a person can become addicted to immediately, but I never thought one of those things would be another person. I didn't even know I was addicted.

THIRTY-THREE

I've thankfully been pretty busy in the week since Marley left. Karl had me over helping with some fence repairs, which always turns into a dinner invitation. I knew exactly what he and Nancy were doing, but I let them think I wasn't in on their scheme. The Dalmatian puppies have taken up a lot of my time, and they are endlessly entertaining. The cluster headaches I've been getting, however, are far less entertaining. My neurologist wants me back in for another scan next week, but I haven't committed to one. When I told her that it was probably because of the extra work, she suggested I may want to hire some help, and it took me right back to that last conversation with Marley. But admitting that I need help is admitting defeat, and frankly I'm sick of feeling like I can't live up to even my most basic expectations.

Sophie's job ad brought in a lot of applicants, and I've scheduled interviews with a few who seemed like a good fit. I'm trying to view this as a new experience that will only make what I do better. With help I could offer more; hell, I may even be able to focus on building awareness about the rescue. One of the applicants has a degree in communications, and Sophie said she's really good at social media, whatever that means.

I'm sitting at the island still stirring my coffee, going over my interview notes, when my door bangs open and Karl walks in carrying a fucking calf. If there is one thing that's going to snap you out of a stupor, it's seeing your neighbor walk right into your kitchen carrying a baby cow.

"Karl," I say, sitting up straight and blinking at the man. "Why is there a cow in my kitchen?"

"Mom had twins and didn't want this guy."

"I'm sorry to hear that, Karl, but that doesn't answer the question as to why it's in my kitchen, which is in my house... which is typically not where one would find a cow."

"Don't worry about the whys, Bennett. Just know that this guy is going to make an excellent addition to your pack."

"I'm sorry, did you just say my pack? A pack is made up of dogs, Karl. That's a cow."

Karl looks down at the calf. "Yes, I thought we had established that this is a cow. Keep up."

"Keep up? I don't think we're even running the same route."

Karl sets down the calf, who immediately curls up on the floor. It's actually kind of cute, but I'm not about to acknowledge that.

"Listen, I've got a bunch of babies right now, and I don't have enough time to deal with a calf no mamma wants. So either you take him, I find a rescue, or we let nature take its course."

Fucking hell, he knows I'm not going to let that last one happen. "What am I supposed to do with a calf?"

"Well, at this stage, he won't be much more work than those puppies you've got. And hey, he matches them. Maybe they'll adopt him into the family. Think of it as a challenge—we all know how you like a challenge. Anyway, I've gotta get back, or Nancy is going to tan my hide." He waves and walks out. I jump up, nearly trip over the calf and follow him out onto the porch. "Actually, there's more."

"If it's more livestock, I'm going to have to decline," I say, defeated.

"No, just some stuff for the little guy. Some bottles of milk and a blanket. Nancy probably already sent an email with all the relevant information for keeping this guy fed and happy." He comes back from the truck with a large bag and hands it to me. "Don't think too much about it, Bennett. And give him a name."

I watch him drive away before the chill of winter chases me back into the house where there is still a baby cow curled up in my kitchen.

I slide down the front of my cabinets and sigh. "What the hell just happened?" I say to the calf, who blinks at me with his gigantic cow eyes. I have to admit the addition of a black-and-white cow around the same time I've taken in Dalmatian puppies does seem kind of perfect. But still, what am I going to do with a cow?

I grab my phone from the counter and open my email to find that Nancy had indeed emailed me a list of instructions. Keeping him warm and well-fed seems to be the most important thing. So basically the same as the puppies. She also lets me know that this is temporary but doesn't say for how long. But I do feel a sense of relief knowing I likely won't have to figure out how to care for a full-grown bull.

I put my phone down and slide closer to the little guy to run my hands down his neck. Eventually, I move him in between my legs so he's resting his head on my thigh. So far he's just like a dog, just a bit bonier and definitely smellier. Despite the overwhelming dread I'm feeling about keeping this guy alive, my mind starts brainstorming ways to train him like a dog. Do cows do tricks? Will they come when you call? I grab my phone again and start to Google. And holy shit, there's an entire website dedicated to training cows just like dogs. It may not be the kind of wave I was expecting, but it is a wave, and at this point I'll fucking take it.

THIRTY-FOUR

Three weeks later

It's actually good to be back in my own place. I love Nellie, but no matter what I always felt like I was in the way or too heavily relying on her generosity. I was also getting tired of being asked if I'd talked to Bennett on any given day. Being home lets me do what I want when I want to do it. I don't have to worry about what anyone else wants to eat or feel bad for not being a better conversationalist. But most of all, I don't have to keep lying to her face when she asks how I'm doing. Apparently Nellie really focused on the "He doesn't really have anyone other than his neighbors" part of our conversation. Me randomly staring off into space probably didn't help my case either.

I say I'm fine, but then every night I curl up with Bennett's sweatshirt and stare at my phone telling myself that I can't text or call him. At one point I even convince myself that he's forgotten all about me by now. I do such a good job convincing myself of that that I end up sobbing into the hoodie. The thought of him being perfectly happy without me is both soothing and a special kind of hell. Great for him, depressing for me.

I've only got forty-eight hours to do a proper cleaning of my place before I leave on my first assignment in over a month. I dust every surface and open a few windows to get some fresh air in, even though it's lightly snowing. When I pull my bedsheets out of the dryer and begin to separate them, I notice that Bennett's hoodie had gotten bunched up with them. I've washed the last of him out of the fabric, and I end up sitting on my bare mattress crying for half an hour. When I pull myself back together, I tell myself this version of me needs to take a hike before I leave.

Twenty minutes later I'm at the post office, stuffing the sweatshirt into a box. I end up staring at the open package for a while. I told myself I needed to cut and run, and everything in me tells me to close the box and do that. Except there's a damn little voice telling me to at least stick a piece of paper in with it to say thank you. That is what a normal adult human would likely do. And there is something about Bennett that makes me want to be that adult. So I quickly look around and grab the first thing I can write a quick note on. I borrow the post office's pen and scribble, "Benny, I accidentally washed this. Doesn't smell like you anymore. Thanks. Marley" Then I stick the post-card of a moose standing in a marsh into the box, shut it quickly, and practically run from the building. It's only when I get home that I realize that I may as well have written that I liked him and missed him and wished he was here. I briefly consider texting him, but what would I say exactly? If I text him, that would open the floodgates, and I'm not ready for that.

Before I go to bed, I log into my email and find one from horedairy@gmail.com. I open it to find a picture of a smiling Sophie standing next to Clarice who has a giant red and white ribbon attached to her halter. "We did it. Time to give those horse snobs a show." I reply with a quick "Congratulations, Sophie. What *udderly* fabulous news." For some reason I also let her know I'm heading off to Syria for work before congratulating her again on the win.

I do a quick check of my schedule for tomorrow and ensure all the relevant alarms are set before tucking myself in. It's the first night since I left Bennett's that I don't have his hoodie to snuggle with, and I'm already regretting sending it back. I eventually fall asleep as my mind creates an elaborate plan to break into the post office and steal it out of the outbound mail bin.

I'm triple-checking my equipment when my phone rings the next morning.

"Newsgate! This couldn't wait until tonight?"

"Goddammit, Marley, you know how I feel about that nickname."

"What?" I say innocently. "It's so appropriate."

"Fucking pain in my ass," he grumbles, but I know he's not actually mad about it. "Listen, there's been a change of plans. Karen has us on a flight for two this afternoon now. So you've gotta get a move on and get to the airport pronto."

I glance over at the clock on the microwave. It's 10:30. "She sure knows how to add drama into the mix." I roll my eyes and begin to pack my stuff.

"Keeping us on our toes for sure." I love working with Simon; he's got a wicked sense of humour and yet knows when to lock it away. That's important in our line of work. I, on the other hand, have a hard time locking away the humour and tend to bust it out when I shouldn't.

"I assume she's emailing all the relevant information?"

"Should already be in your inbox, darling. I'll see you soon." He hangs up, and I take a deep breath before going into prep mode.

We're flying into Istanbul and then to a smaller city close to the Syrian border. From there, we'll cross over land with a couple of other journalists, a group of physicians, and medical supplies. I hate traveling in a large group. It draws more attention, and it puts me on edge. And in general people tend to not go about their lives the same way around a big group of foreigners, which makes it hard to capture the real story. Although I will admit that traveling with doctors is better than with people often just labelled as "officials." I can't be invisible when I'm surrounded by guys in khakis, polos, and flak jackets, claiming they're there to save the day.

Simon assured me that we'll be able to sneak away from the crowd and cover some grassroots stuff. This is another one of the reasons Simon and I work well together; we're not in this field for the glory or to get famous. We both want to help facilitate change. It's why we're still doing the job. It's why he puts his life on the line and leaves his son as frequently as I leave my safe little one-bedroom apartment.

I get to the airport with just under three hours until our flight and find Simon on the other side of security. He greets me with a hug and a coffee. We spread out on the floor near our gate and go over a map of the area we'll be traveling to. He also has a few field notes from colleagues already on the ground. We've always done this to some degree, but two years ago a Thai journalist was taken hostage along with two Italian photojournalists after they unknowingly ventured into hostile territory. One of the most dangerous aspects of the job is that friendly territory today may not be so friendly tomorrow, so knowing what's happening around our destination is vital.

When we have another hour before boarding, we grab sandwiches from a chain famous for their Montreal smoked meat, and Simon doesn't waste any time in asking me about my ankle.

"Let me get this straight," he says, putting down his sandwich and clasping his hands under his chin. "You sprained your ankle on some trail and were rescued by a hot football player?"

"And his twenty-one dogs."

"Oh right, can't forget about the dogs."

"Simon, there were twenty-one of them, it was literally impossible to forget about them."

"Mm-hmm, mm-hmm, sure, whatever you say. So did he pick you up and throw you over his shoulder, caveman-style?"

I laugh remembering how Bennett said he'd always wanted to do that. "Despite the threat of that happening, no, he gave me a good old-fashioned piggyback ride."

"Rewind. The *threat* of that happening?" he asks, a perfectly manicured eyebrow lifting high.

I've said too much. "I was resistant to the help, and he told me that I had a choice: be eaten by mosquitos, willingly climb on his back, or let him throw me over his shoulder in a fireman's carry."

"Lucky you. It's not every day one gets told to climb an attractive man." I adore Simon. He's won several awards for serious stories he's done around the world, and yet he's the first to ask for all the juicy gossip. I think it's how he balances things. He needs to embrace the ridiculousness of our so-called drama at home because real drama is harder to sleep with.

"It was not a hardship, I can tell you that." I sigh.

"So, when are you seeing him again?" he asks, picking his sandwich back up and taking a bite.

"Um... well, honestly, I hadn't really thought about it." *Liar*, that little voice in the back of my mind screams.

And up goes his eyebrow again, but somehow it's disapproving this time. "Excuse me?"

"He's the relationship type, and you know I'm not."

"True, you're the hit-it-and-quit-it-to-drown-out-the-bombs type."

"Ouch. Okay, no need for the brutal honesty, Newsgate." It's one thing to say that to myself, but a whole other thing for someone to say it to me.

"Did you discuss it?"

"What?"

"A relationship."

"No!" I laugh like the suggestion is the most absurd thing I've ever heard.

"Did you discuss a casual fling?"

"No. What's your point, Simon?"

"How do you know he's the relationship type?"

"I..." I guess I don't actually know. He screams commitment, and I guess I just assumed.

Simon puts his sandwich back down and then gestures for me to do the same. Then he grabs both of my hands in his. "Listen, honey, take it from someone who didn't 'do relationships.' I wasted years thinking I was saving someone else from having to lose sleep over my job. I know that's where your head is at too. I wasted time dodging a man who wanted me despite that. And in the end, it was him that left. We had all the plans in place for my inevitable demise, and he's the one who was taken without warning, without a plan. I want more for you because this fuck-'em-and-chuck-'em thing you've mastered will never fill the hole of someone to actually love. Getting to experience that is worth the heartache, I promise you that."

I don't know what to say, so I just stare down at our hands.

"Just promise me you'll think about opening yourself up and allowing someone to love you the way you deserve to be loved."

"Okay." I nod, but I don't think either of us believe me.

"Now, how long did you wait until you had sex with him?" Simon's grin returns, and he takes another bite, anxiously awaiting the gossip he not-so-secretly lives for.

THIRTY-FIVE

Sophie sent me an email last night to tell me that Marley was off to Syria for an assignment. I ended up not being able to sleep thinking about all the things that could happen to her. It wasn't until I was mindlessly stirring my coffee this morning that I realized this is why she keeps herself at a distance from people. Or partly why anyway. I hadn't heard from her in a month, other than a box arriving with my sweatshirt and a note that made me think she missed me but also maybe not. "It doesn't smell like you anymore." I repeated that over and over again. The sweatshirt has been sitting in the kitchen since I opened the box, and for some reason, I stuck the postcard to the fridge.

Lloyd, the calf, is settling in well. He spends his days in the pasture with the dogs and then his nights in the stall Karl helped me construct the day after he brought the little guy into my kitchen. Daisy in particular seems to have taken a liking to him. I find their interactions incredibly entertaining and can lose whole chunks of my day watching them. Which is a nice change from losing whole chunks of my day going over the ways I could have changed things with Marley.

You can't very well tell someone you don't want them to leave after only knowing them for a few days. You can't know someone is it for you after such a short time. It just doesn't seem logical. And yet she is there when I close my eyes or walk into a room. It's as if this old house has a new ghost and I'm trying to join her. Her water glass is still sitting on the table next to her... the armchair. As if moving it would erase her completely.

"Hey, Bennett?" Cass, my first-ever employee, calls as I walk into the barn.

"Yeah?"

She walks out of the supply room carrying a blanket I've never seen before. "So I was thinking, it's about to get super cold and Lloyd doesn't have much going on in the way of natural warmth, so what do you think about using this"—she holds the blanket up—"for walks?"

I take it from her and realize it's a dog coat. "I guess we can see if he'd be up for it."

"I'm also thinking it will play well on social media." She lights up. "Oh! I also forgot." She bolts back into the storage room and comes out with two blue wheels. "Martin's snow wheels came in." Martin was one of the first dogs to arrive after I'd hired Cass and Teddy. He had been hit by a car, and when I got the call that it was either euthanasia or a home willing to put up the money and extensive care for him, I couldn't say no. Teddy in particular has worked hard with Martin's physiotherapy and training. The first day Martin had been strapped into his cart, he was off like a shot. The problem was the wheels weren't ideal for the kind of terrain we often walked on. He'd get caught on a root or would hit a rock so hard a wheel would pop off. And while watching Teddy chase after a little wheel as it careened off the trail and into the bush was entertaining, it wasn't ideal for anyone, most of all Martin. With these new wheels, we now have four different sets that can be switched out depending on the time of year and the condition of the ground. He's going to be a rock star out there.

"We could probably do a post on the cart and wheels too," I say, handing the coat back. I head off in search of Teddy.

He's in the feed room with labeled bowls spread out on the counter in front of him. "Bennett." He nods to me without even looking up.

"The new drops for Clarence arrived," I say, holding up a tiny bottle of liquid that cost as much as a small car.

He takes them and immediately adds a couple of drops to his food. "I'm not sure they do anything," he grumbles before sticking them in the fridge next to various other medications.

"I don't think they make things better, but right now status quo is the best case." Teddy just nods as he continues personalizing the dinners that need it.

"Did Cass show you the dog coat she brought for Lloyd?"

"She did." I laugh. "He's going to look ridiculous."

"He already looks ridiculous out there with the dogs, so go hard or go home, I say. Plus..." He gives me a look. "Social media," we say at the same time. "Did she show you Martin's new wheels?" I nod. "Those will play well on the 'gram too. We can do a whole series on caring for a paralyzed dog and finding the right equipment."

We laugh about Cass's obsession with getting things just right for the Instagram and TikTok accounts she created, but I can't deny they serve a purpose. Marley was right—people do in fact love videos of dogs and, as it turns out, cows. Cass shows me every single thing before posting, even though I've stated multiple times that I trust her. I think she just wants to witness my reaction in real time, and nine times out of ten I end up laughing. She's creative, and how much she cares about this place already shows in her work. Teddy acts like he doesn't care that much, but I've caught him watching the videos more than once, and he's contributed a few pictures to the feed. And he will no doubt be the one leading the Martin series.

After checking in with the dogs, I head back to the house to do some homework Cass has assigned me. I mentioned last week that I'd like to be able to educate people on various aspects of our rescue operation. Teddy had already shared some information with her about how things work internationally, and now I'm feeling like the student who hasn't gotten his work in on time.

By the time Teddy and Cass have gone home, I haven't managed to complete my task, but I have managed to think about Marley. I've spent the last month checking my phone every day, feeling phantom buzzing only to discover no new messages from unknown numbers. I find myself frustrated that she seems comfortable about cluing in Sophie on her whereabouts but not me. Then I feel bad because she doesn't owe me updates simply because I wish she would let me know how she is. I'd rather she be focused on staying safe than on me. And yet I know tomorrow I'll feel the buzz that's not there and check to see that there are no new messages, and just like tonight, I'll go to sleep hoping the next day will be different.

THIRTY-SIX

I spent most of the flight listening to *Everything is Illuminated,* a book Bennett had recommended. It's bizarre, funny, and best of all, requires focus, which gives me a break from thinking about the person who recommended it. I managed to sleep for the last forty-five minutes of the flight, and by the time we were boarding our domestic flight to Hatay, I was ready to jump into work. Once we're settled for the night in Antakya, we'll meet up with some colleagues I haven't seen in a while. It's also my first time going back to Syria in a couple of years and I'm anxious to get there.

Simon says we'll be having lunch with a few other journalists at a Syrian restaurant in the city. One of his contacts has also set up an interview with a couple who recently fled the country. Our editor wants us to focus on the people impacted by the continuing conflict rather than the scenery. I was glad that was the direction they wanted to take because I prefer it to photographing bullet holes and crumbled walls for a week straight.

Searching out people to be story subjects does pose a

greater risk than focusing on the conflict as a whole. It puts a target on our backs and requires a great deal more caution on our part, from how we go about finding people and then talking to them. Luckily we're with well-seasoned guides and interpreters and, on this particular trip, two armed guards. I'm less thrilled about the guards as they'll make it harder to move around under the radar.

Simon and I meet up with Naomi Kostenko, a Dutch-American photojournalist, and journalist Connor Moffit. He claims to have no nationality, preferring to call himself a citizen of the world, although his accent and passport give his Irish citizenship away. I've worked alongside Naomi before and even attended her wedding to a guide we'd met four years ago in Ukraine. We'd both been doing a story on the wildlife boom in Chernobyl, and she and our guide Petro had hit it off immediately. On the way back to our hotel, she'd leaned in and told me she was going to marry Petro one day. I'd asked if she'd taken her mask off one too many times in the radiation zone. Lo and behold, they became virtually inseparable for the rest of our trip, and then eight months later I received an invitation to their wedding in Apeldoorn, Holland. Petro is a stay-at-home dad now to their twins, and I'm expecting to see lots of picture updates throughout this trip.

The last member of our little gang is Nizam, a Syrian-Turkish interpreter we've worked alongside before. The restaurant we are eating at is actually owned by his cousin and his wife, which explains the warm welcome he gets when he joins us. Until he arrived we'd all just been enjoying some Turkish coffee, but now that he's here Simon asks him to order for the table. We are going to feast like it's our last meal, which in reality it could be. While no one acknowledges that fact, it's something we all know well. We've all lost people on these types of trips, and we've learned not to take times like this for granted.

The mezze course arrives first with creamy garlicky hummus, baba ghanoush, and a bowl of mixed olives. I live for this kind of food, or really any kind of food I can dip carbs into. When fresh salads hit the table, Simon grabs the fattoush so fast we barely get a look at the presentation before he spoons a huge heap onto his plate. Shish taouk and lamb kefta follow along with a dish Nizam explains is fatteh.

"You know," I say as I clean my plate with a piece of pita, "after the first time I was over here, I got home and went right to the grocery store. I bought all the spices used in Syrian food." I start listing them with my fingers. "Sumac, cumin, Aleppo pepper, allspice, paprika—"

"You didn't have cumin or paprika in your pantry?" Simon asks, sounding somewhat disgusted.

"I had salt and pepper, and I think cinnamon." I shrug. "I don't cook. But it wasn't like I could just pop around the corner for some Syrian food. I figured I'd have to learn." I pop the piece of pita into my mouth and savour the rich, complex flavours dancing along my tongue.

"And what was the first thing you made?"

I dab my mouth with my napkin and glance around sheepishly. "So I bought some hummus."

Nizam gasps and shakes his head. "No, Marley, no. That is not the way."

I laugh. "Trust me, I know, but baby steps. Anyway, I bought this"—I glance at Nizam, looking remorseful—"terrible, awful, an affront to hummus, store-bought garbage, and sprinkled some Aleppo pepper on it and then ate it with—prepare yourself, Nizam—store-bought pita." Nizam dramatically grabs at his chest and feigns death as the rest of the table laughs.

"Everything else remains sealed." I have to wonder if Bennett would make good use of the spices.

Simon thinks for a minute, and I see it click as his eyes widen. "Marley, I was on that first trip with you, and that was eight years ago."

"What can I say? I am single-handedly keeping the restaurants in my town afloat."

"You're not there for most of the year."

"And I make up for it when I am." I smile around a plump olive.

"Oh, leave her alone," Naomi says. "I don't cook at all either. If I didn't have Petro, I wouldn't even eat in my flat."

Soon our conversation turns from food to our plan for the next week. Simon and Connor have both been in contact with members of the rest of our envoy. Nizam expresses some concern with the armed security, and Connor tries to assure him that they won't be obvious. They'll look like members of the humanitarian team. I haven't expressed my true feelings to anyone—in fact, I've barely acknowledged them myself—but I share Nizam's concerns. There's a fine line we need to tiptoe around, and this will make it harder to traverse.

The sun is dipping swiftly, and the chill of late November begins to seep into my bones. I'm half-listening to Connor and Simon exchange stories from the summit in London and half lost in thought. The area is so alive. People are out shopping and sharing meals together. Children are running around as parents stop to chat as they go about their routines. But my attention is snagged by a medium-sized white dog sniffing around a market stall. She's thin, and without really knowing anything about dogs, I would wager she's recently had puppies. She begins nosing under the fabric that is wrapped around the outside of the stall, and just as she gets her full muzzle under, a shopkeeper from across the way runs out waving a towel and yelling. The dog's head pops out, and she moves to the opposite side of the tent.

I think for a split second of what Bennett would do right now. He'd likely follow her, instantly become her favorite thing, and take her and her brood home to his little rescue. I lift my camera and take a couple of pictures of the scene.

"What's his name?" Naomi nudges me.

"Sorry?" I say, my attention snapping back to reality.

"You had this dreamy look on your face, and in my experience that is only brought on by a ma—" She stops mid-word. "Another person. Sorry, I assumed there was a man."

I stare at her for a minute. "There's no one. I was just thinking about how nice it is here. I wish the whole region was like this."

"Mmm," she agrees, but her expression tells me she knows I'm lying. "Hopefully one day it will be. My father was a journalist, did I ever tell you that?"

"No," I say, suddenly interested in where this conversation is going.

"Well, both my parents technically, but my mom only did local stories in Amsterdam. My father on the other hand worked for one of the big American agencies. He was covering a trial at The Hague, and that's how he met my mom. Anyway, he had been to Syria early in his career, and said it was one of the most magical places he'd ever been."

"I can believe that." Even after years of war, Syria held a certain something. It was like no matter how many pillars were lost, the country still maintained its pride in some way.

"He begs me not to go every time I do. After those journalists were kidnapped, he just kept telling me he would have never let me or my sister go after a story there."

"Oh... that's heavy."

"When I asked Petro if he wanted me to stay, he said of

course he did but he thought it was unfair to do that. 'It is who you are, moya lyubov.' My love," she translates for me.

"Oh, trust me, I knew that term real quick being around you two during your first week together." Petro had said it to her in passing one day, thinking she had no idea what he was saying. She'd blushed so hard that it gave her away. Petro then blushed and apologized for being so forward. I didn't see them for three days after that. And that's when I realize something. "How did you know with Petro? You two barely knew each other, and yet it seemed like you had always been together."

"Honestly, I don't really know. He just... felt like home, I guess. You know when you travel somewhere new and you just know deep down that this is your new favorite place? I'd never experienced that with a person before, until Petro." I must look skeptical because she laughs. "Listen, I don't believe in fate or anything. When I got home I did my best to not think about him. But at the end of the day, thinking about him was one thing that made me smile, and in our line of work, I kind of feel like we should grab onto those things. Luckily, Petro was totally fine with me grabbing onto him."

Naomi and Simon were the only two people I knew in our field who had—or once had, in Simon's case—a stable, long-term relationship. Breakups and divorces are incredibly common among our lot. People are gone for long periods of time, and that alone puts strain on a relationship. Add to that how we form strong bonds with the people we're working with, and partners can get jealous. I've known colleagues who have gotten divorced because their spouses refused to believe they could be faithful when they were sharing hotels with the same people for weeks on end. And then in the end, it comes out that the spouse who was home was the one having an affair. Not to say people weren't having affairs on this side too. Toss all of that in with the stress of doing this job, and it's easy to see why doing it unattached is my preferred method.

"You'll get it one day," she says, smiling at me in the way happy people do.

"Whatever you say." I laugh and roll my eyes.

"Well, friends, shall we head back to the hotel?" Simon says, standing and dropping a wad of lira onto the table.

I look out into the market one more time to see if the dog is still around before following the other three back to the hotel, thinking for the hundredth time since I arrived that I should text Bennett and knowing I won't.

THIRTY-SEVEN

In my hotel room, Simon and I go over some facts that are going to help remind us why we're here and what our objectives are. In the early days of the conflict, people were all ready to help, especially after some news outlets decided that censoring certain images was not going to do anyone any favors. After those images were made public and splashed around the world, tones changed. But people seem to think things have cooled off. The country and its millions of displaced people are no longer in the news daily. Occasionally there will be a story about one country's drone being shot down by another country's, and then how a third country made both of them but isn't actively involved in the conflict. But it's all military-focused, and the people have become an afterthought.

Simon also met with both the security officials who will be traveling with us. They are ex-military medics, probably the most ideal types to be traveling with a group of doctors. It puts my mind at ease a bit but not entirely. I'm still not looking forward to heading over with the bigger group. Yet I'm excited to capture the good the group will do if they're actually allowed to. There is a huge chance that we'll get to the checkpoint and get turned back. Just one of the many fun uncertainties about this world.

"All but one has been in the field before," Simon says, pouring whisky into two paper cups.

I take mine, and we toast. This is a tradition of ours the night before we head out. Neither of us is very superstitious, but we've also always come home safe this way, so the tradition continues. "That's good. So between three experienced doctors and the two medics, we won't need to be quite so much on our toes."

Simon peers at me above his cup. "Oh yes, definitely can let our guard down with this lot." He laughs. "Probably don't even need our kit."

I look over at the desk chair where my flak jacket and helmet sit. "That's a relief. That shit is hot."

"'Hey Simon, how'd that photographer get shot?' 'Oh well, she was hot.'"

"To be fair, you know that has definitely happened before. Comfort above common sense," I say, trying to hold back from wincing as the whisky burns my throat.

"Why the fuck do you drink this stuff if you hate it so much?" Simon asks, his head tilted as he studies me.

I shrug. "I don't know. We started drinking it before heading out, we haven't been killed yet, so I keep drinking it."

He nods sagely. "It's flawless logic, really."

"Exactly. It's like a cosmic shield. We must do all we can to return home to... well, you to your son, and me to my unused spices."

Simon scoffs. "I can think of twenty-two someones who would like you to return home."

I ignore him and drink the rest of the whisky in one go. "So what kind of doctors are we traveling with?" I ask, changing the subject with the skill of a seasoned professional.

He glares at me but gives in. "Two are OB-GYNs, one is a general surgeon, and the first-timer is an ophthalmologist. Apparently, he's got a lot of shit to lug around."

"I mean, that's awesome, but also yikes," I say, dramatically sitting back. "A lot to lug around always means everything takes longer. I hope he's got everything well organised so the guards can get through their checks quickly."

"Impatient, Marley?"

"Simon, I've been out of commission for over a month. I've been going stir-crazy waiting to get back out there."

"I know, babe, tomorrow. Speaking of, I'm going to call the offspring before I crash." He stands and tosses his cup in the trash. "See ya in the morning, kid." He ruffles my hair as he passes.

"Night, old man," I say, my eyes locked on a nondescript spot on the wall.

I chuck my own cup in the trash and prepare for bed. I take a long shower, something I plan to repeat in the morning, because who the hell knows when I'm going to get to have one again. And then I climb under the covers with my phone.

I fire off an email to Izzy and Nellie to let them know that I love them and I'll be out of contact soon but not to worry. My editor has their information if there's news. I know they hate that little bit of info I tack onto the end of every pre-trip email I send. They don't know that last week I updated my will and that all funds are to be left to the Morgan Estate Rescue. I know Bennett's grandfather was worth a fortune and he doesn't need the money, but at the end of the day, it's a gesture I'm just too chickenshit to make in person.

There's another email from Sophie.

Marley

Thanks for letting me know you'll be away for a while. Good luck out there. We'll be thinking of you.

We miss you.

Sophie

And at the end, she attached a couple of pictures. Yogurt chasing one of the cows is definitely going to be printed when I get home. I miss that little guy. I'm so busy focusing on the image of that little white dog that it takes me a minute to realize what the second picture is: Bennett and I at the fence the day we had gone to the Hores' for breakfast. Seeing it takes my breath away, and I can't think of anything to do beyond lock my screen, plug my phone in, and roll over to go to sleep.

I can't sleep, though. The image is pasted to the inside of my eyelids. It's a mix of the shock of seeing that picture, taken without me knowing, and the reminder that everything that took place a month ago was real. Bennett's standing behind me, one arm braced on the fence, the other wrapped across my chest. I'm laughing, my head tipped to the side, him smiling down at me. It's pure joy captured in a single frame. Eventually, I give up and roll over to grab my phone again. I end up falling asleep staring at the image, tears soaking the pillow and telling myself that this is totally normal.

"Christ. You look rough," Simon says when I open the door the next morning.

"Didn't sleep well," I grumble, turning back to grab my gear.

"You ok?" he asks, sounding concerned.

"I've been better" is the only answer I can muster. "I'll be better after I get some coffee in me."

Simon doesn't try to make any more conversation as we make our way to the hotel dining room. I can't say the same for everyone else in our party. Two of the doctors immediately introduce themselves, both looking like they had the best sleep of their lives. I hate them instantly. The general surgeon comes over after Simon, Naomi, and I have found seats. He looks young and like he could have played on a football team with Bennett. I mentally slap myself for thinking that.

The eye guy has yet to make an appearance, and I hope that this isn't a sign of things to come from him. I'm on my second cup of coffee when he comes rushing in with apologies to everyone. He's middle-aged, has a heavy French accent, and is dressed way too well for where we're going. But he's friendly and makes Simon's morning with some harmless flirting.

"No one has flirted with me in an age." Simon fans his face and sits back while the eye doctor heads to the table with his colleagues.

"Maybe it's because you say things like 'in an age,'" I mutter into my mug.

Connor eventually joins us with a plate of fresh fruit and a glass of water. "It really baffles me how you don't drink coffee," Naomi says, taking a sip from her third.

"It's not that I don't want to," Connor says defensively. "My digestive system doesn't want me to." He rubs his stomach. "And this bastard is very persuasive. Also, I do it for all of you. Imagine if I needed the driver to pull over every mile so I could shit my brains out."

Simon, who was about to take a bite of egg, slowly reverses course. "Must you talk about such things at the breakfast table?"

"Simon, I've literally seen you eat chili next to a cart horse with projectile diarrhea without batting an eye," I say, shoving the last bite of eggy toast into my mouth.

"I've literally eaten while... well, you know." Naomi gives us all a knowing look.

I peek over at the table of doctors and wonder what we must sound like to them. Although if anyone is used to shit talk, it's going to be a table of doctors, except perhaps the eye guy.

"Oh, I nearly forgot. Look at these munchkins." Naomi holds out her phone to show us a series of pictures Petro sent of the twins.

"Better than what I got from my kid," Simon says, pulling his phone out and showing us sock-covered feet crossed on a coffee table, a hockey game on in the background. "This is my son's idea of rebelling. Putting his feet on the coffee table."

"I'd show you the pictures I got last night, but, well… that would be a serious breach of privacy." Connor winks.

"Adorable. Funny. Gross," I say, pointing at each of them.

"No cute pictures of dogs or anything?" Simon asks, 'resting his chin innocently on his hands and batting his eyes at me.

I look at him like he's lost his mind and laugh nervously. "Not sure why there would be." I check my watch and declare it's time to get going a bit too enthusiastically.

Naomi catches up to me before I get to the minibus. "What was that about?"

"Just Simon being Simon."

"Surrrre," she drags the word out as she tosses her bag in the back of the bus.

The border crossing goes way smoother than any of us expected. And while the guards gave us a bit more of a look than the doctors, they didn't delay our trip.

"Let's hope that's a sign of things to come." Connor says as he slips his passport back into his vest.

"That was so easy," the one doctor says, turning back and smiling. We're all staring back at her in horror. "What?" she asks, clearly confused.

"If I walked into a hospital and said something like, 'Sure is quiet in here tonight,' what would you do?" Simon asks from the seat beside me.

The doctor doesn't answer, but her expression now reflects ours and she slaps a hand over her mouth.

"So are there other things we should not say while we're here?" the eye doctor asks Simon.

"Basically anything that implies things are going well," he replies while still looking at the doctor that may have just jinxed our trip.

"Okay," he says, turning back to the front.

The guilty doctor is still shaking her head and mouthing "Sorry" so Naomi reaches up to squeeze her arm. "It's ok. Just please don't ever say that again." She nods and turns back to the front. Naomi looks back at us and mouths "Fuck."

Nizam is pointing out the windows at villages as we pass letting us know how many people live there now versus how many lived there before. He makes sure to remind us that Syria has the highest number of displaced people in the world, and so those who call one place home now likely came from some-where else and somewhere else before that.

It's quieter than the last time I was here. Fewer people pulling carts full of all their worldly possessions, fewer cars filled over capacity with people trying to get out. There was always uncertainty about life here during my previous visits, but now it feels even more uncertain. Like the peaceful exterior is a mirage hiding the suffering beyond. I feel an odd sensation zipping up and down my body. Like my skin is coming alive but not in a good way. I lay my head back and close my eyes, trying to clear my head of the buzzing that's taken over. The image that begins to form is the one Sophie sent, and I give in to it. It was the kind of picture that, if it had been of two strangers, would make me hope they were as happy today as when the image was captured. The kind that shows two people meant for more than a few days of bliss. The bus stops suddenly, and I'm rocked out of my thoughts.

The bus driver yells sorry then says something in Arabic. Nizam quickly translates. "Don't worry, friends, it's just a few cows."

I can't see from where I'm sitting, but I look out the left window when we're moving again and see a small boy chasing after two skinny black-and-white cows. They look nothing like the massive cattle on the Hores' farm. I snap a few pictures out my open window as we pass.

About an hour and a half into the trip, the driver pulls over. There is a woman waving frantically next to a car. The driver and Nizam get out to speak to her. When Nizam comes back, he says there is something wrong with the driver. Two of the doctors, along with one of the security guys, get off the bus, and Simon and I follow. When my foot hits the dusty road, I feel the buzzing come back. I do a quick survey of where we are, and the buzzing only intensifies.

The town we've stopped beside is quiet. There are some buildings that have seen mortar damage, but things remain intact for the most part. It's the quiet plus the state of the place that has the hairs on the back of my neck standing up. So I do the one thing I know how to do. I lift my camera and start shooting.

I capture the doctors attending to the man who they've pulled from the car and laid on the ground. The general surgeon has his fingers on the man's neck and is checking his watch. Nizam is bent down, quietly translating. I step back to get the whole scene. The village and medical work being done in what appears to be the middle of nowhere works for me. I like the contrast of the composition. I also like how the sound of my shutter quiets the buzz. This is me, I think. This is what I do.

When a loud crack fills the air, we both freeze. I glance back to see that the woman is clearly panicking. I turn my camera on her now. She's pulling at the man I assume is her husband and gesturing to the car. Finally, he slowly stands and, with the help of the doctors, walks to the passenger side. The woman jumps behind the wheel and speeds off down the road in the direction we were coming from. The last image I take is of the car almost invisible behind a cloud of dust. Nizam is waving to us frantically to come back, and so we run. Another crack fills the air as we step back on the bus. I don't know where we are right now, but I have a feeling it's not friendly territory.

"Were those gunshots?" the eye doctor asks.

"Probably," Simon replies matter-of-factly.

The look on the doctor's face tells me that while he may have been told about this place, he was not fully prepared for it. And I can't blame him. You can be as prepared as possible, but being in the thick of it is a completely different experience.

"Don't worry," Connor says, leaning forward. "Most of the time it's just posturing."

I can tell by the way the doctor smiles that he's not comforted by that little tidbit.

We drive for another three hours before we arrive at our destination. It's a small hospital on the outskirts of a town that's almost entirely rubble. People who are treated here must have to travel from great distances because I doubt there are many, if any, that could live in any of the buildings nearby. We help carry in bags of supplies, and it's obvious the minute we walk through the doors that they are in desperate need of them.

The hall is full of people in various states of distress. All sitting or lying on the floor. Doctors in white coats crouch next to people to check their papers.

"My god," the general surgeon breathes out from beside

me. I'd learned that he'd done stints in refugee camps, but he hadn't been in a country at war, let alone an actual hospital building.

"You're not in Kansas anymore, doctor," I hear Connor say as he walks past him, shouldering two duffle bags.

"Oregon," he says quietly.

"Sorry?" I ask, looking over at him.

"I'm from Oregon."

I adjust the bag I'm carrying. "Well, you're not there, either." Then I follow Connor, careful not to step on anyone.

After I add the bag I was carrying to the pile in what I assume is a makeshift operating room, I pull out my camera and head back to the hallway. Sometimes I worry that what I do is intrusive. And in a way it is. I take pictures that will be shared with millions, but without the pictures, people don't know or they don't believe, and so things don't even have a chance of getting better. Or maybe that's just my Western ideology. I'd rather think that what I do has the power to change things for the better, even when I'm frustrated with the entire system. Nizam joins me and asks permission from various people for me to get a bit closer. I shoot their wounds and injuries and capture portraits that convey just how bad it is. Simon joins us and starts recording short interviews with Nizam's help. We are thanked the same way the doctors are, and it makes me feel a bit gross.

At one point I find myself staring at the back of the doctor I thought had a similar build as Bennett. From behind, all that's different is the hair color. Would Bennett have done work like this at some point? I bet he would have. I could see him in this environment more than I could see him in a hospital back home. When the doctor turns and I get a view of his profile, the illusion is broken.

"This is one of the worst I've ever seen," Naomi says when

I join her, Connor, and Simon outside as they walk away from the hospital. "I mean, it's not what you expect when the fighting has decreased so much. It looks like they were all just caught up in the middle of a war."

"Technically, they are still in the middle of a war," Simon chimes in.

"I guess that's true."

"Did you find anything out about the town?" I ask, putting my camera to my eye and getting a shot of the rubble before us. Then I hang back and get a shot of the three of them walking toward it. When I lower my camera and watch them walking, the buzzing returns.

"You always ask questions, then immediately disappear," Connor says as I catch back up to them. "The town is all but abandoned. One of the nurses said we may find packs of dogs, but that's probably it."

This is something that shouldn't come as a surprise. Packs of dogs roaming places like this are common, no matter where you are. But I have a very different view of packs of dogs nowadays.

"Packs of dogs, you say?" Simon grins and looks over at me. I don't respond, with words anyway, but I think my middle finger says all I need to say.

We don't find dogs, though. We don't find any life at all. There are signs that there was once life here. A shoe abandoned on cracked pavement, bits of paper, a child's toy. Everywhere I look there are signs that people once called this place home. But it also looks like someone tried to wipe it off the map. The buildings are only echoes of what they once were, and I find myself wondering what the point of coming here was.

Connor sits on a chunk of cement, careful to avoid the rebar sticking out, and lights a cigarette.

"I was hoping you'd given that up," Simon says, sitting upwind of him.

"Always easier to talk to people in some places if you can offer them a cigarette and smoke alongside them," he says, inhaling.

One of my mentors had said something similar, but it wasn't something I wanted to do. I never wanted to get closer to people in that kind of way. It's hard enough sometimes to photograph strangers in dire situations. I'm not chomping at the bit to become friends with them too, even if it's all for show.

"Why the hell are we here?" I say looking around, confused.

"Karen said the Syrian government has been trying to convince people it's safe to visit again," Simon says, looking around like she had told him the roads were paved in diamonds.

"The main cities, maybe," I scoff.

"I recently worked beside a young Syrian journalist." Naomi stretches her fingers down to her toes. "She said there is an illusion of normalcy returning to some cities, but she has a hard time buying into it."

"Can you blame her?" I say, gesturing to our surroundings.

"No," the three say in unison.

"I sure as shit am happy I don't understand it either," Connor says, crushing the end of his cigarette under his boot. "The privilege of getting to go home, even after a shitty work trip, is not lost on me."

THIRTY-EIGHT

When my head hits the pillow that night, I have no trouble falling asleep. I do dream of Bennett, though. Well, the dogs more so than Bennett. I'm still in that shell of a town in Syria, and this time there is a pack of dogs. Yogurt leads them through the rubble, smelling, playing, and barking at each other. I watch them from the outskirts and laugh. They look so happy, and I begin taking pictures because it's not a place that has seen happiness for some time. A movement to my right draws my focus from the dogs, and Bennett steps out from behind a crumbling wall. He looks at me, and I wave. I can tell he sees me, but he doesn't smile or wave. He doesn't look too pleased to find me there. Then I notice that the dogs have gone silent. When I look back at them, they're all staring at me too, and then they charge, teeth bared, fur on their backs sticking up. When I look at Bennett, he's walking away, and I yell his name, hoping he'll come back. He doesn't slow his pace, doesn't look back, and I think I should run but my feet don't seem to want to move. I can hear them getting closer, and Bennett seems to be disappearing into the distance. I look back at Yogurt leading the charge, and accept my fate.

"Marley." Someone is saying my name, and I can feel gentle pressure on my shoulder. "Marley. Wake up."

My eyes snap open, and I'm looking directly into Naomi's blue ones. I blink a couple of times, erasing the image of the charging dogs. "I'm cold," I say, slowly sitting up.

"You're covered in sweat, no wonder you're cold." She hands me a bottle of water and then gets up to grab a towel from her pack. "Here."

I drink then use the towel to dab at my damp skin before murmuring a thank-you and laying back down.

"Is Bennett the guy?" Naomi asks, sitting on the edge of my cot.

I swallow and nod.

"Do you dream about him a lot?"

I shake my head. "I hadn't dreamt about him at all, actually."

"Was he okay? In your dream, I mean?"

"He seemed fine." I laugh nervously. "Me on the other hand, I was about to be mauled to death by a pack of rescues."

"Rescues?"

"That's what Bennett does, he rescues dogs. He runs a rescue from his property. They're actually the ones who found me with the sprained ankle."

"Before we leave this place, Marley Cunningham, I want to hear that whole story. But right now let's try and get some more sleep."

This afternoon, the four of us and Nizam are heading to a town about an hour east of here that's still at the heart of the conflict. The land is the knot at the middle of a tug-of-war, and we're hoping to meet up with a local journalist who is risking her life to cover how fighting between the powers that be impacts the lives of everyday citizens.

I close my eyes, but I don't fall back to sleep. Truthfully, I'm not sure I want to. I don't want to see Bennett's back as he walks away from me again. I don't want to imagine a different scenario where the pack did in fact maul me to death. Instead, I pull out my phone and look at the picture Sophie sent. That's the Bennett I want to remember. Frankly, that's the me I want to remember too.

When we say goodbye to the doctors, they barely look up from their work. I recall a time in this country when that was all of us. When we didn't have time to acknowledge the normal pleasantries of life because we were too busy working. So far this has almost felt like a vacation compared to that.

Nizam tells us that we need to keep our heads on a swivel in the town we're heading to now. We're going to meet the local journalist at a café, but she has asked that we appear as normal as possible. That means no helmets, no press badges, no flak jackets.

"Dominic is going to be pissed about this," Connor says quietly to Naomi. "If something happens to us, he won't get the insurance money if they find out we weren't in our protective shit."

"Shut up, Connor," Naomi hisses. She's damn good at her job, but in hostile territory sometimes it doesn't matter how good you are at your job. Being good at your job won't shield you from a bomb blast. We're all uneasy about removing these things that we wear for different levels of protection. But we also understand. We already stick out as Westerners, and drawing more attention to ourselves could be dangerous for those we meet with. Protecting a source is paramount to Simon and Connor, and it's a reason they've been as successful as they are.

Karima is not what I was expecting at all. She's young, and yet she comes across like someone who has been doing this for longer than any of us. Tea is already set out for us at a table towards the back of the cafe as well as a plate of various Syrian desserts.

"Welcome to my home," she says, holding her cup up.

"Thank you for inviting us," Naomi says, copying the action.

Simon doesn't waste time with pleasantries. He knows how valuable time is when you're in a place like this and so he jumps right in.

"Karima, how old are you?"

"I am twenty-five." I do some quick mental math. She would have been around twelve when the conflict started.

"And you graduated from The London School of Economics and Political Science a year ago?"

"That's right. My family had fled Syria a year after the war began. We first went to Turkey, and then we were able to move in with my uncle's family in London."

"What made you want to return?"

"This is my home." None of us will likely ever know what that is like. To choose to leave your home is one thing; to be forced to leave in order to survive is another thing entirely.

Simon and Connor both ask questions about being a woman in Syria in general and then apply that to being a journalist in the country.

"It's one of the most dangerous jobs I could do. The extremists hate us, the people are afraid for us, and covering things is difficult. But nothing worthwhile is ever easy," she says casually as she sips her tea.

"What does your family think of you being here?"

Karima laughs. "Oh, they hate it. But my father always

says, 'Karima will do what Karima wants, and if she wants to make Syria a better place, then she'll do it.'"

"Having a vote of confidence like that must be nice," Connor says, scribbling in his notepad.

"I'm blessed to have them as my parents. And their faith in me gives me the strength to get through the harder days."

As Connor and Simon ask more questions, Naomi and I shoot photos. Naomi is focusing on the bigger picture of the scene while I'm cropping the scene up into smaller pieces. I aim for Karima's hands wrapped around her tea. Her gaze, soft and intense at the same time. Her lips in a smirk that reminds me of Bennett. Karima's confidence is contagious, and I hope she changes the fate of her nation, her home. I snap a couple of wide-angle images, the three journalists shrouded in a cloud of smoke in the somewhat busy cafe. It adds a certain atmosphere to the image that the more zoomed-in images don't.

"I am one of many," Karima is saying as I move to join them back at the table. "The SWFP is growing every year, despite the danger it poses." I've heard of the SWFP, the Syrian Women's Free Press, and I am in awe of their work. So many of the photojournalists were housewives or students when the war began. Their husbands fought for one side or the other, or they watched their family disappear one by one, but instead of turning their backs, they threw themselves into the frontlines of journalism. The amount of courage that takes is remarkable for anyone, but for women, it's tenfold.

I think about how my passion for this work has dried up, and then I look at someone like Karima and feel silly. My privilege has been showing itself to me in a big way. Maybe I'm coming at this work with the wrong lens. It still means something to share what's happening in the world. It means even more to support those like Karima to carry on doing work that will, hopefully, one day make Syria a safe place for their fami-lies again.

We finish our tea and treats, and Karima says she wants to take us on a walking tour of the town. This will be the riskiest part of our day in the town, taking in all we can without looking like we are building a story. We may have left the clothing that identifies us as press behind in the bus, but we still stick out. We put on tourist hats and do our best to look interested in the sights and smells rather than the stories hiding down alleyways and behind closed doors.

Unlike the abandoned town next to the hospital, this one has dogs wandering the streets, alone or in pairs. Most look like they've spent their entire life begging for scraps. I'm distracted by one I'd classify as a puppy, but it could be the shadows it keeps passing through and the malnutrition. It's light brown with black splotches on its face and one white paw. I stop and squat low to take some pictures of it. I've never done this before this trip, taken pictures of stray animals. The puppy eventually takes an interest in me and approaches cautiously. I hold my hand out and try to coax it over more. The closer it gets, the easier it is for me to see that the dog is indeed very young and clearly hungry. I have an apple in my little day pack and pull it out, take a bite, and pull the piece out of my mouth as a peace offering. After a couple of sniffs, it gobbles it up and licks every essence of the fruit off my hand. I repeat until I have only a quarter of the apple left. I look around expecting people to be watching and judging me for feeding a stray, but when I gaze out I'm filled with dread. Everyone has stopped, and they appear to be listening for something. I do the same and that's when I hear it, a high-pitched whistle off in the distance. People start to scatter and I know I need to move too, but my feet won't budge. It's like my dream all over again. I'm scared, terrified in fact, and my last thought before the world around me erupts is that if I die I won't get to tell Bennett that maybe I want to try for something more.

I'm thrown back and hit the ground hard enough to have the wind knocked out of me. As I try to catch my breath, I'm sucking in dust and heat, and for a minute I think this is it. I pull my shirt over my nose and mouth and begin counting slowly to even out my breaths. Looking down, I do a quick check of my body and see I'm not bleeding from anywhere major. I've got some scrapes, but it's nothing a Band-Aid won't solve. I can taste blood and my tongue hurts a lot, so it's safe to assume I bit it. As the dust falls and clears, I begin to see the world in front of me. Bodies are everywhere, but most are moving, albeit slowly. The building that had been at the end of the street is gone, smoke and dust rising from where it had stood, and I wonder if that was an intentional strike or just a casualty of someone flexing their muscles. My ears are ringing, and it sounds a bit like I'm underwater. When I look to my right, Simon is running towards me, yelling, but it's hard to make out what he's saying.

When he gets to me, he drops to his knees and begins checking me for wounds.

"I'm fine, Simon. Just had the wind knocked out of me."

"Your forehead is cut, and you've got blood coming out of your mouth, Mar." He's panicking.

"I bit my tongue. Really, I'm okay. Where are the others?"

"They ran down the next alley. Karima said the building they hit was a known rebel safehouse, although no one had been in it for a while."

"So fucking dramatic," I say, using Simon as an anchor to stand slowly. I am a little woozy as I get to my feet and clearly don't hide it well.

"Whoa, steady there," he says, holding onto both my shoulders. "Take your time, we're in no rush."

"There was just an attack. I hardly believe we aren't in a rush." Then I realize that this is the perfect time for me to be doing my job.

My thoughts must pass across my face because Simon says, "Nope, don't even think about it. Naomi is over there snapping away. Your wellness is my main concern right now."

"You're bad at your job then," I joke. Then I remember why I was so far back from them and begin looking around frantically. "There was a little dog... Did you see it?"

"I've seen loads of dogs, Mar."

"This one looked like a puppy, brown with black and a white paw." I break away from his grasp and stumble towards where I'd last seen the dog.

"Nope, not right now, we need to get you to a doctor." Simon grabs me as Karima and Connor run up.

"I've got a friend who can take a look at her. This way." Karima turns in the direction we came from as Connor and Simon each take one of my elbows.

"What are you looking around like that for?" Connor asks, following my gaze.

"There was a dog, apparently," Simon says.

"There are loads of dogs," Connor replies, clearly confused.

"This one was a puppy, I think. Bennett... Bennett would..." I am suddenly feeling incredibly tired, and I'm not sure if what I said made sense. I catch the look on Simon's face before everything goes black.

THIRTY-NINE

About halfway through the first week of my Marley-less existence, I started a list called "Things to Tell Marley":

1. Yogurt has been sitting in your chair every night since you left.
2. Jason got out again. This time they found him just standing in the river. Karl roped him and got him back home quickly. They still don't know how he's getting out. I suggested that it was maybe time for a cow cam.
3. I keep expecting you to come through the door. I wish you would.
4. The puppies I picked up the day you left are doing well, and they're chewing absolutely everything they can get their little teeth on.
5. Karl brought an orphaned calf over. Actually, maybe abandoned is the right word. His mom didn't want him, which is really sad. I worry that he knows she didn't want him. Who knows what cows know? I

actually like having him around. Don't tell Karl, though.

6. I wish you'd let me know you're okay.

7. I should have told you the day you left that I asked Sophie to place an ad for help. I don't know why I didn't.

8. I ended up hiring two people because they both seemed perfect for the job. Teddy is very level-headed, a tad closed-off, but really good with the animals. Cass doesn't shut up, and she keeps things lively around here. I think you'd like both of them.

9. Clarence is having some respiratory issues. I'm worried he's not going to last until summer, but I'll do what's best for him when it comes down to it. The vet says he's okay "for now."

10. Last night I slept in your bed and then felt weird about it. I don't understand how I miss you so damn much. I don't understand how I miss you more than the people I knew my entire life.

11. I made spaghetti last night, but you not being here has ruined the sauce for me. I'm kind of mad about it, actually. I mean, you've tried it—imagine not liking it anymore.

12. The kitchen is coming along nicely.

I don't think I'd realized how much time the dogs took up until I started making progress on the kitchen. Karl has been over helping now and then, and every morning I come down I'm hit by how much has changed.

"Do you want us to put the food here or in the dining room, Bennett?" Cass asks as she carries in the box Nancy brought.

"Not there," Nancy calls out from the doorway just as Cass is about to put the box on the island. "Take it right into the dining room." I look up and catch Nancy winking at me. I know she can't know why I'm a bit sentimental about the island, but somehow she seems to know that I am. I'm both grateful and disturbed by this realization.

"Everything's on the table already, thanks, Cass," I say as she walks by me.

"This is looking great, Bennett," Nancy murmurs quietly as she hugs me. "Karl's pictures have not done the work justice. Then again I'm shocked I could tell what he was even taking a picture of the way he takes them."

Karl comes in on Teddy's heels in time to hear Nancy's quip. "She says it like she's got any kind of skill. Did you know until these fancy smartphones she never took a picture where at least one person wasn't missing a head? Photo decapitation."

"Maybe," she says, releasing me and moving to take the bag Karl's carrying as he takes his boots off, "that was an artistic choice."

"Whatever you say, my love." Karl smacks her butt as they walk towards the dining room.

Teddy is standing just inside the door, shaking his head. "You'll get used to them," I say, gesturing for him to follow after them. "At least that's what Sophie keeps telling me."

Nancy has prepared a late harvest meal for everyone, and it feels like a nice way to celebrate our first month together. When I look around the dining room table, I wonder when the last time this many people sat around it was. It would have been while both my grandparents were still alive. It's louder than I've grown accustomed to, but the sounds are all joyful, and I wish that Marley were here to see it. But at the same time, for the very first time since we met, I don't feel like she has to be here for me to exist happily in this moment.

I smile to myself before grabbing my glass and standing. "I just wanted to say a quick thank you to all of you. Cass and Teddy, you've surpassed all my expectations and have made me wonder why I didn't do this hiring thing sooner. Karl and Nancy, I know a lot of what you do is because you made some blood pact with my nan, but I appreciate you sticking with it."

"She said she'd haunt our bedroom if we weren't there for you, and I just didn't want to take the chance that she'd see and hear things that would haunt her back." Karl raises his glass to mine.

Cass's eyes are wide, and she's staring at the turkey in the centre of the table. "You okay, Cass?" Teddy asks, leaning in.

She raises her eyes to Karl and Nancy. "Sophie said your place was haunted." She looked back down. "That's how she'd explain away noises at night—and once in the barn."

My eyes slide to Nancy who is downing her entire glass of wine.

Karl, on the other hand, looks proud of himself. "Sophie likes to pretend she was the product of immaculate conception. And let me tell you, there was nothing immaculate about her conception."

"Karl!" Nancy shrieks while the rest of us groan.

I make a mental note to add tonight's dinner and Hore anecdotes to the list of things for Marley. I swear I can hear her laughing while the rest of us squirm.

FORTY

Opening my eyes in the darkness of a cool room, I can hear murmuring coming from somewhere but can't seem to orient myself with where I am or where it's coming from. Then I feel that strange sensation again, and I'm in full flight mode. I sit up fast and swing my legs off the thin mattress, and then without warning, I puke. I look down to see a pair of hiking boots splattered with bits of undigested apple, and I'm immediately transported back to a pair of running shoes and a sexy-as-sin smirk in a Canadian forest.

"Lay back down, Mar." It's Naomi's voice now. "The doctor thinks you've got a concussion." Then it comes back, the puppy, the whistle, but most of all the intense fear that glued me to the spot.

Simon slips into the dark room followed by Connor, Kamira, and a man I don't know. "Marley, this is Dr. Ayad." I nod and let him do what he needs to do as I answer all his questions. After a few minutes, it's just Simon and me.

"I've never seen you like that before," Simon says, shaking his head. "You just froze and had this look on your face... It was like you were watching everything play out right before it did."

"I was scared," I say quietly.

Simon leans in. "Sorry?"

I swallow and look at the ceiling, I'm embarrassed to admit it, and saying it again is almost painful. "I was scared."

"Who the hell wouldn't be?"

"I've never been scared before, Simon." I look at him, trying to share how much it freaks me out, just with my eyes.

"Maybe you have a reason to be scared now." Simon shrugs. "I was never scared until I met Vincent. Don't even get me started on what I go through every time I'm about to leave Ant for another trip."

I glare at him. "Simon, this has nothing to do with a guy."

"You were distracted, Marley. You were taking pictures and cooing at a fucking dog." His sudden change in tone feels like a slap. "I have never seen you scared, and I have never seen you pay attention to a dog before. You asked where the dog was when I got to you. That was your main concern. Don't tell me this guy you met has nothing to do with that."

I don't respond because I know he's right. I know that every word that has come out of his mouth is the truth, but I'm not ready to admit it yet.

After a while, Simon leaves because we're just sitting there in silence. We've never not talked to each other, and I hate it. I despise that I can't admit to him that he's right. I'm with two people who have made this life work while maintaining loving relationships, and somehow I think that they are the exception to the rule while I am very much the rule.

Nizam comes to sit with me and tells me the others have headed back out with Karima. She still has some things to show them and some people for them to talk to. I like Nizam—he's a nice guy, and his stories are fascinating—but I still wish I was out there with the others. I ask if I can have my camera, and Nizam winces.

"It's, um... Well, when you were blown back, it sort of smashed when it hit the ground."

"Fuck," I mutter. I only brought the one out with me because multiple cameras would have given me away as more than an average traveller.

"I'm sorry," Nizam says quietly.

I reach out to rest my hand on his shoulder. "It's not your fault, Nizam. Tell me about your family. I need a distraction."

His face lights up. "Well, you met my cousin Ali and his wife. My mother and father live in Istanbul. We left Syria when I was ten. My father says he didn't know what was going to happen, but he could tell something was going on and that it wasn't going to be good. He's a professor at Istanbul Technical University. My mother is a private language instructor."

"Did she teach you English?"

He nods. "She did. I hated it when I was young." He laughs. "But I guess she was right to make me learn it."

"I wish I knew another language." I pout. "We had to learn French in school, but all I know how to do is conjugate verbs, and if you tested me on it right now, I'd probably fail."

"You know the basics in Arabic."

"I think you should know hello, goodbye, thank you and please in the language of the place you're going. But it definitely doesn't mean you know a language. Even then, I have to refresh my memory before I arrive. I also have this irrational fear that if I say 'please' really well, someone will think I know the language and keep going. Then I'll just be sitting there like a deer in the headlights."

Nizam looks confused. "I don't know this term?"

"Oh, like when a deer runs onto a road, it will be transfixed by a car's headlights and kind of just freeze where it is."

"Ah!"

"Keep telling me about your family."

Nizam goes on to tell me he has two siblings, an older sister and younger brother. He lives with his brother and his wife. His sister is studying in the US, and he's hoping to go visit her soon. He talks about his family like they are the sun and moon, and I'm slightly envious that I don't have that. He asks me about my family, and I tell him we aren't that close.

"Is it because your job scares them?"

"No, they don't really care what I do, I don't think. We're just a family of independent people. It makes my job easier, actually, knowing that if something happens to me, people will be able to carry on like normal."

If I took a picture of Nizam right now, I'd capture the most perfect image of shock. "I'm sorry, Marley, but I think that is the saddest thing I have ever heard."

I laugh awkwardly. "Yeah, well, that's life, right?"

"True. Life is often sad," he concedes, "but"—his index finger pops up—"the love of others makes even the saddest things easier to get through."

Well, fuck, talk about a gut punch. I can't help but think about who I'll have on my side when I'm truly sad about something. Do I really want to deal with something alone? I keep thinking about protecting others from something sad happening to me, but what happens when I'm the one having to cope? Apparently it just took a bomb blast, some harsh words from my oldest colleague, and this guy Nizam for me to have micro breakthroughs.

When Simon and the others get back, they tell me we have to stay the night. The one road we would be taking on the way back is considered hostile territory at the moment. Where is safe and where is not changes like the tides here. Dr. Ayad is relieved we're staying so he can monitor me overnight. Naomi goes with Karima to sleep at her apartment, and the guys are set up in a room down the hall from me.

I meet Bennett in my dream again. This time I'm back on the trail near his home. The forest is so quiet except for the soft sound of a gentle breeze in the trees. Bennett is standing at the opening of the trail, smiling at me. He looks good standing there, his face dappled in sunlight. I start walking towards him.

"What took you so damn long, sweetheart?" he asks when I finally reach him.

"I was scared," I say, not daring to reach out first.

"Was?" he asks.

I bite my lip and nod, and he finally reaches for me. He takes my face gently in his hands and brings his lips to mine. But just as I expect them to meet, he sticks his tongue out and licks from my chin to my forehead.

"Oh my god, Bennett," I gasp, batting at him.

Laughter fills my head as the licking continues. My hands finally make contact with something soft and wiggly, and my eyes fly open. Two thoughts hit me at once: I was dreaming and Bennett definitely didn't lick me, and I am no longer dreaming and there is a puppy going to town on my face. A little brown-and-black puppy with one white paw to be precise.

Everyone, including Dr. Ayad, is crowded in the room as I slowly sit up and take in the scene. I reach for the little ball of fluff and pull him into my chest. I join in on the laughter as his licks tickle my neck. But my laughter quickly turns to sobs, and soon I've got my face buried in the little guy's fur.

"Is crying a symptom of a concussion, Doctor?" Connor asks.

"Not typically," he whispers back. "But extreme emotional reactions are associated with trauma and exhaustion. Also extreme joy. It's hard to say which she's experiencing right now."

Honestly, I couldn't tell you. I am relieved that this guy is okay. I'm sad because I want to be waking up with Bennett and not a room full of people who aren't him, and I'm afraid of what comes next.

The puppy is trying to wiggle out of my arms, so I let him go and look up at everyone, pulling myself together. Dr. Ayad hands me a tissue and then several more when he realizes one certainly won't be enough. I look at the puppy who is covered in my snot, and I'm reminded of how I did that to one of Bennett's shirts. A couple more tears trickle down my face at the thought. I don't understand how I can miss him so much and how I've managed to keep that so far buried for so long and how all of that's coming out now.

I look down at the puppy and then back up at everyone. "How did you find him?"

"I took the memory card out of your camera, and then we walked around showing people a picture of him," Naomi says, holding her own camera up. "There was a lot of pointing and some swearing. Apparently, he's quite a little menace."

"We found him yesterday afternoon," Connor says. "Then Karima and Simon took him to a vet. He's been microchipped and vaccinated. We're just waiting for the documents that will allow him to travel to Turkey."

I don't say anything. I just sit there staring at them.

"Is she alright?" Nizam asks, leaning forward and waving a hand in front of my face.

"She looks like she's in shock," Connor says.

"She's processing," Simon says firmly. "Sometimes her brain needs a minute to catch up."

That snaps me out of it, and I give him a dirty look. "I don't know why you just told me all of that."

"Well, we assumed you'd want to take this guy home at some point."

"Why would you assume that?" I've caught Simon off guard. "Did I say I wanted to?" Everyone is quiet and looking around at each other. "I can't just take a dog home, Simon. I'm not there half the time. What the fuck am I going to do with a dog?"

Simon just stares at me. Then he nods once. "Right." He turns and walks out.

They're all still staring at me so I look down at the puppy to avoid their eyes. This is a case of first saying *thank you, what a thoughtful thing you did for me* and then finding a way to fix everything after the fact. As I sit there staring at the pup, I realize that everything that happened between the blast and going to sleep last night has led to this moment. Simon and the others tracked down a street dog, got it vetted, and started the paperwork so that I could potentially give it a better life in Canada. And not just in Canada, but obviously with Bennett. That is ultimately what Simon is directing me to do, to take this dog on bended knee back to the man who consumes most of my thoughts these days. To make the most of the time I have to make things right with the people I care about most. To give me the chance to find the kind of love and joy that Simon got, even if it's only for a short time.

"I am the worst," I moan, burying my face in my hands.

"Well, you aren't the best right now," Naomi agrees tactfully. "But there are still worse people."

"That bugger had us traipsing around this town practically begging people to help us find that damn dog, Marley," Connor says. "I don't even like dogs."

I look up at him. "Who doesn't like dogs?"

"I don't."

"How didn't we know that?" Naomi asks, clearly as shocked as I am.

"Because of this exact scenario. You're all looking at me like I've lost my mind."

"Haven't you, though?" I ask.

"I'm going to find Simon." He turns and leaves.

"Marley?" Dr. Ayad says. "I'm going to bring you some breakfast. No allergies, right?"

I shake my head. "No. Thank you."

Naomi sits down beside me, and the puppy jumps up at her lap. His entire body wiggles with the force of his tail. "He's damn cute," she says, scratching behind both ears. "Will you really leave him behind?"

I look from her to the dog and back again. "No, probably not."

"Why do I feel like there is more to this story?"

"Because there is, and there isn't." I throw my hands up. "I don't know. I feel like everyone around me is turning into Yoda but with better grammar."

"You're too young to give up on your dreams," Naomi says as though she didn't hear me. "You're also too young to write off loving someone or being loved by someone. I think Bennett is your other half, but you're afraid of the adjustments you'll have to make in order to fit together."

I think of the ways Bennett and I fit together and all the ways that would require adjustments. It wouldn't require much—more so on my side than his. Assuming that he even feels anything near what I feel. I'm suddenly regretting never truly reaching out after I left; that stupid note I included with his sweatshirt doesn't count. Who would want to allow someone like me to fit into their life?

"I can see all the arguments playing out across your face, Marley." Naomi bumps her shoulder into mine. "All the what-ifs that end with you being alone and sad."

"Everyone disregards what-ifs as though they're unique.

But I know you thought about them too with Petro. I know we all think about them the minute we step foot back on a plane."

"Yeah, but those are all the negative what-ifs. Let's ask the positive what-ifs for a change, shall we? What if Bennett feels the same way as you? What if he's waiting for you? What if he dreams about you as often as you dream of him? What if he's the one?"

I can add it to the list. What if I never sprained my ankle? What if he hadn't been out with the dogs? What if he'd never been injured? What if the road hadn't been out? What if I'd been closer to the explosion yesterday?

"Take the dog home to Bennett. Be honest with him and yourself, and open yourself up to the possibility of being something more than this." She holds up her camera. "You're a phenomenal photographer, my friend, but I guarantee with love in your life you'll only get better." I don't exactly know what she means by that, but I'll have to take her word for it right now.

I nod. "Okay."

"Good. Now go find Simon. You owe him one hell of an apology," She's not wrong, I do owe him that.

"Am I even allowed to go wandering off?"

"Apparently you can if you go slowly. You've got a minor concussion, so if you get lightheaded, sit down immediately. The doctor doesn't want you to leave the building, though. Simon's up one flight of stairs so it should be alright."

I nod and rise slowly. "Wish me luck." I say, hoping I don't need it.

FORTY-ONE

Things to Tell Marley

13. Yogurt caught a rabbit today. I must have stood there for 10 straight minutes just staring at him. It was fine, not even a puncture wound, thank goodness. I don't know if I could ever look at him the same way again if he'd killed it.

14. Teddy was telling us about working with some arborists abroad. He trained here and then decided to do some traveling, picking up odd tree jobs in different countries. I'm not sure how legal it was, but he's got some good stories. I bet you'd have a lot to talk to him about.

15. I had my first therapy session in a while today. We talked a lot about you.

16. Remind me to tell you about the team dinner we had last week, specifically Cass, ghosts, and the Hores.

17. I have adopters all lined up for the Dalmatian

puppies. It's going to be weird when they're gone, but I think it's for the best. I don't need to add puppy training to my tasks right now.

18. Sophie was home over the weekend and showed me some pictures of you photographing the cows. You looked like you were in your element. Maybe livestock photography is a possibility.

19. I went into town today to grab supplies. I may have gone a bit overboard on things for Lloyd, and then I felt guilty about that so I got more than I needed for the dogs. On the call later with my therapist, I mentioned the spree and he suggested that maybe it was me hoping that if they have everything they won't want to leave. ~~If I'd had more to offer, would you have stayed? I don't know what more I could have offered~~

20. I found Jason in the dog field today. Karl is now convinced that Jason just wants to be where the dogs are. The dogs were happy to discover the patties he left behind when I let them out. No one is allowed to lick me for another week at the earliest.

21. The kitchen is done. Well, almost done. I think you'd agree it's an improvement. ~~There are some other projects I'd like to start now but~~

22. I actually watched the news tonight, hoping they'd have a story on Syria. I don't know if I'm disappointed that there was nothing or happy.

23. What you do terrifies me, but I'll support you no matter what. I should have told you that when you were here.

24. Why isn't this getting easier?

25. Is it pathetic that I'm holding off starting other projects in case you want to help with them?

26. We lost Clarence today. I buried him next to an old oak tree at the back of the property. The house is eerily quiet at night without his snoring. I kind of hate it.

27. Daisy stops at Clarence's grave every day before and after our walks. She eventually catches up to us, but I don't rush her. Funny how I never noticed her pay much attention to him while he was here.

28. I fucking miss you.

FORTY-TWO

Simon and the other guys are on the roof. When they see me, Connor and Nizam issue quick "See ya's" and bolt. Simon sits looking out over the town, drinking tea, looking like he doesn't have a care in the world.

"This place suits you," I say, sitting in the seat Connor had vacated moments earlier.

"Have you come to admit you were wrong and I was right?" He hasn't looked at me yet, but I can hear the smirk in his voice.

"Maybe."

"Sooner or later, everyone comes to tell me that."

"You're too cocky for your own good."

He looks over at me and smiles. "Vincent used to tell me that."

"Well, then I'm in good company, I guess."

"He also used to beg me not to go back out into the field. Every time I got back from an assignment, he'd ask if I was ready for that evening news job he'd heard about being available, and I'd shiver and gag. But every time I left, he'd hug me and tell me how much he loved me and how proud he was to call me his husband." I can see it all playing out. Vincent was the overtly affectionate one in their relationship, but when Simon let his guard down a little, you could watch him melt for him in real time. I remember once upon a time wondering what that kind of love would feel like.

"If you'd known your time would be cut short, would you have taken that evening news job?"

Simon thinks for a minute. "No."

"Really?" I ask, absolutely shocked.

"I'm not sure I would have been the partner I was if I was around all the time. I don't know what I would have replaced the adrenaline of this job with." This makes sense to me on a visceral level. "Our relationship worked so well because the time we got together was intense and we were always making up for the time we spent apart. It's the same with Ant. I'm not sure our relationship would be as strong as it is if I was watching over him all the time. If I could have seen Vincent every day all day I would have, but I'd still need this." He sweeps his arms out. "This is who I am."

He sounds like me now. "I've been questioning if this is still who I am," I say quietly, standing and walking to the edge.

"Are we talking about the whole independent woman thing or the photojournalist thing? You do realize, my dear, that you can be more than one or two things, right? Who you are isn't your job; your job is part of who you are."

I turn and lean my elbows on the low wall. "I was lost in thought about my future when I twisted my ankle. I felt so burnt out after my last assignment, and I was questioning whether or not it was even what I wanted to do anymore. Did I still have the passion for it?"

"Ah. And how have you felt about this trip? Has any of the passion returned?"

"Some." I shrug. "I don't know. I've been kind of preoccupied."

"Maybe that's because you need to actually explore how you're feeling instead of running away from it."

"Maybe. But I—"

Simon cuts me off. "No buts, young lady. I guarantee I know what's been going on in your mind, and I bet you've been going around in circles trying to justify every little feeling you've had that keeps you from doing the very thing you want to do. And that thing is to clearly take that puppy back home with you and show up at that man's door and beg him to take you both in."

I stand there and stare at him, blinking slowly. "That's a bit dramatic for my tastes, but something along those lines."

"Excellent. And just so you know, I won't be letting you back out of this. You could have died yesterday, Marley. Does he even know where you are?"

I look down at my feet instead of at him. "I assume his neighbor may have told him, but he wouldn't have heard it from me."

Simon is looking at me with wide eyes. "Wait, why does his neighbor know where you are?"

So I go into the whole story about the Hores, and he laughs throughout. I am shocked I haven't told him before now. Simon loves a fun name. When I get to the part where Sophie sent me the updates about the cows and the picture of Bennett and me, Simon jumps back in.

"So let me get this straight. You told the girl you took cow pictures for that you were going to a hostile country without telling the guy you spent a week falling for? Marley, you may actually be broken."

"I never claimed that I wasn't."

The others eventually join us on the roof. Dr. Ayad

brought up a tray of food that was supposed to be my breakfast but that I happily shared. I have a minor headache so I'm given some ibuprofen for it and told to keep hydrated. But other than that I'm cleared to wander around with the others. I feel absolutely naked without my camera, and I have this odd anxiety that I've never experienced before. But I focus on the good what-ifs rather than the what-ifs you're almost expected to have in a place like this. Especially after what happened yesterday.

We brought the puppy along because a medical facility is really no place for an animal that isn't house-trained yet. And I've been alternating between fighting with him trying to eat his new leash and carrying him around. Luckily everyone has taken a turn carrying him, including Connor. I have a feeling that he won't be as anti-dog as he claims to be by the time he flies home.

Karima introduces us to a couple of other journalists, and we spend about an hour talking to them about their lives here. One had been shot and was kidnapped five years earlier. The fact she is still doing what she does astounds me. The more we talk to these women, the more I find myself finding a purpose in this profession, even if my passion has waned. Even though I see this sort of stuff all the time, it's not lost on me that I get to go home while these women *are* home. They can't just turn off the TV. They are in the thick of it. This is their reality. And if doing what I do helps ease some of their burden, then that's my purpose.

That night as I'm falling asleep I realize what I put myself through in order to come to the conclusion I'd already come to, but this time I'm listening to my instincts. I've always been good at doing that for work, but apparently not in my personal life.

Word comes through around nine a.m. that the road appears to be safe so we can head back to the hospital today. I am relieved to be leaving this place but sad to say goodbye to our new friends. We have to stop a couple of times to let the puppy, who doesn't have a name yet, use the facilities. In his case, the side of the road. At least we can see if anyone is approaching for miles in every direction. We make it back to the hospital without a single incident, hostile or puppy-related.

We're spending one more night at the hospital before we head back to Turkey. I am checked out again when we arrive, and I feel bad for technically jumping the line. I'll make it up to them by purchasing some supplies for the waiting room. The eye guy is amazed I got away with not having any damage done to my eyes, and come to think of it, I am too. Really, I got lucky in many ways. It could have been so much worse.

I find myself antsy to get home. Every minute seems to drag, and I'm becoming irritable. Thank goodness for the puppy. I decide to focus on naming him rather than on the clock and the location of the sun.

Naomi and I take the dog for a walk while the guys work on their articles. I tell her more about Bennett and how things evolved while I stayed with him.

"I expect an invitation to your wedding. And that guy"—she points down at the dog—"better be walking down the aisle with one of you."

I'm kind of surprised to not feel terrified about the prospect of walking down an aisle. It's amazing how much a person can change after a near-death experience.

"So we can't keep calling him that guy or the dog. Any names dancing around that head of yours?"

I shrug, and she gives me a look that says to just tell her. "Okay, Bennett and I joked about our names being characters from classic literature. His whole name is very Jane Austen because his mom was obsessed with her. And he made the connection that there's a Marley in Dickens."

Naomi scrunches her nose. "Hardly the same sort of characters. Were you named after Jacob Marley, an evil old miser?"

"Ya know, I never asked, but I would put my money on no."

"Okay, so it's a reach but it's actually kind of cute, so I'll allow it."

"Anyway, I was thinking maybe a name from another Dickens classic. Although those seem like they are pretty popular dog names."

"He was a street dog so clearly you'd have to go with one of the characters from Oliver Twist," Naomi says.

"Actually, no," I say. "I was thinking of Pip from *Great Expectations.*"

Naomi looks down at the pup. "Pip the pup. I like it."

When we get back to the outbuilding, we have dinner and chat with the doctors about the last couple of days. They are all exhausted but feel good about the work they are doing. The eye guy is already planning a return trip with more equipment and hopefully one other doctor to help him out.

Before we call it a night, I write Pip's name into his little passport and pack it next to mine. Then I take him out one more time. The night is cool and silent, and when I look up it's like I can see the entire solar system. This country and its people deserve so much more than what they are getting from those in power domestically and abroad. But I am so happy to know people are fighting for their homes by sharing the truth with the world. I only hope one day they are shown the same devotion for the sacrifices they make.

The countdown back to Bennett, back home, is on.

FORTY-THREE

"That's it, sweetheart," I praise as Marley sinks down onto me. Her being on top is new, but I'm not complaining about the view. I never truly understood the term "breathtaking" until her.

"I've missed this," she breathes out as she starts a slow rhythm that's making me clench everything to ensure this feeling lasts as long as possible. "I've missed you," she says as she reaches for my hands and guides them up her body.

Even in our current state, she feels too far away. I sit up so we are chest to chest. "You feel so fucking good," I murmur. "I never want you to leave again," I say between kisses.

She doesn't respond with words but smirks and pushes me back down, taking control. Her rhythm increases, and I watch in awe as she throws her head back, the creamy column of her neck begging for my lips. I'd never considered myself a neck guy, but with Marley, there isn't a part of her I don't crave. She is a delicacy I will never tire of.

"I'm so close," she whispers. I dig my heels into the mattress and hold her hips in place, fully taking over. Giving her exactly what I know she wants. "Don't stop!" Her breathing quickens. "Bennett! Don't fucking stop."

The gentle tones of my alarm pull me out of the dream. As usual, Marley fades, and I wake alone, sweaty and uncomfortable. I've got twenty minutes before I need to meet Teddy and Cass and I use every single one of them before meeting them in the driveway.

"So, either of you know any car games?" Cass's head pops between the front seats.

"No!"

"Yes!" Teddy and I say at the same time.

"Excellent!" Cass ignores Teddy's less-than-enthusiastic response and turns to me. "What's the game, boss man?"

I hate that she calls me that, but I also like how at ease she seems and I don't want to tell her to knock it off and throw off the vibes. "We just called it the Last Letter game. Basically, you pick a subject, like geography. Then someone starts by picking a place, the next person has to then name a place starting with the last letter of the first place."

"Who did you play this game with?" Cass asks.

"A few of us on the team bus would play, usually as a study method."

"Team bus?" Teddy seems suddenly interested.

"Football."

"Baseball." Teddy points to himself.

"No ball!" Cass adds. "So, Last Letter game. Who wants to start?"

"You start, Cass," Teddy suggests.

"Okay, let's see. Isn't it annoying how when you need to think of a place on the spot, nothing comes to you? I'm even blanking on my hometown name. Fucking weird, eh?"

"You can do it. I have faith in you," I say as I merge onto the highway.

A shelter up north that had reached capacity put out an SOS to other shelters for help. In total, six answered with each of us agreeing to take at least three dogs. I figured it would be a good opportunity for Cass and Teddy to see how I do things so that in the future any one of us could make the run.

"Korea. My brother Foster lived there." She claps. "Teddy's turn."

"So many A's." He groans. "Akron."

"Nantucket." Cass didn't waste any time with that one.

"Tulsa."

"Algiers."

"Syria."

Syria. Marley is in Syria. I don't know if she's okay; I haven't heard a thing from her. Sophie hasn't said anything else, and I'm too chickenshit to ask. I don't know if the thought of her reaching out to Sophie is too much, or if Sophie also not having heard from her freaks me out more. All I know is that the mention of a place I've spent very little time thinking about until recently sends my heart rate into dangerous territory.

"Earth to Bennett..." I blink a few times, and realize they are waiting for me to name another place.

"Ugh, sorry." I give my head a small shake. I don't want to play this game anymore. I don't want anyone to bring up Turkey or Damascus or anywhere near where she could be. But I also don't want to talk about it, and I know that if I suggest a different topic or game, Cass will want to know why and she's annoyingly good at getting the truth out of people. "What did you say?" I ask Teddy.

"Adelaide."

"Right, um, E... Essex."

"Oh, fuck, an X?" Cass throws herself dramatically back against her seat. "Does such a place even exist?"

"Yes," Teddy says, and when I look over he's smiling smugly.

"Can I use my phone?" she whines.

"No!" Teddy and I say together.

"Guys, come on! Okay, can I pass?"

"I guess so. I don't really think there are rules."

"Except apparently using technology," she grumbles.

"Well, yes, that's the only rule," I say, looking back at her in the rearview mirror.

"I pass."

"Xaghra," Teddy says.

"Oh, and where is that?"

"Malta."

"No shit! Have you been there?"

"I have." Teddy nods. "I wasn't there for long, though. That's an A for you, Bennett."

We play until I pull into a rest stop to grab some food. I get back to the car first and find myself pulling up the photo Sophie sent me. I'm lost in Marley laughing and don't notice when Cass and Teddy have gotten back.

"Whoa, who's the hottie?" Cass asks, looking over my shoulder.

I lock my phone and mutter "No one" before accepting the burger Teddy is holding out to me.

"Didn't look like no one," she teases as she buckles her seat-belt. "Is she your girlfriend? Or *was* she your girlfriend?"

"You know she's not going to stop, right?" Teddy says with a mix of sympathy and curiosity. He's the type that acts like he's above gossip, but at the end of the day, he's the first to lean in to hear some.

Maybe if I talk about her out loud that will somehow get her out of my system. Or it will make missing her ten times worse. "Not my girlfriend, never my girlfriend..." And then I proceed to tell them about how one day I was out for a walk in the woods when suddenly there she was, my Marley.

"Wait, she just left and never even texted you?" Cass asks.

"She sent a postcard... and my sweatshirt back."

"Ouch," Teddy whispers.

"But—" Cass starts.

"Ya know what, I think that's enough Marley talk for now. How about another game?"

"Two truths and a lie?" Teddy asks, surprising me and Cass into stunned silence. "What? I haven't always been a grump."

"You go first then."

"I have been to the top of Mount Kilimanjaro. I have over sixty plants in my loft. I have never been in love."

"There is no way you have that many plants." Cass laughs.

"Nah, I think he definitely does." I've seen his resume, so the plants kind of check out with his Environmental Studies and work experience as an arborist. "I think you've never been to the top of Mount Kilimanjaro."

"Both wrong. I've been in love, but only once."

"Tell us right now!" Cass practically squeals.

"Let's just say she was perfect and I fucked up and if I could go back and do things differently I would without a second thought."

"How'd you fuck up?" I ask, curiosity getting the better of me. Also, something tells me he wants to talk about it. Why bring it up if he didn't?

"My life went to shit, and instead of talking to her, I ran away." I've been on the other side of that situation.

"Like to another city?" Cass asks.

"Like to another province and then another country. I never even said I was leaving, I just upped and left."

"How old were you?"

"Twenty-two."

"Have you looked her up at all?" Teddy shakes his head. "What's her name? I'll do it now. Maybe she's single, and this can be your shot at redemption."

"I'm not telling you her name. It's been a decade. She's moved on, and so have I."

"Bullshit!" I say. "You just told us you'd go back without a second thought. No one who has moved on says shit like that."

"That's true," Cass agrees.

"Cass, can you make a note for me?"

"Sure."

"29. I think you should come back and help us track down Teddy's greatest regret." Cass laughs as she types it into her phone. "What's your biggest regret, Cass?"

"Oh, I don't have any regrets." She beams back at me in the rearview.

I know she's not lying either, and as we continue towards our destination, I wonder what a life without regrets would feel like. Mine has been made up of little ones all culminating in the biggest one of all: letting Marley walk away.

FORTY-FOUR

One Week Later

My journey home takes longer than expected mainly because Simon insisted I move my flight back a few days to give myself more time to recover. The last doctor I saw told me I should be okay to fly, but it was that "should" that put Simon on edge. Rescheduling my flight for him was the least I could do after he tracked Pip down for me. It also gives me time to finish editing and submitting the images I took along with Simon's article. He submitted a long article for the paper on humanitarian efforts in Syria and then co-wrote a piece with Connor on the Syrian Female Journalist Network for a North American news magazine. The one side trip we all considered a bonus ended up being the one we were most excited about.

There were also things I had to do to prepare Pip for the flight. I needed a carrier, food, a travel-safe water dish, pee pads, and another trip to a vet to get something that would keep him calm. At the airport, I got to keep him with me until we were about to board, and then one of the staff came to take him for me. Watching her walk away with the carrier was way more emotional than I had expected, and I willed myself not to cry. I failed.

I had also gotten myself something to keep me calm on the flight. My anxiety about seeing Bennett again had grown by the day. I'd been playing out every possible scenario I could encounter when I got to his place. Would he even be home? Would he invite me in? Would he tell me to leave? The worst thing I could imagine would be arriving to find a woman there. I mean, that wouldn't be a bad thing for Bennett, and part of me would have to be happy for him. But for me, well, that would be the icing on a triple-tier cake of suck.

My dreams have also been very Bennett-centric. And while we never seem to come together in the way I want to, he hasn't walked away again. I've never been someone who analyzes dreams and I'm not about to start, but I must admit it does put my mind at ease that he only walked away that one time.

When the flight lands in Toronto, I have to go to a special section so a vet can do a quick check of Pip. I'm almost more nervous about this than I am about seeing Bennett. Even though two vets have given him the all-clear already, I worry that standards may be different here in Canada. In the end, though, he's given the okay and a quick clean-up before going back into the carrier.

Izzy sends a text to say they're waiting outside, and I get everything sorted before walking as fast as possible. I'm only guilty of desperately wanting to hug my friends, but I may as well have just gotten away with bringing something illegal into the country.

Izzy screams and Nellie whoops when they see me, and then I see Nellie's eyes go immediately to the carrier and I'm suddenly invisible. I had given Izzy a heads-up that I had a travel companion, but I knew Nellie's reaction would be way better in person than in an email.

"Whaaaat is that?" Nellie says, rushing towards me and dropping to her knees in front of the carrier.

"Pip, Nellie. Nellie, Pip," Nellie spares me a glance before sticking her fingers right through the bars.

"Oh my god, aren't you just the cutest little thing? Hi, Pip. Oh, what sharp little teeth you have."

Izzy comes over and one-arm hugs me. "It's good to have you back in one piece. Shall we leave them to it and get your bag in the car?"

"Sounds like a plan," I say, gently putting the carrier down and walking to Izzy's car.

After I put my bag into the trunk, she throws her arms around me and squeezes. "Fuck, I was so worried about you. When you said there had been an accident, I was imagining so many things."

"I'm fine, Iz, just a minor concussion," I say, patting her on the back. "I may succumb to strangulation soon, though," I gasp.

"Oh shit, sorry." She releases me and then grabs my face, searching my eyes.

"Iz, what are you doing?"

"Checking your pupils."

"Why?"

"Because I'm a doctor, and it's what doctors do."

"You're a psychologist."

"Yeah, which has to do with the brain, so I'm checking your brain." She pats both sides of my face and nods. "All clear!"

"Thanks, doc." I turn back to where Nellie is still on her knees cooing at Pip. When I look up, I see one of the parking enforcement people coming over to us. "Time to get going, kids. We're about to get told off."

"Oh, let me sit in the back with him," Nellie says, pulling the carrier from my hands and rushing towards the car.

"Fine by me." I shrug and get into the passenger seat.

"Izzy, did you know? You had absolutely no reaction," Nellie asks from the back.

"I knew Mar was bringing a companion, and I assumed it wasn't a man she'd just met since she's about to rush up to Bennett's and confess her undying love."

I look over at her, wide-eyed and mouth open. "How... I nev — You can't kn—" All the words die before they fully leave my mouth.

Izzy reaches over and pats my knee. "You said on the phone that you had been scared for the first time ever, and you mentioned having dreams about him." She spares me a quick look before navigating out of the airport pickup area. "The only thing that changed between this assignment and your previous ones was that you had experienced something resembling a relationship. Mar, you really underestimate how well I know how brains work." She looks too smug about that. "Plus, your reaction was a dead giveaway. If you weren't planning on doing just that, you wouldn't have reacted nearly as dramatically."

"When are you doing it?" Nellie says from behind me.

"I don't know. Tomorrow, maybe?"

"Have you talked to him at all?"

"No," I say, feeling somewhat ashamed as I pull out my phone. "I could text him and make sure he's actually around."

"Oh, don't do that," Nellie says. "Just show up."

"I don't know. I'm not sure I want to put him on the spot."

"You would get a very clear answer pretty quickly if you surprise him," Izzy throws in. "Although bring the dog, just in case."

"To win him over?"

"No, in case he rejects you. You can brush it off and say you were bringing him another rescue."

"But he's *my* rescue," I say, offended.

"But *he* doesn't *know* that," Izzy shoots back.

"So, what, if he rejects me, then I have to give him my dog? That seems like a real shitty deal for just me."

"If he rejects you, that's a shitty deal for him, Mar," Nellie pipes up. "But he won't reject you. He's going to take you in like he takes in all those adorable dogs."

"I'm not a homeless or abused dog, Nellie. I'm a human being. I don't want to be rescued."

"Not even a little bit?" Izzy pouts at me.

"No, it's weird. I'm a grown-ass independent woman, I don't need some man to save me."

"We all need saving once in a while, even if it's from ourselves," Nellie says quietly. I'm not sure if that's meant for me or the dog.

I should embrace the fact that everyone in my life seems to be so gung-ho about making sure my love life is as fulfilling as my professional one. But it's hard for me to admit that they're right. That what I've been avoiding my entire life is what I may actually need.

"I'll come with you tomorrow if you want," Nellie says.

"I'd come, but the kids have a dentist appointment and Tom has three surgeries and both our parents are away," Izzy adds.

"It's okay, Izzy. Nellie, you don't have to, but I won't say no to the company."

"Perfect. But we're taking my car. I'm shocked you made it there and back last time."

"Tom was also shocked."

"Why are you slagging on my car?"

"Maybe because it's a piece of shit," Izzy says as she merges with the northbound traffic.

"I don't need anything fancy if I'm not here to drive it most of the time. Plus, it's a deterrent for thieves."

"That's an excellent point," Nellie says. "No one would waste time trying to steal that thing."

The rest of the trip plays out like it usually does when they pick me up after I get home from an assignment. I ask about Izzy's kids and if anyone has woken up in any of Tom's recent surgeries. So far he's got a perfect no-wake-ups streak. I completely fill them in on what happened, and Izzy's response is to pull over on the side of the highway and burst into tears.

"Izzy, I'm fine. It's okay," I say, resting a hand on her shoulder.

"No, it fucking isn't," she yells at me. "You could have died, Marley."

"I could have died during any previous assignment. Hell, I could die tomorrow. Any of us could." I sound a bit like Nancy now.

"Don't even put that into the universe," she says angrily. "None of us are going to do that because I will kill you if you go and die tomorrow."

I hear a snort from the back seat. "That doesn't even make sense, Iz."

"It makes plenty of sense," she says, looking at Nellie in the rearview mirror.

"Don't die because if you do I'm going to kill you. On what planet does that make sense?"

"It's a saying." Izzy wipes her nose on her sleeve and then pulls back onto the road.

Izzy isn't the emotional one in the group. Usually that's Nellie's job. Izzy is the practical one, and I'm the emotionless one. Or I was until just over a month ago. They're off arguing about different sayings and how they make sense and don't, and I'm okay with no longer talking about the many ways tomorrow is not guaranteed.

Nellie insists that I stay at her place tonight for logistical reasons, but I think it's because she's not ready to say goodbye to Pip. We stop quickly at my apartment so I can drop off my dirty clothes and grab something suitable to wear tomorrow. I stand in front of my closet for way too long trying to figure out what one wears to confess their feelings for someone. In the end, I grab a pair of dark jeans that I feel good in and a mustard-colored sweater. In all likelihood, I won't even have a chance to take off my coat so what I've got on top won't matter. Even if he invites me in, most of the time he saw me in clothes that were hanging off my body because they were his, and that didn't seem to stop him from wanting me. I finally tell myself to shut up and throw the clothes in a tote along with fresh under-wear, pajamas, and some hygiene products.

The first thing we do when we get to Nellie's is walk into the backyard and open Pip's carrier. He comes flying out and then slides to a halt. Then he's sniffing the ground and taking tentative steps through the snow. He lifts one foot high and licks it then repeats with his other one. This goes on for a while before he realizes no matter what he does the snow is going to keep getting on him. Ten minutes later we're all running around with him and laughing, even I-never-want-a-dog Izzy.

I take a picture of Izzy on her back laughing as Pip licks snow off her forehead. "Boy, it sure would be a terrible thing if Tom saw you having fun with a dog."

Izzy's head snaps in my direction, and she jumps to her feet. "Marley, don't you dare."

I hold my phone up. "Don't dare what? Press this button here that says... I think it says send." I smile wickedly and hit it.

Izzy goes to run at me, but she's not wearing appropriate

winter boots and she slips on the mix of snow and grass and goes down. Pip thinks it's a game and is on her in seconds.

My phone dings, and I look to see a reply from Tom. "At least let him know it's your dog and not a surprise for him," Izzy huffs.

FORTY-FIVE

Grey morning light filters through the blinds in Nellie's guest room. Pip is still asleep at my feet so I don't move. I want a minute to collect my thoughts. Today's the day I own up to some very big feelings. Today's the day that could change absolutely everything. I hope Bennett sees me and smiles that big, beautiful smile. I hope he wants this, us, at least half as much as I do. I have so many hopes, and I'm trying not to entertain the doubts that lay in wait at the corners of my mind.

Eventually, my bladder forces me up. Pip follows me into the bathroom and sits watching me. I've never shared a space this intimately with a dog, and I wonder how normal it is. Is it weird that a dog is watching me pee? I mean, to be fair, I've watched him pee many times. Pee on the grass, on a carpet, in a van, on a vet... I shake my head because it's too early for these kinds of discussions with myself.

I pull on a pair of sweats and a sweatshirt and pick Pip up to carry him outside. I know he's capable of walking there, but I don't trust that he'll make it from the bedroom all the way to the back door without finding the perfect place to pee inside.

Nellie is already up and sitting at the kitchen island, sipping her coffee and reading with a half-eaten chocolate chip cookie next to her. She looks like an ad for cozy in an old sweater from a university she didn't go to that has seen one too many laundry cycles, a messy bun high on her head, the tail feathers of a blue jay tattoo just peeking out of her sleeve. If I looked down at her feet, I'm certain she's got her knee-high slipper socks on too. I offer a good morning as I walk past her and set Pip down in the snow. He looks up at me like he thinks I've lost it, but then nature calls and he's off sniffing. I close the door before he has a chance to change his mind and go pour myself a coffee.

"Whatcha readin'?" I ask, joining her at the island.

"A historical fiction that you'd hate."

"Why would I hate it?"

"It's set during the First World War and basically on the battlefield."

"Ah." I nod in understanding. I refuse to read books that take place during conflicts. I need to fully escape, so battlefields are an instant no for me.

"How'd you sleep?" she asks, closing the book and pushing her glasses onto her head. I shake my head, knowing she's going to be swearing soon while she untangles the nose pieces from her hair.

"I slept. No dreams, surprisingly."

"That's good." She looks over at the microwave clock. "I thought we could leave around nine."

It's 7:30 now so that gives me plenty of time to get physically ready while I work myself into a state of mental stress. "I have a feeling I'll be driving back alone tonight." Nellie grins at me.

"Please keep your expectations in check, friend. I'm already freaking out." I stand and let Pip in after I hear a high-pitched bark from outside. He comes flying in and slides right into the fridge. "Wet paws, little man." I laugh and pick him up. He's freezing but seems happy. "I think he's going to be just fine here." I smile up at Nellie, who looks suddenly elated. "In Canada, I mean."

"Okay." She holds her hands out. "Give that little terror to me and go shower."

By nine I'm ready to go. I decline a travel mug of coffee because I don't want to be the first thing I say to Bennett to be "I really need to pee." Been there, done that.

Nellie manages to entertain me with stories from work. She's a librarian at the university in our city, and it's amazing how the current generation either has it all figured out or needs help with the most basic things. Seniors in the area also use the library for various pet projects, and I love when she has stories of the students and seniors helping one another out.

When we are about ten minutes from Fire Route A, I start to fidget. Nellie reaches over, takes my hand, and squeezes. "It's going to be amazing, Mar."

I nod. The best-case scenarios I keep playing in my brain *are* amazing. But the more I realize how badly I want those to come true, the more powerful the doubts get. Bennett's had so much time and space away from me.

The minute she turns onto his road, my heart begins a desperate attempt to escape my chest. We follow fresh tire tracks in the snow that lead into Bennett's driveway. A little hatchback is parked between Bennett's SUV and a truck I don't recognize. There are footprints leading to the house and out to the barn, but that's the only sign of life I see. No dogs in the field.

"You good?" Nellie asks as she parks behind Bennett's vehicle.

I look around and nod. "Yeah, it's just real now. Just...give me a minute." I sit there, staring at the little car. I don't know why it has captivated me so much. Maybe because the fresh tracks are from the truck. There were none leading to the hatchback. "Okay." I breathe out slowly and wrap my scarf around my neck before slipping my gloves on. "Wish me luck."

"You don't need it, but for your sake, I'll say it. Good luck, Marley."

I slip out of the car and follow the footprints that lead to the door. There don't appear to be any lights on in the house, but I knock anyway, then step back and shove my hands in my coat pockets. When no one comes to the door, I make my way to the barn. I can see that there are lights on in here. When I open the door, I'm hit with the overwhelming stench of fresh cow shit, which is unexpected. I make my way in, stepping around the dog beds spread out all over the place. That's when I hear murmurs coming from the end of the barn. Just as I'm nearing the end, the murmurs stop and a head pops over the half wall of a stall. I scream and fall back as she does the same. Then I hear footsteps from the floor above and someone coming down the stairs. A man that isn't Bennett appears over me, followed by the face that had popped over the wall.

"You must be Marley!" the woman says as she reaches down to help me up.

"Um," I say, feeling slightly disoriented as I swipe my hands down the back of my jeans. "Yes. How do you know?"

"I'm very nosy, and I saw Bennett looking at a picture of the two of you one day on his phone and I was like 'Soooo, who's the hottie.' and even though he said 'no one,'"—she does an excellent impression of a grumpy Bennett—"I eventually got it out of him. I'm incredibly persistent." She looks exactly like the kind of person who would be incredibly persistent. A ball of energy contained in a stocky five-foot-six frame. I like her immediately.

"That is one word for it," the man says, widening his eyes at me. "I'm Teddy," he says, sticking his hand out for me to shake. Teddy is the woman's polar opposite. Tall and lean and almost rigid, although his wild brown waves don't quite fit the formality of the rest of him.

"Marley, but I guess we established that."

"I'm Cassandra, but call me Cass," she says, shaking my hand next.

"I'm sorry, I don't mean to be rude, but who are you two?"

"We work here." Cass smiles proudly at me.

"As in..."

"We work for Bennett."

"You work for Bennett? Bennett Morgan? The man who owns this place?"

I must look lost. "We help run the day-to-day operations of Morgan Estate Rescue," Teddy clarifies.

"Since when?" I hope I don't sound accusatory, but what the hell is happening?

Cass breathes as she makes a show of thinking. "We both started about, what was it, Teddy? A month ago? I don't know, it's been a whirlwind. Lots of new dogs came in after the first big snowfall, and it's been pretty nonstop since. I've spent the last three nights sleeping in the office." That explains the lack of tire tracks.

"Bennett actually hired people?"

"Yep. And we were only going to be part-time, which was fine, but who doesn't want a full-time job in this economy, right?" She nudges Teddy. "I'm guessing you're probably here for Bennett, right?"

"Um, yeah." I nod. "Judging by the lack of dogs around, I assume he's on a pack walk?"

"Yeah, he left about thirty minutes ago. I'm sure you could catch them on their way back if you head out there now." She looks down at my feet. "Although maybe not with those boots. What size are your feet?"

"Nine."

"Perfect. You can wear mine." She turns and disappears through a set of doors.

"She's a lot when you first meet her, but she means well," Teddy says, quietly watching where she disappeared.

Cass comes back down the corridor, carrying a pair of boots that are far more appropriate for the amount of snow currently on the ground.

"Thanks," I say while I slip mine off.

"This is the best day," she says almost giddily. "Bennett was kind of in a weird mood this morning so this should cheer him up."

"Or I'm about to make things worse."

"Not a chance in hell." It seems like something Cass would have said, but this time it's Teddy. And his vote of confidence actually makes me feel better.

I take off towards the trail, following the tracks of two dozen dogs and a man. There is something kind of great about heading down the trail to find Bennett when it was the trail he found me on. It's where things began, where I realized things would never be the same. It's quite literally the path that led me to the most unexpected destination. Physically and mentally.

When I finally see Bennett, he's standing with his hands on his hips, just watching the dogs run around in front of him. He hasn't heard me and neither have the dogs, so I take my phone out, pull up his number, the one I've never used, and type a simple,

Hi

I see him feel his phone buzz and then pull it out of his pocket. A reply comes.

BENNETT

Who is this?

Turn around

I can see him tense, and just as I'm about to open my mouth, he turns. We stand there just staring at each other. He looks so damn good standing there all decked out for winter. This man wears the seasons very well. I hope I get to see him in spring and summer too.

"Marley?" I see his lips move, but no sound comes out.

I draw my lower lip between my teeth and nod, and that seems to do it. One minute he's stuck in place, and the next his strides are eating up the distance between us. The minute I'm within arms' reach, he's pulling me to him and I hold on for dear life. When he finally pulls back, he takes my face in his hands and studies me. At this moment, I'm reminded how much I like the way he looks at me. I can feel his tears against my skin, but seeing them causes my own to finally spill over.

I point at his face. "I hope those are happy tears."

"I didn't think I'd see you again. I think they're tears of relief."

"I'll take them." I'm about to kiss him when all the dogs surround us, including a few new ones. Bennett lets me go, and I drop down into the chaos of fur and tails and god-awful breath. That's when I notice that one of the dogs is slightly awkward-looking and wearing a blanket.

"Bennett?" God, it feels so good to say his name in his presence. "Is that a...cow?" I say, pointing at the calf standing with the dogs as if it belongs there.

"That's Lloyd," Bennett says so matter-of-factly that I burst into laughter.

"I'm sorry, did you just call that cow Lloyd?"

Bennett smiles that Bennett smile. "Well, that is his name."

FORTY-SIX

When I got the text from the unknown number, it felt like my heart stopped. When I turned and saw her there, it felt like I could take a full breath of air for the first time since she left. Even after touching her, I still couldn't believe she was standing in front of me. But then she said the thing about Lloyd's name, and I could no longer doubt my senses. She's here, she's real, she came back.

Once the dogs have had their time in her spotlight, I pull her back to me and watch as she drags that damn lip back between her teeth for the second time. I can feel my most primal instincts come to the surface, and all I want to do is drag her to bed or whatever surface is handy. I have never felt anything like this before, never once has someone made me feel like I'm on the edge of losing control. I manage to keep myself in check though as my eyes trail over her face. She's slightly more tanned than she had been when she was here. Freckles play across her skin, and I brush my thumb across her cheeks before tracing the recently healed cut above her right eyebrow.

I must be frowning because she raises her hands to my face and runs her thumbs along my forehead. It's this touch that completely undoes me. A surprised laugh bursts from her as I haul her up against me, her legs instantly wrapping around my hips as our lips finally meet.

I have a fleeting thought of her being here to tell me it's okay to move on, or that she has, or that there was never anything to move on from at all. But the way she kisses me back pushes those concerns from my mind.

We kiss until one dog, definitely Yogurt, starts to whine, and it gradually morphs into a chorus as others join in. I rest my forehead on hers and just relish in the reality that we're once again sharing the same air. I pull back because I need to look at her again. She's looking at me the way I had thought I'd only dreamed about, adoration mixed with disbelief, like she can't believe I'm real but she's damn happy I am. I never want her to stop looking at me like that.

We both loosen our grip, and she slowly slides down my body until her feet meet the ground. It's the very best kind of torture I can imagine.

"Take me home, Bennett," she says, reaching out her hand for me to take. We never got to do this before, and I'm taken aback by how right her hand feels in mine as we head toward the house. But really, I shouldn't be. Everything with Marley, even the silences, feels right. The only thing that hasn't felt right was when she was gone. When her ghost was the only thing left of her in my house.

We take several breaks on our way to the barn to make out, only breaking apart when the dogs remind us that maybe they don't want to be standing in two feet of snow.

When we're about halfway back, Marley sighs. "I have never wanted the ability to teleport so badly."

"It's incredibly inconvenient that they haven't come up with some way by now."

"Right?" Marley exclaims. "Although..." She smiles wickedly at me. "The anticipation is half the fun."

FORTY-SEVEN

We get back to find a somewhat stiff-looking Nellie standing at the barn door with Teddy and Cass. Pip is playing around in a snowbank larger than him that he keeps disappearing behind it.

"Who is that?" Bennett says, pulling me towards Pip with the enthusiasm of a child on Christmas morning.

"That would be Pip." I let go of his hand and snatch my wild child off the ground just as the other dogs notice him and begin to swarm.

"Let's go into the barn. The dogs can stay out in the field for a bit longer," Bennett says, gesturing to the door, eyes glued to the ball of fluff in my arms.

Cass and Teddy round the dogs up and get them in the field before joining us inside. I set Pip back down and plunk myself onto one of the dog beds. Bennett does the same and coaxes Pip over to him.

"He was a street dog in Syria," I say, watching Pip begin to gnaw on Bennett's fingers.

"Sophie told me," Bennett says quietly. "Not about the dog,

about Syria. Why didn't you tell me you were going?" he asks, unmistakable hurt in his expression.

I look up at the others who have joined us, and Nellie seems to catch how uncomfortable I am with sharing in front of strangers so she asks if they can give her a tour of the property. Teddy seems to catch on right away, probably because he's barely taken his eyes off of Nellie, but Cass needs a couple of nudges.

When I hear the door close, I take a deep breath. "Bennett, when I left, I never thought I'd see you again. I didn't think I wanted to." He looks like I slapped him. "Oh, no, I don't mean it that way. I mean that it was hard for me to admit that I did want to."

"Um..." he starts.

"I need to get this out." I cover his lips with two fingers. "At some point in my life, probably watching my robot parents interact, I had decided that I wasn't a relationship person. That part of my life seemed figured out. I had gone for a walk that day to try and figure out what I wanted in my career, which at the time was my entire life. And then I was here and you were, well, you, and I got this glimpse of what a relationship could be like. Going to bed next to someone and waking up with them was something I had never done before. It's not something I actively wanted. And I remember thinking that it was going to feel so strange, sharing that space. But then it wasn't. It felt... I don't know, right. Everything with you felt right, and that terrified me because I barely knew you. And I thought if that's how it felt after less than a week, it would only become more intense the longer it went on. Remember when I told you I wasn't afraid when I did my job?" Bennett nods. "I froze." I swallow. "When I needed to act, I froze. For the first time in years, I was afraid, and not afraid for someone else, I was afraid for me. The last thing I thought was that if I died"—I wipe the tears that have gathered—"if I died, I would never get the chance to tell you that I loved every minute of time we spent together. That I thought of you daily. That I regretted sending your sweatshirt back with that stupid postcard. How I hated that my stubborn brain kept me from reaching out. That your smile was like coming home. I was afraid you'd never know how deeply I felt for you and how much you changed my life in a matter of days." I'm crying now, huge tears streaming down my face. "I didn't want something to happen to me and leave behind someone who cared for me half as much as I cared for them. I didn't think that was fair."

Bennett is squinting at me like he's trying to sort out everything I've just said to him. "Marley." He pulls me closer. "What happened out there?"

I blink a few times, and my vision clears. I swallow and nod and manage to get out a choked "An explosion. There was a whistle and then an explosion."

He doesn't say anything for a minute, just stares at me. "I know your job is dangerous, Marley. But life is unpredictable no matter where you are or what you do. If the choice is having you and worrying about you versus not having you and worrying about you, I'm going to pick having you any day of the week. And I know falling for you happened fast, but life is short. We should probably go hard while we can." He takes my face in his hands and brushes away my tears. "What made you come now?"

"I got tired of playing the what-if game with only bad outcomes and started playing it with only positive ones. "

Bennett smiles approvingly. "That sounds like a better game. Definitely more productive."

I reach up and gently guide his hands off my face so I can hold them. "I'm not perfect, Bennett. In fact, one could argue that I'm pretty damaged."

He squeezes my hands. "You're not damaged, Marley. You're human. And like all other humans, you've got baggage." He tilts his head, his gaze holding mine. "But the nice thing about baggage is you can always unpack it. I'd like to think that this is a great place to unpack."

"I'm scared," I whisper as more tears fall.

Bennett kisses them away. "Then let's be scared together, sweetheart."

"You're going to have to be patient with me."

"Fine with me," he murmurs as his lips meet mine. I sink into him, and I can already feel the fear begin to dissolve.

Pip chooses that moment to give a frustrated little yip and makes us both laugh. "He's gotten used to being the centre of attention." I sigh, reluctantly sitting back. "I was distracted by him when it happened. The explosion," I clarify. "When Simon found me, the first thing I asked was if he'd seen a puppy. I thought he was dead. But Simon found him and took him to a vet while I was under medical supervision. I was so mad at him when he said he was mine and I could take him home. It was obvious to everyone else but me how badly I wanted to be back with you. It took several different people giving me words of advice to finally admit it."

Bennett reaches over and plucks Pip from my lap. "So I have this guy to thank for getting you back then?"

"I think I would have found my way back to you eventually, but you can thank him for getting me back here sooner."

"Why Pip?"

"Figured I'd stick with the Dickens theme."

"Ah, from *Great Expectations*." He looks up at me. "What?"

"Nothing, it's just really hot that you know that."

"What else do you think is hot to know, because I'm a big fan of learning."

I tap my chin, thinking. "I've always kind of thought bull riders were kind of hot."

"Damn." Bennett sighs, his head thunking lightly against the wall when he tips it back. "I think I'm out already. Pretty sure that's on the list of things I'm not allowed to do on account of the repetitive brain trauma I've sustained."

"I'll find a way to come to terms with that then," I say, taking Pip back and setting him on the ground. "At the end of the day, I'll survive on your smile and knowledge of literary classics." I move so I'm straddling his lap and just stare at him. I find love in those hazel eyes as he gazes calmly up at me. "I think I'm in love with you, Bennett John Edmund Morgan."

"I was wondering if you'd come to the same conclusion as I had."

"What? That I was in love with you?"

"Exactly." He laughs against my lips, his hands pulling my hips closer to him as we rock into one another. His hands slip below my sweater leaving goosebumps in their wake.

"Ahem," a voice cuts through the sounds we're making. "Sorry to interrupt, but it's colder than Sir John Franklin's corpse out there," Cass exclaims, shivering dramatically.

I look down at Bennett with one eyebrow quirked. "She was a history major," he says, shrugging.

"When you say Sir John Franklin, you are referring t—"

"The captain of the Franklin Expedition, yes." Cass nods.

"Right, of course. That's a deep historical cut."

"Thank you," she says as if I just gave her the best compliment.

"So..." Nellie says, leaning against the wall and crossing her arms. "I'm going to assume I'll be heading back alone today."

I look back at Bennett again. "One hundred percent." He grins at Nellie before looking back at me. "Did you bring any clothes?"

"I did not."

"Wow, you had that little faith in us, eh?"

"Well, I just didn't want to assume. I mean, you could have needed time."

"Oh, he's had all the time he needs, I think," Teddy says from beside Nellie.

"The stuff from Sophie is still here. I can drive you back to get anything else you want or need. Or we can just buy you all new stuff, although I kind of want to see where you've been calling home all these years anyway."

I'm stuck on the fact that after a month Sophie's clothes are still here. "Why didn't you take the clothes back?"

"Wishful thinking, I guess."

"Hoping I'd show up without a change of clothes?"

"Exactly." He pulls me into him, seeming to forget about the audience.

"Okay, anyway, perfect," Nellie says, pushing off the wall. "Guess that's my cue to head out." She walks over and hauls me to my feet for a hug. "Call me if you need anything, alright?" When she lets me go, she drops down to scoop Pip up. "Don't forget about your Aunt Nellie. And you." She points at Bennett. "You're doing great. So just keep doing exactly what you've been doing."

"I'll do that," he says, standing to join the rest of us.

"I'll walk you out," Teddy says, tipping his head towards the door.

"You can take off, Teddy. Thanks for coming in early," Bennett calls after him. Teddy answers with a nod and a quick, almost nervous glance towards Nellie.

I can't help but notice the shade of pink she turns when she nods and follows him, only giving me a wave over her shoulder before disappearing through the door, eyes very clearly fixed on Bennett's employee.

"Twenty bucks says those two have a quickie in her car before she leaves," Cass says with a grin.

"Oh, that's not really Nellie's style," I say, leaning back into Bennett as he wraps his arms around me from behind.

"I'd have said eye-fucking wasn't Teddy's either, but it was getting uncomfortable out there. When they saw each other, it was like they couldn't decide whether or not to fuck or fight. Then they disappeared inside the barn for a bit. When they came out, I'd say they'd settled on fuck." She says it so thoughtfully it takes me a minute to make sense of what she's implying. "Anyway. Want me to let the dogs in a few at a time so they can meet the new addition?"

"That would be great, Cass, thanks."

"So," I say looking up at him, "two employees."

"Turns out you're not the only one who knows how to take advice," he says, planting a kiss on my forehead.

"So, if you have help now, I guess that means you have more time for other things."

"Such as?" he asks.

"I think I'd rather show than tell." I smile up at him.

"I do enjoy a demonstration," he says, kissing me like we have all the time in the world.

FORTY-EIGHT

All the time in the world sounds great, but I'm quickly reminded that space and time are two very different things, and just as Marley is melting back into me, the barn door bangs open and Karl and Nancy step in.

"I knew petting the dogs was part of the job description, Bennett, but I didn't know your employees were encouraged to do that to people too," Karl says, laughing as he walks right up to Marley and pulls her out of my arms and into his for a back-breaking hug.

Our confusion must show because Nancy adds some much-needed context. "Teddy is making out with some woman in a car in your driveway."

"Yes!" Cass shouts from behind us. "Pay up, boss man," she says, holding her hand out towards me.

"I never took that bet, Cass. And Teddy's off the clock. I don't care who or what he pets in his off time, as long as it's consensual."

"Oh, it definitely seemed consensual," Nancy says, hugging Marley with a bit less force than her husband, but not by much.

"I'm so glad you're back. Now this guy won't have to bring him any more baby animals." She gestures between me and Karl.

"The only true way to distract Bennett from his sorrow is with adorable baby animals. Worked like a charm."

"Yeah, you weren't very subtle about it, though," I say, gently pulling Marley back into my arms.

"Didn't stop you from taking them all in." Karl's booming laugh fills the barn.

"Wait, how many?" Marley asks.

"Lloyd, a couple of kittens, and a young deer," I say nonchalantly.

"A deer?"

"He went to a wildlife rehabilitation place after being here for a couple of days. I already had my hands full."

"Anyway," Nancy interrupts, "I'm sure you two have lots to catch up on, so we're going to take off. I've left a lasagna and an apple crisp on the porch. Bake both at 350 for an hour. That gives you time to be doing some... reacquainting while dinner cooks." She winks, waves, and drags Karl out.

"She's as subtle as a thunderstorm," Cass says, shaking her head. "Bennett, I can finish up everything here and deal with some of the emails that came in overnight if you want to go show Marley what you've done in the house."

I thank her and take Marley's hand to lead her out of the barn and towards the house. I grab the bag Nancy left by the door before opening it and ushering her inside.

"Bennett!" she breathes out as she slips her boots off and takes a look at the kitchen.

"Karl thought I needed more animals to keep me distracted, but this probably helped more."

"It's... well, it's fucking perfect is what it is," she says running her fingers along the white marble counters and taking in the dusty blue cupboards. Everything but the appliances and one other thing in this room is different. The island counter doesn't match the rest. When she notices, she turns to me with one eyebrow raised.

"I wasn't quite ready to replace that yet." I follow her towards it, caging her in from behind as she smoothes her hand across the surface. "I've got a butcher block piece for the island, but I wasn't ready," I whisper, dropping my lips to her neck.

"Bennett," she says quietly, turning to face me before slowly pulling herself up to sit on the counter. She guides me between her legs and hooks her ankles around the back of my thighs, pulling me into her. "It's perfect. I love it."

"I love *you*, Marley," I say, kissing her deeply. When I pull away, she's laughing. "Is loving you so funny?"

"Not at all. It's just... Well, this whole scenario is kind of funny. I feel like I'm stuck in a book or a dream or something. It doesn't feel real."

"Anything I can do to make it feel real for you?" I ask, leaning in and placing my lips on the skin just below her ear.

"I can think of a couple of things that might help."

And then I fulfil one of my greatest desires as I hoist her over my shoulder and carry her up to my bedroom. She giggles the entire way but stops the minute her back hits the mattress. She props herself up on her elbows and openly admires me from the bed. I let her look for a minute before my patience melts away and I crawl over her, pushing her back down gently.

I start at her neck and kiss until I get to her lips, then I drag my teeth over and off that damn bottom lip. "Feel real yet, sweetheart?" I whisper, reaching down to unbutton her jeans.

"It's starting to," she squeaks.

"Good." I grin against her skin as I slide the zipper down.

"Oh, and Bennett?" she says, her hand reaching down to still mine.

"Yes, Marley?"

"Don't you dare be gentle with me," she commands as she reaches for the hem of my shirt and rips it off.

"Yes, ma'am," I say before following orders.

"Is it weird that your employees know that you fucked off to go... well, fuck?" Marley lies back, breathing heavily, after round two. At some point while we were cuddling, I heard the sound of tires on snow and figured that it had been Nellie and Teddy leaving.

"It wasn't until you said it out loud." I laugh nervously.

"It's been good, though? Having help?"

"Yes. I definitely haven't had as many headaches, which I must admit has been nice."

"Good." She kisses the skin over my heart before laying her head down again. "One of my what-ifs was what if I hadn't sprained my ankle, I would have eventually made my way back to my car, and that would have been it. We never would have met."

"What a tragedy that would have been," I reply, playing with her hair.

"I never would have gotten out of the cycle of stubborn independence, and you would have never hired anyone."

"The rest of it all matters, sure, but I think the whole not meeting thing is what I dislike most about that timeline. I am sorry you had to be in pain for us to meet, but it was kind of worth it in the end."

"Oh, I'd sprain both ankles again in a heartbeat if it meant having you just like this."

A beep sounds from below us, and she sits up and scoots to the edge of the bed. "As comfortable as you are, I have gone too many weeks without Nancy's sauce."

"Oh my god. If you had never sprained your ankle, you would never know the joys of that Hore's sauce."

"Don't you dare joke about such a thing, Bennett John Edmund Morgan."

Once we've gotten dressed, something I argued against until Marley made the excellent point about people around here having very few boundaries, Marley hops on my back for old time's sake.

Sitting at the island next to her feels surreal. If this is a dream, I never want to wake up from it.

When we are done eating, we stand together doing dishes. "I love this," Marley says as she dries the last plate.

"Doing dishes?" I ask.

"Doing dishes with you, laughing with you, eating with you, existing with you." She slips the plate into the cupboard and turns fully towards me, reaching for my hand. "You're the best thing that's ever happened to me, Bennett." She smiles shyly.

I thought hearing her say she was in love with me was the highlight of today. But as it turns out, being not just someone's best thing, but *your* someone's best thing, is the greatest thing of all. I pull her into me so I can just hold her and appreciate how of all the paths I've taken in my life, the most unexpected one quite literally led me to her.

EPILOGUE

Marley texted to let me know she was through customs. She'd been gone for two weeks on an assignment in Poland. At least, she was working out of Poland. I've learned that could mean she's traveling across borders, but she doesn't always know for sure until she's on the ground. I've learned a lot about her over the last several months. Neither of us was under any illusions that we truly knew one another after five days. Marley had kept her apartment when she got back, but after the first month, she announced while giving Lloyd a bath that she was going to give it up. She had suds up to both elbows and was lathering his neck when she looked over at me and with a very straight face and said, "I think I've decided to officially moooove in." We celebrated in my office, which is no longer a Marley-free zone.

She's had short trips here and there, but she's only had two long trips since she came back to me. Each time she comes back, we exchange notes just like we'd done without planning to the first time she came back. Hers are always in the form of photographs, mine in list form. Her notes are obviously more beautiful, but I do believe mine are funnier. For the first two months, she was working on a book one of her editors had pitched her. It was by revisiting old images and telling the stories behind those images that she began to rediscover her passion, and when she told me she wanted to go back out, I was all for it. The look in her eyes as she was talking about a proposed trip was what sold the idea for me. When we'd met, she seemed so defeated about her job. As if she was just going through the motions. After she'd come back, I'd asked what her dream was, and she had said to make a difference. I know what it feels like to have had a dream of making a difference and to think that dream is impossible. My path may have changed, but my goal has remained the same, and with the rescue, my dream is intact. I wanted Marley to have that as well.

Marley realized she could tell stories without putting her life in harm's way. She and Simon are working together on a book now to tell the stories of displaced people impacted by conflict around the world. She travels to virtually conflict-free places to capture striking portraits of individuals and families and occasionally their pets, and while we know tomorrow is not guaranteed, she feels like she's helping to make a difference. Their work will hopefully shine a light on why helping people in crisis is never a one-and-done thing. She has made me see that you cannot simply remove someone from trauma and expect that trauma to remain within the border in which it began. Trauma travels in the minds and on the bodies of people.

I'd asked if she wanted to stay overnight in the city, but she is anxious to get home and see the animals. I'm not upset about that at all. Every time she goes away, Pip seems to need a lot of cheering up. He's a bit like me in a way. Cass says it's like Marley was drawn to him because of some cosmic force, and

Teddy says that we're both just needy and Marley is who we're needy for. I hate to burst Cass's bubble, but I have to take Teddy's side on this one.

Teddy sent me a message as I was pulling up to the arrivals pickup, letting me know that Nellie had arrived with Izzy and her family and they were getting the house ready. I had wanted to hold off on the belated birthday party, but the others had insisted. I think Nellie is always looking for an excuse to come by for some dog and Teddy time, although she'd never admit to the second part. Izzy told me in no uncertain terms that they fully expected us to disappear at some point to begin making up for being apart for so long. Nancy sent me a picture of the finished cake, although it's a veggie lasagna because we all know Marley would rather have a full meal made with Nancy's sauce than an actual cake. It's also veggie because shortly after Marley came back we both decided that it was hard to enjoy beef when we had Lloyd out frolicking with the dogs. It was like he knew what we'd done when he saw us.

We are on the same page about most things, especially when it comes to talking. I'd told her I wanted us to share things no matter how good or bad and that her messes were mine now and vice versa. She'd accused me of butchering a Vance Joy song but appreciated the attempt. The only thing we've really argued about is the damn kitchen island. Marley insisted that I needed to update it to match the rest of the kitchen and that my sentimentality was weird. I reminded her that there are a lot of other things I could be weird about. That being said, Karl and I finished the island last week. I can already hear Marley saying, "Was that really so hard?"

The only other thing that has changed about the house other than the addition of a few art pieces Marley has picked up on her travels are the copious number of pictures of the two of us and our growing pack. She's always taking pictures, which shouldn't surprise anyone, and it seems like a new one is added weekly to the living room wall. "When in doubt," she'd said to me one morning as she straddled my thighs and pointed her camera at my very satisfied face, "take the damn picture." The one Sophie took of us from those first few days is framed and sitting on the dresser in our room.

I pull up to the exit just as she walks through the sliding doors. Her dark hair is immediately caught by the wind and whips around her head. I jump out of the car and assume the position. I know two things are about to happen: 1. When she is about fifteen feet away, she's going to drop her bags and run and jump into my arms and kiss me real good. 2. We're going to get told off by the guy in the safety vest for not getting out of here fast enough.

We manage a whole two seconds of lip-locking before a whistle is blown. Those two seconds are always worth the reprimand.

Marley pulls back and smiles the way she only does when she's truly happy, her hands still cupping my face.

"I missed you!" she says, searching my eyes and pulling that damn lip between her teeth. It never gets old, and I doubt it ever will.

She gives me another quick peck just as the whistle sounds again, longer this time, and then jogs back to grab the bag she dropped. I give the guy with the whistle a polite wave and get in behind the wheel as Marley tosses her bag into the back. I take her hand the minute she's seated and kiss the finger I hope to place my nan's ring on one day soon. Preferably when we don't have a house full of people.

"Thanks for coming back to me," I murmur against the back of her hand. It's the same thing I say after every trip. She smiles at me before reaching with her free hand to grab the back of my head. Her lips meet mine for a quick yet passionate kiss. When she sits back, she looks over at me and says one of my favorite things.

"Take me home, Bennett."

ACKNOWLEDGMENTS

Thank you to...

Cassandra for holding my hand from the first paragraph of draft one until I hit publish. I could not have done this without your encouragement and supervision. I'm so lucky to call you a friend and even more grateful that I get to say I'm related to you.

Alex and Jamie for always being willing to read bits and pieces as I wrote and then suffering through the first draft.

Jen M, Natasha, Jenn H, Canadian Erin C, American Erin C, Joshie, Jess, Marie, Whitney, Kati, reading an unedited manuscript is always a gamble but I'm glad you were willing to gamble on me.

Sarah, editor extraordinaire, I am so glad I was pointed in your direction. This book would never have gotten to where it is without your talent for digging deeper. It wasn't easy but it was more than worth it. I'm so glad Jenny nudged me in your direction.

Jenn Kavanagh Photography for making me feel comfortable on the opposite side of the camera. Working with you was a dream.

Hannah for never sugarcoating a single moment of this journey but for always being there with the perfect encouragement and words of understanding.

Elodie for every voice message and video call to help me

navigate the world of self-publishing. It meant a lot that you took the time to do that for me.

Vanora, Jaima and Matt for your guidance and patience. I adore discussing the ins and outs of self-publishing with you.

Carley Fortune who wrote "Keep writing!!!" in my copy of Every Summer After, so I did.

Every single Bookstagram friend who said "I can't wait to read your book." Your support has been priceless and I'm beyond grateful to you all.

Mary-Jo & Linda, listen, I didn't love the idea of you two reading the spicier scenes but I made peace with it quickly and I'm so grateful to both of you for reading and encouraging me from the beginning.

To Pippin for the mid paragraph snuggles, headbutts and constant supervision. I'm sorry I turned you into a dog in the book.

Ally, finding you on one of my many trips down an unexpected path was life changing. Having your support throughout this as well as your incredible artistic talent has been a dream. Thank you so much for bringing Marley and Bennett to life for me.

Kailey, for always being there to cheer me on even when you were dealing with life throwing all it had at you. Your strength is inspiring. Please note I wrote this whole book in 1st person for you.

Mom & Dad, I am the person I am today because of you. Through the best and worst you have supported me. Being your daughter is a privilege.

And last but certainly not least, to Sean, the love of my life, my calm sea, my helping hand, my Bennett. You have stood by me cheering along every dream I have and I can only hope this one truly shows what I am capable of with you by my side.

People like to scoff at instalove but I knew before I met you that you were the one and so let them scoff, we know the truth. Meeting you was the best thing that ever happened to me.

ABOUT THE AUTHOR

Megan McSpadden dreads talking about herself almost as much as seeing a snake on a hike. But she knows we all must do hard things so here it goes.

Megan lives in Hamilton, Ontario with her husband, two dogs, two cats and unruly garden. When not writing she can usually be found photographing families (don't worry they pay her to do it), yelling at her beloved Toronto Maple Leafs, dreaming of traveling somewhere else or cooking something her husband will ask her to make again but knows she won't because Megan doesn't do recipes.

Megan enjoys writing romance that will make you laugh one minute only to cry the next. Don't ask why because she doesn't know.

Stay tuned for Nellie & Teddy's story, coming 2024!

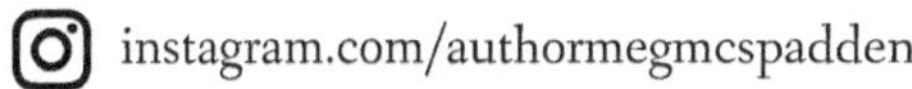 instagram.com/authormegmcspadden